A CAT
AT
THE
END OF
THE
WORLD

T0283982

COPYRIGHT © 2022 Robert Perišić
TRANSLATION Copyright © 2022 Vesna Maric
DESIGN & LAYOUT Sandorf Passage
COVER DESIGN BY Dejana Pupovac
PUBLISHED BY Sandorf Passage
South Portland, Maine, United States
IMPRINT OF Sandorf
Severinska 30, Zagreb, Croatia
sandorfpassage.org
PRINTED BY Kerschoffset, Zagreb
COVER IMAGE Cat and Kittens
(F. S. James. Macy Collection. ca. 1896, cat. no. 120)
courtesy of The Met Collection API.

Sandorf Passage books are available to the
trade through Independent Publishers Group:
ipgbook.com | (800) 888-4741.

National and University Library Zagreb
Control Number: 001140769

Library of Congress Control Number:
2022938968

ISBN: 978-9-53351-399-7

Co-funded by the
Creative Europe Programme
of the European Union

This Book is published with financial support by
the Republic of Croatia's Ministry of Culture and Media.

The European Commission support for the
production of this publication does not constitute
an endorsement of the contents which reflects the
views only of the authors, and the Commission
cannot be held responsible for any use which may
be made of the information contained therein.

A CAT AT THE END OF THE WORLD

ROBERT PERIŠIĆ

translated by Vesna Maric

SAN-
DORF
PAS-
SAGE

SOUTH PORTLAND | MAINE

PART I

1. The Voices

Scatterwind

A BOAT TRAILER is rusting in the grass. Over toward the houses are four rubbish bins. There is a deserted fish-can factory across the road. A single small cloud in the sky, very slow. I brood in the heat, such rest. And then I hear those two. I know that I know them. My memory is good, but it's in the wind. They have sat down below, in the shade.

I have good hearing, so good I can sometimes hear myself among the leaves. When I turn around suddenly, I also hear the sounds I accidentally drag behind me. When I am moving, mid-sway, it can be confusing, those sounds, the voices I carry, that hook on to me like burdock. But the heat vibrates without my breeze and I can hear them clearly.

They fed the hungry colony one summer, perhaps last year. They are looking for the one they fed. It seems they have found something else. They are talking about something she found. It does look old, she says quietly. You think so? he says.

I move closer and look. The coin seems familiar, but my memory is far. She found it behind the wall, over there among weeds by the broken chair.

Something flashed then. From the depths, an entire boat surfaced, long rotten in time.

From the Other End

AS HE WENT toward the end, his memory of the beginning improved. He spoke of a poison, a mild one, and the day he'd chosen. He poured water into the wine and said, "I don't know why, Kalia, I now remembered the moment I left El. Have I told you about it?"

"No," Kalia said.

Arion repeated stories, and repeated the words he'd used inside those stories. Kalia didn't mind because he did the same thing. They sat by the sea in the middle of the cove, facing the way out of the bay; to their left, on the slope, the town was sprouting.

"Yes, I had once abandoned El," said Arion. "That was at the beginning, when I noticed that I was getting used to him. And I didn't want to get used to him. It was when I ended my war.

"I saw then that I didn't know where I should go back to. The question had not presented itself for a long time, but it appeared then: Where was my home?

"There was something confusing about the fact that I had come to love El. There was something in it that I had not foreseen. It was as if I was changing. But I didn't want to be different. It was not through my will. The fact that I had come to love El was annoying me—I wanted to tear myself away from it. Why do I need this, to have someone to worry about? Is he hungry, where is he, I worried, but I didn't want to worry. This was not for me, it was a kind of love felt by an old woman, I thought. I never would have said then that I loved El, I would have said look at this silly beast, the way it's making me run around. As if he'd made me love him, he'd fooled me into it. And then I made the cut. I left and abandoned him. I left him in the care of an old woman in Syracuse. I gave her some money for his food. I knew, as I was giving her the money, that she would use it to buy herself food, perhaps pay off some debts, because she was poor. But I counted on the fact that she'd always give him something to eat, because she was a good person. All I wanted, Kalia, was to go on my way. I went home then, to my polis, Taranto. That's a colony that was built long ago, like Syracuse. You've heard of Taranto, Kalia? Have I already told you about it?

"No, eh? Taranto is a Spartan colony, the only one they ever built. It was special, our colony. The Spartans sent the children the Spartan women had with foreigners there. Those foreigners had lived in Sparta and fought wars for Sparta, but the Spartans did not grant citizenship to these mercenaries, or to their children. There were many of those foreigners, and there were enough of their children to found Taranto. Sparta had never formed a colony before or after. They didn't feel like forming colonies, they just wanted to get rid of us. Yet they did form a colony for us, apoikia, a home away from home, to make it all easier. That's when you see what a colony is, Kalia. It's not much different here on Issa; we were all a surplus in Syracuse. Like the ones they sent to Ancona. Some were in Dionysius's way, some were democrats, or spent, mumbling soldiers, or they were Pythagoreans, or a tacit family of a traitor, or an embittered sister of a dead soldier. Or anyone who hadn't yet been bought—and why not sell him now?

"And then there were those who were mysterious, like you, Kalia. It was the same way here, if you look well. Things were clear only in Taranto. The Spartans hid nothing because they were like athletes: they had neither the time nor the patience for making things up. Taranto had already become powerful when I was born, although it wasn't exactly known who we were, only that we were not those who we were meant to be. This made things strange, the fact that we were all illegitimate Greek sons and daughters. And we were also foreigners in the place where we'd arrived; there we were Greeks. Foreigners, of foreigners, on foreign land. That was my birth polis. It's no wonder that some philosophized, even those like me, although I did not realize for a long time that this was what I was also doing. And, as I said, I had to go back there and check something in Taranto, that's what it seemed like to me. I had memories from there, but they weren't clear.

"My mother died when I was little, I don't remember her. I don't remember her, at least not in the kind of memories I could recall, although I wonder if that's the entirety of memory, because sometimes in my dreams I have the sensation that I remember her, and although those dreams are more often beautiful than bad, I don't like them because I am gripped by cold upon waking from them. And Father took another wife, who was perhaps not exactly good. I say perhaps, I always say perhaps, because I am not sure. Was my father's wife good? That is what they asked me. I said that she was good even though I had no idea why I was saying it. Perhaps it was so they would stop asking. How should I know what a wife should be like? What the one my father married should be like, with whom he had other children, my sisters and brothers? How should I know what she should be like? She was the way she was. I didn't know any other. Perhaps she was good—she claimed to be. She said she was too good. Perhaps that sounded like a warning.

"She sometimes said that I would see what others would be like if they were in her place.

"That sounded like a warning that she might leave. But she didn't leave. And I didn't see any others, so I didn't know if she really was as good as she said, and if others were better. Once she said it at dinner, 'I'm too good, I'd like to see you with another.' Then I asked Father, 'Is there another woman?' 'Why?' he asked after a silence. I said, 'Just to see what she might be like.' He started to laugh, really he laughed too hard. I didn't laugh, nor did my father's wife.

"This was before I understood that some things are said in the way that one should not take them to be true. This thing that I should see how I would fare with a different woman—this, in fact, did not mean that I should see how I would fare with a different woman. It was only then I realized that what people say could mean the very opposite of what is being said. Especially when it is said by someone who is good. They actually don't even have to be good. They are good because they speak.

"For example, when I tell this story, you, Kalia, think I'm the good guy in the story.

"Who would be the good guy in my story, if not me? You see, it pays to speak. But, you know, you can't stop some people. They talk all the time because they think that this will make them look like the good guy. Just give them time. The ones who talk the most are the most suspicious. Still, you get to know them a bit and their lie becomes more familiar than the truth of those who are silent. The problem with those who are silent is not that they might tell a lie. The problem is with the truth, and what to do with it. You can see it in the way they frown as they think.

"It is rare for a bad person to lose their mind, while those who are concerned with the truth, they can go mad. That is why in the polis we prefer to choose politicians who lie, it's safer.

"I always considered why some people are silent and was always on the side of the silent ones, perhaps because I too often chose silence. Still, don't believe me while I speak. I am, Kalia, mostly concerned with myself in this story and that is very suspicious. Because the I depends on the story.

"You know, since I arrived in Issa, I could tell each of my stories the way I wanted to. I could do this because there was no one here who knew me. You know, the people who know you, they don't let you liberate yourself of the I that always postures in front of them in the same way.

"I always postured so that I looked strong and unbreakable. I did not tell stories in which I didn't appear that way. You can lie to those who know you and to those who don't. But the lie to those who know you is deeper. It's hard to get out of. In fact, you'll tell the truth more easily to a passing stranger, even if you tell a little lie along the way. You can even lie about your name, and the rest can be the truth. You tell the truth a lot less to those who know you. They know you and tell the truth about you. And then you do the same in return. And there is a whole other world above the truth. That is the most unbelievable world, and it is the very one in which we live. That obscures a clear perspective, Kalia.

"I think Simon told me about all this. Have I mentioned Simon? No? What I remember from him is that we don't know others. And then we don't know what we are like either. Because maybe I was bad, maybe I made my father's wife angry, maybe I was horrible even though she was too good. And really, I don't know if I was bad, if I was ungrateful, because I didn't know what I ought to have been like, and I didn't know what she was like, or what others might be like in her place. Do we know what others are like—are we better or worse than they? Take a better look at them and you'll see that in their eyes, everything is different. I saw, but only later, that almost everyone thinks they're good, too good. I, however, didn't think this, so it seemed that something was wrong with me. I didn't think I was good, and that word itself was strange to me. Maybe because it was good, too good.

"And then, what was I like? I wanted to be on the outside, although it may be impossible to be outside of the good and bad in words; it is hard to be outside unless you have a great wall, and even if you do have it, you'd be peeking over it. I was not good, that's entirely possible. But in order to be bad, I had to, I guess, have done some deeds. I did those only later, but it was still unclear at the time. I simply didn't know what I was like, so that I sometimes thought I was good, and sometimes I thought I was bad. Perhaps I even thought I was bad more often, but then I'd think, I can't be the only bad one, while everyone else is good. There was something in me that told me that it was not right for things to be this way. Then I told myself: I may be naughty and at fault, let them say that, but I am still good, maybe even too good.

"When I think about it now, I was not the only one to see it in this way. Simon helped me with this. He could have been my grandfather, but he was not, he was our neighbor in Taranto.

He would sometimes see me fighting with other children, the times when I thought I was right, and sometimes when I was down, when I thought I was wrong—then he would talk to me, as if in jest, but seriously. He looked at me seriously, even though he often made jokes, which sounds strange overall, but this is exactly how it was. I would go to the sea often with Simon. What I know about fishing today, I learned from him. Including that a fish needs to be killed, and not left to thrash about. It is not all right for it to be dying for a long time so that others could see it was fresh, he told me. Because if one day someone leaves us to thrash about, that would not be good for us, and we would resent those who watched us in this state.

"I don't know what you think about this, Kalia, perhaps I am only a fool who sells dead fish?

"Simon played the flute and taught me to play; he told me about harmony in music and mathematics. I learned from him the word cosmos. He told me about the Counter-Earth, which makes harmony with our Earth, and while it cannot be seen in itself, it is visible through harmony. I don't know if this is simply the same picture seen from the other side. He said that all of this is in the flute and that it is best sensed through playing. Still, what mattered to me the most was the fish. I wanted to bring fish home. I proudly took home the fish Simon gave me as his assistant, because I would have the right to speak as someone who is good.

"Simon only told me that I was not bad. He told me that it still remains to be seen, what I am like.

"Simon once told me that he wasn't just a fisherman. I was already not a child by then, and Simon was already sick. It was only then, at the end of his life, that I realized he was hiding from something. I was already at that age when you say you know everyone in town, and you greet everyone like an old friend, and Simon, I remember, asked me: Are there still any Pythagoreans around? Among you, the youngsters, are there any left? He was as old as I am today, and maybe he forgot what not to talk about. I asked what a Pythagorean was, and as soon as he saw that I didn't know he said that there must not be any left and I shouldn't ask around. He asked me to promise not to ask around and I promised, because I didn't care either way. I had other things on my mind.

"It was only later, when I left Taranto, that I came across that word in Syracuse, where soldiers and those who did not eat meat sometimes drank together—I met all kinds of people, Kalia, and I'd ask about Pythagoreans as an aside, and I'd prick up my ears, and I saw that I was, having listened to Simon so much, perhaps a Pythagorean myself. I had all this in my head. But it was nothing more. Because inside me was rage, an excess of unbearable strength, and I was not like Simon, I did not bend toward harmony. That confused rage was why I was not able to understand myself when I stopped being a soldier in Syracuse. That is why I went back to Taranto.

"I had almost forgotten about Simon and then when I arrived in Taranto, I heard that he had died.

"I went to Taranto because that is where I became the one who later fought the Carthaginians, for Syracuse, the one whom Simon could not help, at least not then, when we were spending time together. But, you know, some people help you only later, when they have been dead a long time. I went on the path of my rage, Kalia. I looked for the story I never told because I wanted to appear firm and unbreakable. And for that same house in which my father's wife had fed me. She didn't beat me, didn't touch me. She fed me. The children she had with my father, she caressed. She still asked that I call her Mother, repeated this, as if it might fix everything, or at least make the missing parts invisible. Sometimes you must make invisible that which is missing, make invisible that which isn't there in the first place. But its absence must not be evident—that is the higher level of invisibility. It can make your head spin.

"She had asked, so I called her Mother, sometimes, as if trying it on for size. Maybe that's the reason I became repelled by the word. It made me dizzy like in that game where you spin around. Later, whenever I heard 'mother' said, the aggrandizing and celebration of it, I felt anxious. I knew that this word should mean something good, which made me even more anxious if I thought about it, so I didn't want to think about it. Funny enough, it was only later when Miu became a mother, here on Issa, only then I could see it in a new light—the word mother. Only then did I feel care. And I was already old. I don't know, Kalia, if that's a comedy or a tragedy. Maybe it's a comedy after all. Now I feel almost like a mother myself, but it was a long way to get here and very roundabout. It now seems to me that the word's bitter taste had spilled over to the entire Earth. And it was that way later, that when I came to see the word mother in a good light, the taste went further, into life.

"Later I wondered what it was that she'd wanted to achieve by having me call her Mother. I don't know if it was a performance for my benefit. My father sat there as if there was nothing strange about it. Perhaps it had been a performance for him. He, like me, participated in the higher level of invisibility. When, later in Syracuse, I heard that he had died, I felt more angry than sad. Because I never got to talk to him about the invisible.

"Back then, when I was leaving, I didn't know what to say about it. And I didn't know where I got this great desire to leave home. But it was a great relief when I went to Syracuse. It was a great relief when I became a warrior, for Syracuse. I could kill the Carthaginians, I could be angry, I could be bad, yet still be good, for Syracuse. I came as a mercenary and became, with time, almost a Syracusan. Like my ancestors, the mercenaries, only I was a Greek from Taranto, and the Syracusans were Greeks, and everything was fine, we could hate the Carthaginians together; I could have children in Syracuse, only I didn't want any. Because I was used to being tough and sharp, I was hard and fearsome, and I got used to being like this, so it irritated me when I witnessed someone's love; I thought it mawkish. I was irritated by the sight of people being affectionate, it annoyed me to see families, annoyed me when a soldier told me about his kids. It irritated me to see someone caressing a child.

"Once a friend, a former soldier, invited me into his home and welcomed me as a brother. We really were like brothers. But when I saw his family, all that mawkish love, I thought—not immediately, but after a lot of wine, which we drank like brothers—I thought, he is a traitor.

"It was lucky that he was still in good shape because when we finally wrestled, and when I wanted to strangle him—and I wanted to in my drunkenness—he managed to wrangle himself out of my grip. He ran into his house—and it was night already—and from the house he yelled, 'Go, go, and never come back!'

"You see, Kalia, that's what I was like. I nearly killed a friend because he left me alone with my rage. No one could handle me, Kalia, no one except other riders who go beyond, over there among the others, to break their defenses. I loved horses, the most beautiful animals, who sweat just like us. We can run the longest, us and horses, because we sweat, while others cool down through their mouths, pant, and when they have to stop, we catch up with them, we who sweat. I got along with them. While trotting, in our balance as the trees rustled; while galloping, in every common move. Maybe I had remained a warrior for such a long time because of the horses. I may have had a horse anyway, but I'd have needed to have a stable, a house, land; even if I thought about this, it was a distant possibility. I buried my horses.

"Now I feel closer to donkeys. I used to consider donkeys inferior because you could not attack with a donkey. There were never enough horses and a donkey would have served against pedestrians if it was willing to move. But it didn't want to attack, there was no way. You could only use it to transport food. Once our donkeys, who were bringing us food, sniffed out a fire ahead of us, and stopped. We knew our soldiers had crossed that way already, but the donkeys didn't trust us. They dug in their hooves, and one of my soldiers, who was worse than me, started whipping them. There were five donkeys, and being whipped like that, rather than move, they lay down on the floor. He whipped them, until they started to bleed. And then he whipped their blood. Then something rose up in me, and although I too was angry that the donkeys had stopped, I put a knife to his throat to make him stop. He looked at me in the same way he'd looked at the donkeys, as if he'd stab me the first chance he got, and since I didn't like this man much, I realized there was no other solution so I killed him like a fish.

"Later on the soldiers, his and mine, testified that he'd attacked me. Perhaps they were afraid of me, or perhaps they really were on my side. Despite all this, I thought donkeys were an inferior species. We were something else, up there on the horses. A horse was not afraid and trusted us. Now I think the donkeys had very good reasons. Along with every other animal that doesn't trust us.

"But I wasn't always like this. A youth like the one I was might say that I have simply lost my strength. One can say a lot of things, Kalia, but I now know that I behaved the way I did out of rage and no one could tell me straight: you fool. If someone had dared, I might have killed him. That's why no one said anything to me. We were the center of all power, everything radiated from us.

"All this time I had Simon on my mind, I realize this now. I don't know what it is that includes, or excludes, what you have on your mind. It could have been the fact that I had already been wounded so many times. But I was recovering anyway. Then I met El on the enemy tower of a defeated city. He said nothing, did nothing, but he ended my warring years—I know I've told you this already, and I know exactly when. But I hadn't told you then that later on I didn't know what to do with El, whom I had wanted to bring as a trophy to Syracuse. The fact that we had made friends was not part of the plan. So I made up for it with silly curses, as if defending myself from it.

"It was unclear, as you can see, what I was looking for once my war was over. That's why, because of that lack of clarity, I went back to Taranto for the first time after many years, and left him in the care of the old woman whose house I'd lived in long ago in Syracuse, as a young man. I had to go to Taranto. Everyone goes back somewhere in the end. And

ROBERT PERIŠIĆ

then, arriving in Taranto, sleeping in their house, I did not have a good dream. It was as if I was falling into something. I didn't know what it was, and though I wouldn't admit fear, it made me feel very young again. I felt the anger of a little boy in a man's body. I didn't know this little boy still existed.

"It was not what I wanted to find, I was looking for home, and I didn't want to leave straightaway although I didn't feel well in my father's house, who was no longer alive, although my brother was there with his family and my father's wife too, who was too good. I looked for an opportunity to talk to her alone and that's when she complained they did not respect her, they hardly gave her food, they couldn't wait for her to die. There was no gratitude.

"She thought it strange that I didn't have a family. 'You too are getting old,' she said. 'Are you going to stay alone?' I saw she was afraid I had come to stay for good. But she also seemed not to care. I watched her. I saw her life had gone by, and mine nearly too.

"I could have stayed in that house. I had cleaned up a room for myself, it had an entrance from the courtyard and I didn't have to be crowded in with them. I could have taken up even more space because they feared me. But the house held nothing for me. I was forcing myself to stay, slept there several nights, waiting to get used to it. I couldn't wait to leave.

"One morning my father's wife was sitting down in the yard, warming herself in the early sunshine. I said I was going to go to Syracuse and that I would bring back a beautiful animal that catches mice and repels snakes. I told her I'd be back. I didn't want them to feel relief straightaway. 'Tell me: Were you good to me back then?' I asked her, pretending to be casual about the question. She looked at me as if I'd only just arrived. 'I was good,' she said. 'But you didn't love me.' We were entering higher invisibility again.

"That house disgusted me. I understood in Taranto that this is where my feeling came from. That's why I don't have a human family. But the fact that I understood it didn't change how I felt. I couldn't find anything new in Taranto, and our talk remained unfinished. There remained no possibility of finishing it, so I left her house then, and on the way to the port I stopped by Simon's house, where an old woman I didn't know now lived. 'If there is a flute in the house, I'll buy it,' I told the woman, and she brought it out, brought it out immediately, as if it had been arranged, although there had been no arrangement. She gave me Simon's flute and said, 'He told me to give the flute to the one who asks for it.' She pushed the money away. 'You must be the student he talked about,' she said. 'We fished together,' I said. 'That must be someone else.' She looked me up and down and said, 'Simon has been dead for years and no one else has asked.' I left Taranto and wondered why Simon believed in me. And if I were the one he had believed in or whether I should return the flute? Because I knew that I was not the way Simon would have wished. He had left the flute to me, except I was not the one.

"It's unusual when someone believes in you, Kalia. I left Taranto followed by the shadow of the one Simon believed in. For me, I could see, the only home was far from home. When I returned to Syracuse, the old woman said that El had wandered away right after I left. She had looked for him, but he might have followed me. 'Perhaps he hadn't understood at all that he should stick around my house,' she said. I looked for him for a long time, faltered and then looked again, walked this way and that, walked down streets, little alleyways no one walked down—where people and animals stood and watched—into the yards of decrepit huts that rested on wooden stilts, where a rose bush would still be growing. I knew that a cat does not know the difference between a palace and a neglected yard. He could have been anywhere, and in those days I got to know Syracuse again, as a tangled town full of nooks where an animal might look for tranquility.

"I found him, in the end, next to a burnt-down house covered in ivy, where there was some kind of rubbish dump. I saw a cat that looked like El from a distance. When I got closer, I saw that the cat was smaller and darker. But he walked like El. And he was looking back at me.

"He came closer, was dubious, sniffed me, and then, looking into my eyes, meowed hoarsely, and I knew it had to be him. Darker than soot. Shrunken with hunger. When I tried to stroke him, he looked at me askance. I took out two sardines that I'd brought for him; they probably didn't taste so good since I'd carried them around for days, but he came closer and ate. I sat down on the ground. He sat a few steps away from me and gazed ahead. He'd occasionally eye me up and down as if to say: what a failure. I sat next to him, close to the burnt-down house.

"It was not a beautiful place, except for what could be seen in the distance."

Scatterwind

A BREATH, a breeze. Can you hear me, over there by the dump? I throw these words into the silence of a humid afternoon, into the pauses between passing machines, into your middle ear and the rings of your vital spirit, I throw them like a hollow basketball player and a windy ghost who stumbled onto this island several thousand years ago. Yes, I could be more accurate, but I can't get into details right away.

I'm not an ordinary spirit, the way people imagine—a person's ghost or some such thing—but I am from a family of wind spirits, dragged from the upper parts of the atmosphere by some dramatic events since my situation at home was very difficult, so much so that it made me seek out a new base; there were many of us in the family, not to mention the extended family, there wasn't enough wind for everyone and so it goes.

Okay, to be honest, perhaps the fact that I was, as they said, too lively, or alive in a way, had something to do with it—although it's a bit different in our parts. I guess I did not follow traffic rules because I used to get carried away in thought, and I did not know how to think and stand in one spot yet. I would sometimes follow an idea so far that others thought me hard headed, and then one time I wandered so far away that, it could be said, I blew myself away—it is not impossible that my brothers helped me out a bit, but I cannot be sure because I never once glanced back—and then I was also pulled by gravity, down into unknown savannahs where black-and-white animals walked around, which are, I realized later, more or less the only black-and-white things on Earth. I love zebras to this day. In my loneliness at the time, they reminded me that I existed, which was not clear to me, because the pressure had shrunk me by about a hundred times (since then, my family considers me as nothing but a silly dot). And the water's evaporation, this humidity in the air, which I was not used to, initially made me feel, shall we say, stoned. Even though my family was not that much higher up, perhaps another ten kilometers, steamed up like this I never managed to get farther from the superficial troposphere, or, in other words, to the third of the level of my homeland. I think I lost a couple of hundred years attempting to climb up, but I slowly saw that it wasn't working and decided to look for something to do around here.

You see, I have wandered off too far already, and I did say that not everything can be told straightaway. Okay, let's move forward. I am where I am because I once entered a bag, and in the end I boarded a ship, all because I was following a strange bunch that was leaving Syracuse; I helped them out a bit with the wind—because I don't really have any great might, just some wind power—and I arrived with them. I saw that there wasn't much competition so I spend my days here, as well as centuries, as a small entrepreneur: I enter in, out, and around. Others came later, but that's a different story. They don't say hello to me, it's as if I were not here, but that's how it is among spirits—everyone minds their own business. To tell the truth, I can't see them either, I just hear people mentioning them. They used to mention the Greek spirit, then the Roman one, and then there were all sorts of spirits. But they never mention me. For them I guess I am but a silly old air-conditioning unit. This never bothered me because it is true that I am in fact quite technical. With time I even learned to think in one spot. It could be said that I settled down.

Obviously, I learned the human language, I did have plenty of time. Actually several of them. They stick, you learn, whether you want to or not. But I've never said a word until now. I've started speaking because the circumstances are a bit tense, at least in my job, and I have found a way to speak through a surveillance device, which I cannot explain now because I'm using the network illegally.

May it be seen as a mitigating circumstance that I am quite new to speaking. I hope my spirit doesn't get in the way too much. Once upon a time a spirit would have delivered all this in verse, but what can you do—you can't go completely against the times simply to get some attention.

Normally no one hears me and I have to make all kinds of extra efforts.

Only, as soon as I started speaking, I came across some problems. For example, with the I.

It seems that my being invisible doesn't get in the way of telling a story, but even I find this I suspicious—the I that appears while I speak. Because as soon as I say I, it seems that I am pretending to have a body. I'd rather speak without the I, but I don't know how I'd speak without this I. It seems to me that it wasn't planned that way; basically I'd rather speak as an it or a they.... Because what I really am is in between—a sum, a multiplication and some higher mathematics, plus a touch of physics and chemistry. Pressure, balance, circulation. And periodic stillness—all of it has a result.

It's not easy to transmit this through language. Let me put it this way: over where a spirit meets wind, the I is a relative thing, like a breath. This is a very vague description because language wasn't created for me but for humanity and there is no other way, I must be I; because people aren't used to someone speaking and not being I. I see and understand it's not programmed like that. Therefore, as a practical type, I use I purely technically, but I ask for consideration that this I is quite different from—possibly the opposite of—the human I.

And my memory is stored in the wind, which is quite complex. Try sorting things in the air and you'll see—it's a bit of a mess, plus crowded with the voices I remember, then

ROBERT PERIŠIĆ

there are things that have become a bit draughty, which happens easily in the wind, so I need to concentrate. That's why I speak best on humid summer days, when I'm idle, resting on a wall not far from the dump, so if it happens that I repeat myself it's because my memory catches up with itself in whirlwinds. Well, you can understand it better now that people too have started to store their memories in clouds. I will see them in a few thousand years when they have to remember where they stored something. I am saying this so that it doesn't seem that I am messy. All things considered, I am unusually orderly and systematic.

I see that it's going to be a bit complicated in any case, which is why I will stick to tradition and say I, and if I accidentally get carried away and shift genders while speaking, you can put it down to changes in the weather rather than gender, which I don't have. Another thing I find problematic is that I is a very special word that can grow. This worries me because I've seen it happen to people, but I've never understood if that comes from language or something else: that I is, in some way, inspired, but also inflated. I've seen that I can expand so much that it distorts the person saying it, which I've always found funny, although sometimes it is horrible to see.

It bothers me because having not spoken before, I don't know if it comes from the body—which presents no challenge for me—or if it comes from language itself, because if it does, it could cause certain problems. Leaving storytelling aside for a moment, it could lead to changes in the climate, if you understand what I am saying, because it is imperative that I do not get ideas above my station. Climate is very rickety lately and the last thing it needs is me getting overinflated.

As you see, I have many worries, and one of them is working out where I got this desire to speak in the first place. I think that it might even be connected to disappearing, because from what I have seen, everyone who has spoken has ended up disappearing into thin air. It's true that I've wondered lately: Do I have an expiration date? Perhaps my desire is signaling an end, or a sense that I will leave this place? Perhaps higher powers will dissolve me, or expel me from here. Because something is happening, in the distance, approaching from above and below. Weird holes are appearing. I'm often drawn by a void. And that might be the reason I have started to speak.

There are long drowsy periods, those months that come in a sequence when not a single rain cloud passes, nothing I can nip in the bud as the ground stiffens and the rest die inside.

And then there are gusts I have not known before, that come out of the blue, cunningly, while I am drowsy.

I have been doing this job almost two and a half thousand years now and it's never been like this. I can see that someone isn't doing their job, someone up north. I think it must be a right mess up there. Mind you, it's easy for me to talk because my island isn't melting away like the poles. I know, I know, I am talking too much about work. Not everyone is interested. Everyone has their own problems.

2. Some Time Ago

Kalia, Before Knowledge

KALIA LIVED NOT knowing that this is what it was called, that everything is implied in the term "to live." This is an entirely common kind of ignorance that is always forgotten. He lived in a house and an inner courtyard that he could not see from the outside—he did not know it was a courtyard. He learned language slowly, and was starting to understand, through language, that he was living, although it did not explain the miracle. Twelve rooms could be entered from the courtyard—some of which even spread over two floors— but everyone had to go through the courtyard to enter the rooms because they were not connected.

Sabas's house was beautiful, the house of the greatest master, which was evident in the courtyard; it was the kind of place that penetrated your very soul and when you uttered the word "house," this was what you had in mind. This was the house, and in your dreams it will always be the only place.

Everything that happened seemed to Kalia the only way it could ever be. And he was beginning to understand: this sense that you exist, move, and, bit by bit, say words that others confirm.

Kalia repeated the words he liked, arranged them on top of one another, sometimes he couldn't stop himself. Everything was marvelous in that house, and out of reach, and the courtyard was the best place of all; full of light and so many things to look at, touch, crawl on; all those journeys, for example, following a turtle. Was there anything better than being in the courtyard?

Liburna was in one of the rooms; she cooked and fed him so that he could grow. She sometimes measured him and was pleased. He didn't lag behind Pigras, who was a year older; he was on track.

"Just don't repeat words, that's not good," said Liburna.

"That's not good," said Kalia.

Sometimes guests would come for a symposium—to the andron, that was the name of that room where only men entered—and he'd serve them wine. The symposium went on after sunset, into the night, it was one of the most wonderful things: that which lasts beyond light.

Kalia saw guests change fast, but didn't know if it was because of the dark. He didn't know much about wine; he only saw that the visitors were not the same when they came and left the house. So he didn't believe that their demeanor when they arrived was what they were really like either. Rarely would a person become more pleasant, and if they did it was those who did not appear nice at first. Kalia watched

ROBERT PERIŠIĆ

them, watched their words, incredible words, and then he watched them falling over.

And when at the end some of them would funnily roll around on the floor, and when some of them would try to grab his body, Sabas would say, "Leave him alone!"

Kalia watched them falling over as if he were stargazing. Sometimes he, entirely unwittingly, watched things as if they were far away even though they were close. He once said this to Liburna and she got frightened, so he understood that this was not good. Sometimes he would, however, think it might be a good thing after all. Things were sometimes too close, all around him, and there were too many of them. He could only take everything in if he looked at things as if they were far away.

Scatterwind

MY LONELINESS IS quite necessary. Those of us who have, in this or that way, through restructuring, via falling on the Earth and after retraining, ended up working in and around winds, don't generally get to see each other. We don't do symposiums or that sort of thing, because it would immediately get breezy, things would start flying all around. We don't gather because we don't want to risk a serious disarray.

Not that I, as an island breeze, have anything against the breeze from the other island. I am, in fact, always here to cover for him if he goes elsewhere—because I can sense right away if he isn't there—but this has happened quite rarely, once in a hundred years. And he covered for me when I went over to Pompeii, of course not for tourism but for study. But we do it in a way that ensures we don't run into each other. Because if by any chance we did run into each other, it would be more of a collision than an encounter, meaning it would be a storm and there'd be serious damage.

I don't have any other choice than to hang out with creatures who don't even know I'm here. It is, however, possible that some of them do sense my presence, such as Mama from the dump. Sometimes she looks right at me, although I know I cannot be seen. I hang out with her, and others from her colony, because I have known them a long time and they don't change.

Otherwise, everything else changes here, the natives too of course, not to mention these new guys, the tourists: this coming and going like crazy people, that never used to happen.

That was only ever done by pirates in the past, or arsonists, or passing armies.

When I think about it, it's not so bad that all of them turned into tourists. Much has changed.

And maybe I too will turn into something else. The fact that I am remembering things long gone might be one of the signs; the fact that I want to talk about my arrival and who were, actually, my friends.

Kalia, The House

KALIA COULD SEE that Pigras walked around the courtyard differently and that he had access to the whole house, that he spoke differently and stood differently. It was as if Pigras had a strange power. It seemed that the word house had a different meaning for him, as if the house was more his than Kalia's. Still, Kalia lived in this house, so he thought it was his house. Which other house could it be? If someone asked him where his house was, he'd point to Sabas's big house.

When he started to recognize the word slave, he at first thought it referred to someone else, and then he started to understand that the word slave had to do with him: the outer him.

He tried to ignore that word, as if it might disappear.

He wasn't sure what the difference was between him and Pigras. Was it only a matter of playing? Because Pigras had to win every game, otherwise he cried in a rage.

Then Zenobia—Sabas's wife and Pigras's mother—would descend the stairs. If she saw Kalia it seemed that she was looking at the sun and it hurt; that's how she'd scrunch up her eyes and the upper part of her face. Her top lip would lift up and expose her teeth. Kalia knew he had to get out of her sight. That's how it always was. He knew that Pigras had to win.

"That's how it has to be," Liburna told him. "He was born to be a master."

"That's how it has to be," repeated Kalia. "He was born. He doesn't know how to play differently."

"That's what the gods wanted," she said with a sigh.

"We are not gods?" he asked.

"No," said Liburna.

"They don't know how to play differently," he said.

"How do you come up with such thoughts?"

"Come up, how do I come up?" he wondered.

"Can you speak normal?" she asked.

He saw that she was worried. Kalia had to focus, then he said, "I can."

"Do you remember what I just said?"

"He was born to be a master. That's what the gods wanted," Kalia said. "Is that normal?"

"Yes. That's good." Then Liburna added, "You're not as dumb as you look."

Kalia didn't know how he looked. He wanted to ask Liburna how he looked, but didn't know if it was normal.

Kalia had heard the word Syracuse several times and knew it was something bigger than the house and the courtyard. Liburna would say she was going into town and then she'd come back with food. It seemed that's where Syracuse was. Kalia didn't think the house was part of Syracuse, he thought Syracuse was that which existed beyond the courtyard. He'd played there a few times with Pigras, once they even went to the shore where they watched dolphins.

"That's the sea," Pigras said.

It glistened. They watched dolphins jump and dive. Sometimes it seemed like they were friends.

"Is the sea also under?" asked Kalia.

"Under what?"

"Where the dolphins disappear, under."

"That's also the sea." Pigras laughed. "Do you want me to throw you in so you can see?"

Kalia ran back to the house.

It seemed Pigras was his friend, only he was sometimes nasty. It was better when Pigras laughed at him because then he'd slap him on the shoulders and pat his head like a friend might. When Pigras eyed him seriously, he'd hit him harder, on the nape of his neck.

When Pigras attacked him, Kalia could defend himself, run away and struggle, but he wasn't supposed to throw Pigras to the ground. That's how it always was and Kalia didn't know any different. He watched Pigras's movements and made sure he was out of Zenobia's sight, but he didn't fear Sabas.

Liburna once told him, when no one was around, that he should also fear Sabas because if Zenobia noticed that he didn't fear her husband, that would not be good.

ROBERT PERIŠIĆ

Liburna explained everything to Kalia, and she knew a lot. She explained that Syracuse was a big polis, that the Greeks came a long time ago with boats and settled here. "Those among the Greeks who came first, their families still own the most land today—they are gamoroi. Sabas is a gamoroi too. After that came the Greeks from Athens, which was the biggest polis, and they wanted to conquer Syracuse. But Syracuse won—that's how it became big. And now Syracuse is the biggest."

"And our house is also Syracuse?" he asked.

"Yes," she said.

Kalia was glad. *We, Syracuse, are the greatest.* He thought of Syracuse like he thought of the house he lived in, that it was his.

Liburna saw this in his face. She'd had a son once who longed to be a soldier for Syracuse, and he got what he wanted. She said, "But don't think Syracuse is ours because we are slaves here."

Kalia didn't want to hear this and was gazing at something else: he was looking for the turtle.

Liburna also told him, "You know, I am not from Syracuse. I was captured by pirates long ago. They sold me here."

It seemed that Kalia wasn't listening.

"It was all different then, only the turtle was the same," said Liburna.

That caught his attention and he asked, "The same, the same?"

"Yes. I only spoke to the turtle. I couldn't talk to people because they all spoke differently from me."

"The turtle understood you?"

"No, not really. But I knew turtles from back home. They felt familiar. Sometimes it's important to have someone to talk to. Because when you don't, it hurts."

"What hurts?"

"Something... Something you'd like to say."

Kalia was listening intently now, and Liburna thought he'd have a hard time understanding. But if she'd talked to a turtle, she could talk to him. Sometimes it seemed to her that he wasn't all there, but she wasn't sure because at other times he seemed to be very clever.

"And where was your house?" he asked her.

"I'll tell you about that tomorrow," she said. "Not to make a mess in your head."

"A mess in the head, a mess in the head," he said.

"Why do you repeat that?"

"A mess in the head, many things," he said.

She sighed and said, "Yes, many things. I'll tell you everything in time, don't worry."

The next day she told him that she was from Liburnia, which is why they called her Liburna, and that her real name was Menda. She had actually told him this several times already, but he called her the way Sabas and everyone else called her.

ROBERT PERIŠIĆ

"Yes, Menda," she said. "I'd like it if you called me that because that is my real name. That's how I will know it's you calling, and not someone else." She said only her daughter and son had called her Menda. "He is no longer alive," she said, "and she might still be living. She was too beautiful. But too... naive... Sometimes I think you're just like her."

"Why?" asked Kalia.

Menda got lost in thought as if it had been a difficult question. Then she said, "Because you're beautiful."

She didn't want to confuse him further. Once, long ago, she had told him that his mother was dead, and that his father had gone to war and never came back.

Kalia waited for rain and gazed at himself in a puddle. He wanted to see what the word beautiful might mean. But he couldn't see very clearly.

He called Menda Liburna occasionally, but he saw that she was glad if he used her real name.

It seemed to Kalia that Menda knew everything. He learned from her that Syracuse was in Sicily, and that there were other Greek cities around them, but also those in which Carthaginians lived and that they spoke differently.

He wondered how Menda knew all this, and she laughed. She said everyone in Syracuse knew those things, and that she was a mere cook. He didn't understand this. She said there were many people cleverer than she, like those who could write.

"They can make by hand that which they speak, as if they are saying it."

"They can speak through their hand?" he asked.

"Yes, something like that," she said.

"I'd like that," Kalia said.

Menda looked at him. She was afraid it was not for Kalia. But then she thought, *Perhaps it's worth checking if he's stupid. If he learned to write he might even be useful to Sabas.*

Scatterwind

MY PROGRESS IS slow. It has been quite a long time since I started speaking. This language with the I, and my windswept memory—it's all quite complicated to handle.

But I remember one thing very well. I didn't notice language at all at first. Probably because people in general didn't interest me greatly. I passed by without listening to them. I didn't find them beautiful, they were always carrying something around, like ants. Maybe I was wrong, but I didn't consider them to be the chosen species.

I have to admit I found them somewhat ugly. Planted on those two skinny legs, you could easily knock them over in the passing. How they have managed to survive with this pathetic sense of balance, I could not understand. Basically, a ridiculous animal with a bald body. And so many dangling body parts. You can't see it so much with all the clothes on nowadays, but there aren't so many animals with so much hanging off them. For example, their larger cousins, the orangutans and gorillas, don't have so much on display. Those gentlemen look like angels compared to humans. With men and women, everything is outsized compared to the rest of the body. So what else could I think but that it's a species with only mating on its mind? I don't think it's wrong, but for it to be evolutionary progress, well, that didn't occur to me.

I remember my disbelief seeing them at sea. That's when I realized that they knew something about the wind, which surprised me. Because their sense of smell was useless. And their hearing was weak.

My movements are, for example, immediately sensed by animals—they smell and hear me, prick up their ears, and people can only look at animals and wonder what's happening. I thought: not only is this not progress, it is evolutionary regression. These creatures smell almost nothing, can't hear half of what's going on. They just go on and look, look, look, and look, and of course they cannot see me. To think that they'd end up in power, I really could not have guessed. Luckily there were no betting shops at the time, so I didn't place any bets.

So, to cut a long story short, when I saw them setting sail, I was shocked: But how? They understand the winds? There was no doubt about it, you could see they understood things. But how they got to that understanding was unclear to me. Half-deaf, smelling hardly anything, but there you go. It was a riddle, and riddles are rare in my world because things are mainly transparent to me. And it was the kind of riddle that was part of my job description, so I started studying humans and following them, to see what hidden sense they possessed. If they could not smell a third of what an elephant could smell, if they could not hear a third of what an owl could hear? My main impression was that they really had no idea what was going on around them.

And then—out of every other species—who raised sails and hitched a free ride?

I hate to admit it, but that's when they gained some of my respect, and I have been giving them endless free rides for centuries ever since.

Kalia, Letters

IT WAS THE first time Menda tied Kalia's sandals—they'd belonged to Pigras but he'd outgrown them; for Kalia they were new. It was also the first time Menda took Kalia to town. They ventured far from Sabas's house, down crowded streets, and arrived at a market where there was such a lively crowd that it nearly swept him away. Menda had to pull him constantly by the arm. She bought only a few things at the market. They then went inside a knot of streets, and Menda told him to remember the way because once he knew how to get around, he'd go on his own. Behind those streets was another, smaller market; she said this one was for the poor.

"I have to buy everything at the first market," Menda said. "If they gave me money, I'd buy everything at the poor market, but they don't give me money—Sabas comes and pays for my shopping every week. It could all be cheaper but he doesn't want to come here, doesn't want to be seen at the poor market because he is a gamoro."

On the way, Menda told Kalia that they were going to see a man who was smart, but a little strange because he didn't want to walk on the ground. "He thinks the earth will swallow him and walks very carefully, and he'd fought with his family over this so he now lives alone. He has a donkey, in order not to walk, but he rarely rides it," Menda said.

"He's a bit grumpy, because he sits at home all day, but ignore that."

Kalia listened and thought that there were interesting people in town. Menda told him this man would teach him the alphabet, that this was a big secret—he could tell no one about it.

He asked if he'd get to see the donkey.

Menda laughed, as if she knew he'd say that. "Of course, we have something for him."

Menda reached inside the large pocket of her woolen tunic—she had made the same one, only smaller, for Kalia. He too had two deep pockets on each side to keep his hands warm.

She pulled out two big carrots. "No one will notice them missing and the donkey will love us," said Menda.

They arrived at a small house, which was connected to other small houses. One could not go farther since it was the end of the street. There was a small stable with a rickety door rotting at the bottom, and Kalia saw gray legs and hooves.

Menda said, "If you're ever handling a donkey, make sure you're not rummaging around behind him. A donkey can see all around except behind his hind legs."

"He can see everything on the sides?"

"Yes, because his eyes sit that way. Donkeys are good, but if they get frightened of something behind them, they can even kill with their hind legs."

The stable door had a round opening through which, after Menda beckoned, donkey teeth peeked out. Kalia thought he was grinning at him. Then the rest of his head followed, except for the ears, which couldn't fit through. Menda offered the carrot to the donkey and it seemed that the animal smiled with his eyes.

"Can I feed him the other one?"

Menda lifted Kalia. "Carefully. Put your fingers together, hold the carrot by the edge. He won't bite on purpose, but donkeys don't see clearly right in front of them."

"Don't see?"

"Well, we don't see all that well in front of our mouths either."

The donkey pulled up the carrot and chewed, his eyes happy.

"I call him Mikro," she said. "But don't mention that in front of his owner."

Menda stroked the donkey's forehead and Kalia did too, cautiously at first, then with an open palm.

ROBERT PERIŠIĆ

"Are you glad?" Menda said with a laugh. "I am too. I have no use from being loved by a donkey, but it makes me glad all the same."

Then they went into Mikro's owner's house. He was a skinny and smaller man compared to other adults. This was the smallest grown man Kalia had ever seen, but he was very serious, perhaps the most serious of all.

Kalia would have been much happier if they had stayed outside, but he had to sit down here.

Menda told him, "You'll sit here and learn the letters while I finish my chores. If you work well, we will do this every day."

The small man was called Alexandros. After Menda left, he looked seriously at Kalia, then asked in a screechy voice, "Tell me honestly, do you want to learn the letters?"

Kalia looked at the door—his true desire was to feed the donkey, or to be with Menda at the market, in the crowds. But he looked at Alexandros and it seemed as if the man knew this, and thought Kalia didn't want to learn the letters because he was a slave.

Kalia saw this in Alexandros's eyes.

Now when he stepped out of Sabas's house, things were becoming more clear. His desire turned around the longer Kalia looked at him that way and he said, "Yes. I want to learn the letters."

Kalia then went to the market with Menda every day, and he learned the letters. He read sentences, which he had not even known existed, because the existence of sentences had not been visible to him, nor the fact that everything could be broken down into individual letters and then put together again by reading. This made Menda happy. She'd been afraid Kalia was dumber than the rest, but he was not.

And everything was fine until the cat turned up. In a bag.

She ruined everything, Menda said later.

Incidentally, I was also inside that bag.

Scatterwind

THIS STORY MAKES me remember myself, which I am not sure is a good thing, because we scatterwinds normally don't reflect much but rather we simply are, day to day. But here I am, made to reflect by language, language is pulling me back, or rather back and forth, in all directions, and I have to admit that it's a very interesting tool, almost like time travel.

The thing with the sails happened after I had crossed a large desert and emerged at the top of Africa. Of course, I didn't know what its name was, nor did I call any country or continent by name. I think that's the normal thing to do. Africa could be called Europe, and Europe Africa, and nothing would change. I didn't really understand the need for any of it. All the names are actually wrong, I have understood this from the start.

But I'm rushing ahead within the story again, because I am talking about things I didn't even know of in the beginning.

Because, of course, I began to understand the meaning of names only through humans.

At first I thought that they were related to birds because they were so loud, mostly in the day, like birds, so I thought they were mimicking them. I thought it was tweeting, just less musical, which I had expected from humans, considering their diminished hearing capacities. When I noticed that there was a repetition of names I still thought it was simply an attempt at singing out of tune. It took time for me to realize that a name is an invention.

I recall how I found it funny when I realized that they tried to name absolutely everything they could see. As if they were trying to put a spell on everything.

I was listening to all of this along the way since it is not necessary for my work, and so I didn't make much effort. It was all sinking in slowly, with time, and as I said, I had plenty of time.

This was slowing down my so-called education somewhat, because I really can afford to say, "Oh, there's plenty of time, I'll do it tomorrow." Only after a lot of casual listening I saw the whole thing and that it was not about names and naming but about the web. Even though all the names are wrong, you get something out of it at the end: a web in which everything gets caught. I thought then that humans were somehow related to spiders because a spider too secretes that from which it weaves its web.

Language is humanity's web, I saw, and every name is a tiny thread. No single word is an end in itself and it means nothing unless it's part of the web. It is, I thought, a really large song.

And so, I learned human language along the way, and then various languages because as I said, I had nothing but time. During that time some of the languages became extinct. Beautifully woven, large and wide tongues were dying, disappearing like a dead spider's web. And all the languages are large, there are no small ones. There are remains of some, woven into new webs, while some are just threads in the wind.

Only an occasional trace reminds me and sets my memory off into a whirlwind, such as when I found that coin by the rubbish, there on the road to Kamenica, where I brood and talk inside myself in the distance, behind the wall, on a broken chair in the swelter.

Kalia, Miu

THE CAT SHOWED up in the bag that was carried by the young, tanned sailor, who turned up in the courtyard and asked after the master of the house. Kalia called Menda and she went to inform Sabas.

Kalia saw that there was something alive in the bag.

The sailor said, "Inside is an animal they call Miu in Egypt."

"Why do you keep it in a bag?"

"So she doesn't run away. She was with me on the ship. I let her walk around on the deck, but now I have to be careful."

The sailor then said that he'd already brought one, which he'd sold to Sabas's friend. The daughter of that man loves it very much now. They told the sailor, in that house, that they don't need another one themselves, but that Sabas might want to buy one for his son.

"It's the new entertainment for the rich," the sailor said. A pleading sound came from the bag. The sailor laughed. "There, that's why they call her Miu."

When Sabas showed up with Menda, they went to the kitchen with the sailor. Since no one had told him to go away, Kalia sat down on the floor. The sailor closed the door. Sabas said he wanted to see if the animal was healthy before calling Pigras. And he wanted to be sure it was from Egypt because the reputation of his house meant that he needed the original item, not some mongrel.

The sailor untied the bag, laid it down on the floor and said, "She's frightened now."

Everyone watched the bag, and the sailor said that they needed to take care with these animals, since they're very much prized in Egypt. They are under the protection of their goddess Bastet, who is similar to our Artemis, the sailor was saying.

Sabas watched him inquisitively. "How can we tell she's from Egypt?"

The sailor said it could be seen by her behavior. "If you catch a forest cat in Greece, even if you raise her from birth, she'll never be your friend. But the African cat forms an attachment to people. I have brought one to your friends and they know that this is true."

Sabas nodded.

The sailor told him that it was forbidden to take a cat out of Egypt and that he had taken a great risk doing it. "If they had caught me, they would have surely killed me."

"Does that put the price up?" asked Sabas.

"It's really true, master," the sailor said. "If an Egyptian came to trade with you, you'd have to hide Miu. Because if he saw Miu, he'd have to buy her from you and return her to Egypt. It is his sacred duty. You could even earn a profit, but I imagine that is not what you're after. So, the fact that I brought her is an act of great bravery."

"You're a very brave thief and a blaspheme, is what you mean to tell me?" Sabas said hoarsely.

"That's right, sir, I am very brave."

The animal's head poked out of the bag; she looked around to see where she was. Kalia watched her: so tiny. She was sniffing the floor and the air, looked around and up as if looking for the sky, and started toward Kalia's legs with an uncertain step.

"You shouldn't be touching her now," the sailor said, "until she sniffs around to get her bearings." Then he added, "You know, although I am very brave, I have treated Miu with respect because I don't really want to get on the wrong side of the goddess Bastet, even though I don't believe in her. But I wouldn't want to get on the wrong side of the things others believe in, because even when I think it's silly, it sometimes happens that I later have a dream that it's not silly. I wouldn't do this if I didn't have children, and my salary isn't very high. That is the source of my courage, sir."

Sabas now looked as if he really believed that the sailor had come from Egypt. Then he took out a few coins and said, "Will this do?"

The sailor glanced at the coins and nodded.

Menda had been holding back from saying anything, but when she saw the money she said, "Master Sabas, she's such a small animal."

Sabas said, "Every gamoroi house has one now. It's the fashion."

The sailor said, "She's small and young. She needs to be young in order to get used to people. But she grows fast."

Before leaving the sailor also added that Miu still didn't know that this was her home, and it was necessary to keep her inside so she wouldn't escape. They needed to take it slowly with the creature, he repeated, until she understood that this was now her home, because she had just got used to being on the ship.

"When she understands, in four or five days, that this is her home, she won't run away."

Sabas looked at Kalia—Miu had, after sniffing about a little, climbed into his lap.

The sailor nodded, serious. "You see."

Kalia sat motionless, not to frighten the cat.

Sabas watched Kalia and Miu, as if contemplating something, and told Kalia, "She can stay here for a few days, until she gets used to the place, because you're more careful. I see that if I give her to Pigras now, he's impulsive, she might run away."

Scatterwind

I WAS, AS I said, also in that bag. I'd been hanging around Sicily for some time already, where I had arrived through a series of not-so-fortunate events that were then, and later, a big topic of conversation. But I won't go into that now.

Sicily was divided between the Carthaginians and the Greeks, but I, of course, had no problem crossing borders, which were anyway subject to frequent shifts. I could be with the Carthaginians in Palermo—also known as Ziz—in the morning, and by the afternoon I'd be pushing rain to Syracuse. And pushing rain clouds takes longer than handling dry wind. Pushing rain clouds is a bit like boring, slow traffic, like when trucks are going uphill and moaning softly. Sometimes I am also like a shepherd who is herding cattle, because there are always some runaway clouds or those that get distracted. This can be a problem. But even problems, after you've had them for a long time, become routine.

It had become routine to watch the incessant bickering between the Carthaginian and Greek colonies, and the

ROBERT PERIŠIĆ

bickering was frequently turning into warfare. Since I was spending time on both sides, I saw that they were more or less the same as each other, except for the fact that they spoke different languages. The Greeks were, at the time, postulating that language was what separated them from animals, but it also separated them from the Carthaginians. I could see how languages fought their own wars. I also hung around the seas of Sicily, in order to get away from their languages for a while.

I needed some silence. To be honest, it isn't a total silence like in the desert where I could only hear the wind blowing, or rather I could hear myself. I was perfectly fine with the silence of the waves. As far as I could see, few would opt for a complete silence if they could listen to the sound of the waves.

I had come across the ship with the sailor and the kitten by chance, while wandering around the seas, and I felt like a mother wind. Did I say mother wind? There you go.

There is something in those tiny newborns that turns you into a mommy. It could be that they expel something into the air, something hidden in their smell, a kind of message. I am basically, as a female wind, rather sensitive to smells.

Okay, I'll go back to my masculine self now, not to confuse matters, it's all the same to me anyway.

I say, perhaps those newborns send something off into the air that gets stuck to me. Whether this is a message or cosmic order—since it has an effect even on creatures like me—I don't know. It has happened once already, in the very beginning, when I came across zebras. I've been cautious since. But there was this little ball of fur on the ship's deck. For a long, long time I didn't approach animal pups. Sometimes I'd just study them, watch them play, but carefully, from a distance, in passing. But I threw caution to the wind, so to speak. I misjudged. I was too close to that creature on the deck, I suppose, and I stayed around too long. I wasn't aware that it was happening. But when the ship docked in the port, and the sailor bagged the kitten, and when it let out a sorry little voice, I also entered the bag.

I know, it was a stupid thing to do. I really have no tools to mother anyone.

Moody Miu

FROM THE MOMENT they met, Miu behaved as if she and Kalia were friends. She'd sit in his lap and purr, and sometime she'd climb up on his shoulder and lick his ear. He liked stroking her fur and seeing in her eyes that she enjoyed it. Kalia thought this animal was always like this. But after four days, when Miu should have realized that this was her home, he saw she wasn't always like that.

Kalia had gone to the market with Menda, or rather he'd been practicing writing at Alexandros's house, and when they came back they found Pigras with Miu in the kitchen: it seemed they were playing. Then Pigras, as soon as he saw them entering, picked up Miu as if he wanted to show her off to Kalia and Menda, as if they were seeing her for the first time.

"She's been in the kitchen long enough, now she's coming with me!" he said and in order to emphasize his words, Pigras victoriously shook Miu.

The fact that he shook the cat wasn't to do with her, thought Kalia, but because of him and Menda. He was showing them that Miu was his property. That's how Pigras played, as a master, because that's how he was born.

And then Miu bit his hand. She bit him as hard as she could, and also scratched him with her claws as he was dropping her.

Kalia couldn't believe how Miu had changed.

Pigras went quiet and then started shouting. "You haven't prepared this animal! You haven't prepared it!"

It sounded as if he was talking about a meal.

"I'm sorry, young master," Menda said. "They say she's moody."

"I'll kill her," said Pigras, sniffing. "Where has she gone?"

Kalia was afraid for Miu, but then he saw that Pigras wasn't in a huge hurry to find her.

"Don't kill her, young master," Menda said. "Your father paid for her. I could see it was too much money, but he paid. I don't think you should kill the animal without telling him."

"I'll sort it out," Pigras shouted, and then left.

"You see," Menda told Kalia when Pigras had gone. "I knew we shouldn't be taking this animal. I could see it in her eyes."

"Why?" Kalia asked.

"Mischievous eyes," Menda said.

"She's only looking."

"But she's looking straight ahead," Menda said. "She's not humble, tame, like a cow or a dog. It's a wild animal, stay away from her."

It was the first time Kalia thought that Menda didn't know everything.

"You're on Pigras's side?" Kalia asked her.

Menda looked at him. "What side, what are you talking about? It's his cat."

"The sailor said we should be gentle with her."

"You've become as rude as the animal," said Menda. "She also frightened my turtle."

"She was just sniffing it."

Miu crawled out from somewhere and looked up at them, seemed frightened by the tone of their voices. Then she climbed into Kalia's lap.

"This is not good," said Menda.

Kalia saw that he'd made Menda angry and was afraid. What would happen if Pigras had heard him? But he hadn't heard him, Kalia knew. Because Pigras wasn't one of those who might hear something and keep it for later. If he'd heard him, Pigras would have come back in immediately and hit him. Then Kalia would have to hide behind Menda. Kalia often hid behind Menda's wide hips and knew every-thing that would come next: Menda had to tell Pigras that he was clever, and that Kalia was stupid, and she'd remind Pigras that he was a noble and good young master. At such moments, she was simultaneously protecting Kalia behind her and speaking in soft tones and moving her hands gen-tly, which calmed Pigras down, and even slightly hypno-tized him.

Kalia was now holding Miu in his arms as he trembled inside, even though he wasn't feeling cold.

"This is not good," Menda said, watching them.

Kalia held the mischievous animal, which would, according to the sailor, grow bigger.

Scatterwind

ONCE UPON A TIME, I was present at the birth of a zebra. She stood up her its long, wobbly legs immediately. That was the first time I got a feeling for life on Earth (because in the beginning it seemed to me that there wasn't much of a difference between the movements of clouds and earthly creatures). I got this feeling with the little zebra, which was also a kind of birth for me. I had been, until then—if I think about it—a mere technical phenomenon and it was possible that my getting a feeling for life was a kind of technical error. But that's how it happened and I could never reset myself to my original setting, even though I tried.

At that point I didn't know what was happening to me. I just found her funny. That's where my silly contribution came from. The entire time she was growing up she seemed to do nothing but make her close relatives laugh—and I became one of them—and so even today, if I accidentally laugh, I laugh like a zebra.

I visited the zebra her whole life; so she always lived in a pleasant breeze and loved me even though she didn't know me. Everything I could do for the zebra and her mother was to direct the wind away from the predators, and give the zebras the advantage of sensing them first. I hadn't named her because I didn't know names then. When one day later she lost her strength, stumbled and fell, two young leopards spotted her and killed her quickly, and ate her body. If I could have killed them, I would have. But I have no body, to bite and hit, I only have a lot of time.

I followed those two young leopards. I wanted to harm them. I directed the wind so that it would obstruct their hunting. It would blow from them to their prey and the prey would sense them. It would blow from them to their prey even before they saw the prey. They couldn't smell anything, moved around in vain. They were getting weak quickly. Then I left them alone for a while. I saw then that they weren't very good hunters. It seemed that their mother, who was meant to teach them to hunt, hadn't done a very good job. Perhaps something had happened to her and she couldn't finish teaching them. They were, I could see, two helpless brothers. I watched them: sharp teeth and claws, yet they caught nothing. They couldn't eat grass like the zebras, they needed meat. Half-grown, long, skinny. One brother was still strong, the other one was weak and stumbling. Several hyenas had their eye on him, waited for him to collapse.

They followed him silently. It took time. He gazed at the sun, at his brother. Might he catch something?

His brother watched him: Should he leave him alone and go hunting? Then the stronger brother saw some antelopes on the horizon and started toward them. The exhausted brother tried to go with him. Then he sat down, there was nothing in him, in that savannah sun, and the hyenas watched him, waited for him to put his head down, to fall asleep, which seemed like a very attractive idea.

My revenge did not taste sweet. I left the savannah then. I went north. I never saw zebras again.

Kalia, Useless Things

"WHAT CAN YOU do, he was born to be a master," said Menda, consoling Kalia when Pigras had been nasty to him. "That's what the gods wanted," she would add, so that Kalia would accept it.

And perhaps because he'd accepted it, he found it easier to take, it felt ordinary.

Menda had said all this, however, because she thought Kalia would suffer if she had told him otherwise. Menda was born free, and she was planning to tell Kalia very different things one day about all of it, but she knew for now that this was the best way.

Then Kalia saw that the gods weren't helping Pigras at all when it came to Miu accepting him as her master, or even as her friend. Kalia had at first felt uncomfortable for Pigras so that he gently scolded Miu and handed her over to Pigras, but she would just wiggle out and go back to Kalia. It wasn't because he was afraid of Pigras's ire. He was worried for Miu and there was a confusing fear in him about what it all meant.

He saw that Miu went against everything he'd ever been told: that Pigras was born to be a master. He saw Miu walk all over it. And walk all over it calmly. It now appeared that Pigras wasn't actually born to be a master at all.

Kalia told as much to Menda and she got angry; she said that Pigras was born to be a master, that the gods had wanted it and that one shouldn't either question it or think about it.

Pigras had, in the meantime—because he'd been told in the other wealthy households that it was the only way with cats—tried to win over Miu and be nice to her. He was trying to please her, stroked her, and took her scratches, which he wouldn't have done had he not had a great desire to win her over from Kalia and prove something to himself. The fact that Miu sat in Kalia's lap and licked his ears, while she treated Pigras as if he were a nobody, drove Pigras into a tearful rage. Some might say that she treated Pigras like trash, but this wasn't true since Miu was a lot more interested in trash than in Pigras.

Pigras had, however, decided to be nice to Miu, so he took all his rage out on Kalia, whom he'd push into the mud, or hit "accidentally," as if it had been a joke, and Kalia wasn't allowed to frown because then Pigras would say, "What's that frown for?"

Kalia waited for Miu to stop coming to him and accept Pigras as her master. That would be best, he thought, because he saw that Pigras would rather throw out the animal than let her be Kalia's cat.

He regarded objects close to him as if they were at a distance, especially an approaching Pigras. Not because Pigras would hit him, but because it had been easier to withstand him before, when he had believed Pigras was born to be a master. He could see now that this wasn't the case. Whatever Menda said, the truth was plain to see.

Menda watched Kalia, worried—he appeared vacant. Still, when Miu jumped into his lap, a smile would appear on his face.

Things spiraled after that. Pigras was getting worse, and Menda took Kalia into the kitchen, saying she needed help, and closed the door so, she said, the cat wouldn't come in, having brought him bad luck.

Again, Kalia thought he didn't understand words properly. Such as good and bad luck. Miu's presence had brought on many of Pigras's punches. But he felt different. He used to think that he was worse than Pigras, but Miu gave him a different feeling and that feeling now lived inside him, confused, like good and bad luck.

She would sometimes fall asleep on top of him, as if that sleep signified the joy of trust.

That's why he asked Menda why she'd said that thing about the donkey. He remembered. Why did she say there was no use from being loved by a donkey, but that she was still glad for it? And why did she tell him about the turtle? Menda waved her hand, as if she was sorry she'd said anything in the first place. No, she never should have told him that useless things could be good. That is how masters could afford to think about luxury, but not slaves.

Scatterwind

I SAW HOW it was with cats. They came when people started farming. While people walked around gathering their food, they were only accompanied by dogs. I understood my first story then, which they told in one of the now-dead languages, as they walked.

They said how some people had once found an abandoned lair of baby wolves; the mother was not there. The people probably would have killed them immediately had they not found them funny. They were play fighting, chasing each other, nibbling on one another. Each time, someone would win; they all won and lost equally. Everyone knows what a game is for— to learn to win and lose. I saw that everyone had to learn this. And those who grow to be the strongest, they also get old and lose their power. That's a game.

The baby wolves played and people found it funny, they saw themselves in the pups. They didn't kill the animals and they went up to the women, they were hungry. Among them was one woman whose child had died, but she still had milk in her breasts. She adopted the wolves. She found a way to feed them her milk without it hurting. They protected her later.

Little wolves look like dogs, they don't yet have that elongated snout or a lethal gaze. Dogs are like this because dogs are the children of wolves who have remained children. There was no one to raise them as wolves. Dogs are the children of wolves who were adopted by a woman.

That was the story told in a language that no longer exists. I heard other stories later, about how a hunter tamed an adult wolf, but I don't really believe that one. It's hard to tame a grown animal, and one is too few to make a difference. I believe the first story more because pups had to grow affection for humans as their mother. But who am I to say? I only know that because I witnessed it: dogs were man's first friends.

The dog belonged to a woman in the beginning. The woman could feed the wolves, the one whose child had died, and they were looking for a mother, and that kind of search is always the same. They were always on the go then, only setting up camp for a short period of time. The first dogs went behind the one they considered to be their mother and they protected her.

I saw dogs walking with people for thousands of years, and only when the humans settled, the dogs finally had somewhere to chase the sheep around and toward. The sheep were afraid of dogs because they thought they were wolves, and dogs pretended to be wolves, they found it entertaining, and when they'd herd the sheep for the humans, sheep could see that humans could protect them from the wolves. Dogs laughed joyfully. They are still laughing because sheep still think of them as wolves, even though they have never seriously bitten them. Dogs are happy with this because they are the children of wolves who love to play at being real wolves; it's just a game, the way pups play. But sheep have no time for thinking, they run in the direction the dogs herd them in and then dogs are humans, they are the ones who were adopted by a woman, those who are pretending to be wolves. Such dogs tamed sheep.

I wanted to talk about cats, but I always forget that you can't do it all at once—such is language.

Dogs were the first to accompany humans, and cats were the last. That's why they embody nature the most.

Miu And The Servant

PIGRAS ONLY MANAGED to lure Miu to the master's part of the house by offering her food—and this part of the house was bigger and brighter. But then she would run back into the kitchen and the dark shed where Kalia slept. The fact that Pigras was merely putting up with her so he could retrain her, and best Kalia, she seemed able to sniff out.

Pigras didn't understand how such an animal might be retrained. He asked around in other houses, but no one knew. There was no way to train them, they said, because if someone bothers her, punishes or hits her, she doesn't love that person and avoids them, that's all. You had to be nice to her and wait for her to warm up to you.

Pigras waited, gave her meat and fish, she didn't refuse, would eat it all up, wait around to see if more was coming, and then she'd leave to find Kalia and lie before his feet, looking around as if lazily checking that the world was still in perfect order.

ROBERT PERIŠIĆ

"This animal has no gratitude at all," Pigras complained to Menda, who nodded. "What does she think? I think she thinks I am her servant!"

Kalia watched this and saw that Menda almost laughed. Then he thought perhaps she did like Miu a little bit.

"But how could she think that, young master," Menda said.

"She doesn't think. It's a stupid animal."

"Very stupid."

"Couldn't be more stupid if she tried. I didn't even know there were such stupid animals."

"Me either," Pigras said.

"I don't think you should bother with her anymore."

Menda thought Pigras might give up, that's how exhausted he looked.

"But she thinks I'm her servant!" Pigras shouted.

He put his head in his hands. Menda was afraid that he'd hit Kalia again, perhaps even Kalia and Miu both, but it seemed he was spent. He was stronger, but he couldn't win.

"Young master, are you in pain?" Menda asked him, worried. She waved at Kalia to move to the kitchen.

"I hate that animal," said Pigras. "I have hated it from the first day."

"Oh, ignore it, she doesn't deserve..."

"I can't, I can't ignore it," said Pigras. His breathing was rough, as if he were inhaling rage and exhaling misery.

Menda gave him some water. She stroked his head. Pigras sat down on the ground, relaxed, and fell on his back. He raised his knees and stomped on the ground, hollering with pain. Zenobia turned up quickly.

"What's the matter with him?" she shouted.

"I don't know, noble mistress, perhaps he's been stung by a wasp?"

"It must have been some animal," Zenobia said. "I know which one too. He cries because of it all the time."

"Oh, really?" asked Menda.

"He's in love with it."

"Is that possible?"

"It's possible. My child is dying inside, I can see it," said Zenobia seriously.

Menda wanted to tell Zenobia that he didn't love the cat. She was quite sure of it. And she saw that the cat knew. She herself pretended not to love Miu, but Miu still went around her feet. She seemed to know that Menda loved her a little bit. She wanted to tell Zenobia that he hated the cat, that he only wanted to own it; she wanted to tell her that the cat knew this. But it was not wise to contradict her at that moment. She watched the wailing Pigras as his body twisted in pain, his mother embracing him. He was stomping his feet and raising up dust, as if he were a bit crazy.

"This is awful," Zenobia said. "What kind of a curse is this?"

"I will make him a calming herbal tea," Menda said.

Scatterwind

I SAW THAT there were people who were raising their children to be winners. I had never seen such animals before because every animal knows that pups play and fight, that they win and lose with ease. I saw that all young animals did this. There must be a reason, I thought; it must be how they prepare for life, for failures and victories. I saw that it was something the little ones carried inside them, that they already understood games, that they didn't have to think about it. I watched for entertainment, but there was something else there.

I had heard from people that—if you were a foreigner—the most difficult thing was to get a joke. I remembered this because I am not only a foreigner, but I am neither human nor animal. But I developed a sense for jokes over time. I don't know how I got it, but I think it was there before language. I think I got a sense for jokes while I still watched my zebra at play, sometimes alone, sometimes with others. I saw it right away: animals know how to play alone, hopping around, dancing or chasing their own tails. Playing always makes it seem there's someone else there with them. Someone imaginary: a tail, a fly, something invisible in the air because humans aren't the only ones who imagine things that don't exist. Back there at the beginning I thought that my zebra was playing with me, that she could feel me although she couldn't see me. It was possible that she played with a breeze. But perhaps not, because later I saw that such a thing wasn't particularly unusual. If she was bored and there was nothing around, something would be dreamed up in the air. One can already spot the joke there; I saw all those things with my zebra, wondering what it was in the air, if it was me or something imaginary. As I might have already mentioned, I got a sense for life with that zebra, perhaps precisely because she played with the invisible me, so I moved, played, blew down her back and felt her joy. And the joke is clearer when several pups are at play. The joke is immediately obvious, when they play fight in that silly way of theirs. And they know it's a game because they always, I could see, fought without a wish to hurt another, careful not to hurt another, and that kind of care was there already, they didn't actually have to pay a lot of attention to it, they didn't have to think about being careful, they didn't have to hold back to be careful, but that was how they played and this was already in the animal.

If you watch pups playing, you'll automatically learn about jokes. You'll see what's funny. It doesn't come from language, or from people. A joke is from earlier on; an animal who is funny while playing, it's inside it. The animal knows this is a game and that which humans found funny when watching baby wolves at play, that is inside the wolves and inside humans: a language before language.

Game, funny.

Winning, losing.

I saw, because I had time, that this was a small joke—and a prelude to a bigger one.

Kalia, Celebration

THE FOLLOWING DAY, after Pigras had been rolling around on the floor in pain, Menda had a lot of work in the kitchen because there was a celebration. She also had a head full of thoughts, *What will happen to Kalia if Pigras carries on with his madness?*

She had spent the whole night thinking how she might tell Zenobia that Pigras was not all right. Even if he is a master— she could say—not everything in his life is going to turn out as he wanted. That's not how life works. The child had not learned to lose and was not prepared properly. He could turn into one of those madmen who goes crazy because they're not winning and become pitiful. But no one pities them. It would not be easy to say this to Zenobia. She'd have to say it side-ways, so that nothing was clear, and Zenobia would surely fly into a rage anyway. Maybe she could say something to Sabas, perhaps the following day, after the celebration. Because it was for Pigras's own good. The child won't learn to be a win-ner and a leader this way, which is what they have planned.

If Sabas would hear her out, she thought, perhaps this thing with Miu might get resolved too.

She got Kalia out of the way by calling him to peel the vegetables. When Pigras looked inside the kitchen in the late morning, he looked perfectly fine. She said, "I see you're better, young master. You're not in pain?"

"No, not at all," said Pigras, looking jolly.

"You were in a lot of pain yesterday?"

"It was my tooth," said Pigras.

"The main thing is that it doesn't hurt today."

Later on, Miu wasn't in the yard, and when Kalia started looking for her, Pigras walked after him for a while, as if he was looking for her too. Kalia felt, however, that Pigras wasn't looking for her, but was mocking his search. He asked, "Do you know where she is?"

Pigras laughed, as if this was what he'd been waiting for. "I tied her up. I was too nice to her."

Kalia stopped.

"What are you looking at me for? She's mine."

Kalia averted his eyes. He looked down at his celebration sandals, which had once belonged to Pigras.

Pigras added, "You're all mine. From now on, she will be on a leash."

He walked off victoriously.

Kalia sat down on the densely packed ground outside the kitchen. The sun shone on him, but he was looking straight ahead, as if he were in darkness.

Menda came out. "Come on, don't be so sad. It's only an animal."

"And us?"

"Don't speak like that, come on, get up!" Menda lifted him up onto his feet and went back to work in the kitchen. She was preparing more food because of the celebration.

Kalia walked around the yard in circles. The fact that there was nothing that was his was not new, but he still felt that everything had been taken from him. It seemed that everything he could see had already been taken from him and that he was far from everything. Farther than ever, as if he were entering a void. He didn't know what to do with that feeling, so he walked around in circles, in an odd way, like someone who might shut himself up inside these circles. He repeated words in his head and separated them into syllables.

It was a sunny day, and occasional sounds of celebration could be heard from the city because the Syracusans were welcoming the victors, liberators of some city whose name Kalia couldn't remember, and Sabas and Zenobia had gone to town to greet the victors, ceremoniously beautiful and upright. They must have been very happy because Sabas gave Kalia a tiny smile in passing, hardly visible, blurry like something out of a dream that you quickly forget, and that's how Kalia felt, as if he were in a dream where you walk around in circles, and the things around you move even faster.

Soon after, Pigras turned up again. "She scratched me and bit me again, look!" He showed the scratches on his arm. He complained, as if Kalia was supposed to console him and also take responsibility for it. "You will punish her!"

Kalia watched him as if someone who'd been stirred from a dream. Pigras's words separated into single letters. The image of Miu scratching Pigras and resisting him brought him back to reality.

"We'll do things differently now," said Pigras.

He grabbed Kalia by the tunic and dragged him. Kalia felt that Pigras had thought of something bad, but he surrendered to walking. Pigras took him upstairs, to the beautiful part of the house, where Miu squatted in a corner, tense. When she saw Kalia, she meowed in a jerking melody, as if she were posing a question. Pigras told Kalia to wait and went into the next room. Miu's repeated meow now sounded like a question with a howl at the end. *She doesn't understand why I am not setting her free*, realized Kalia, and he stroked her back, which startled her, and then she looked him straight in the eyes as if to see if he was still her friend. Kalia was now entirely present in the moment, his heart pounding in his ears.

Pigras returned with a pair of iron scissors and said, "Cut her claws!"

Kalia looked at him, startled with fear. He looked at the large scissors. Even if he knew how to do it, he'd hurt her with those scissors.

Kalia spread out his arms in wonder, as if in prayer, and stuttered, "I, I..."

I can't, he wanted to say. Perhaps he had said it silently.

"You can't?" Pigras said.

Kalia was catching his breath and nodding his head limply.

"I can, do you want me to do it?" Pigras asked as if he was playing.

Kalia said nothing, was waiting for something, a miracle.

Pigras continued. "But why should I, when I have you? Why should she hate me? I have been so stupid. I am her master and she needs to love me. She needs to hate *you!*"

Kalia watched him. There was drumming in his ears.

"That's why I have you," said Pigras.

Kalia now thought he understood it all. The walking around the courtyard, the void into which he had been sinking, the fact that nothing was his.

"Says who?" Kalia asked, watching the enormous scissors and then Miu on the floor.

"My mother told me," said Pigras, who was not afraid of Kalia at all and didn't have to hide anything from him. "We are good. And we don't have to do bad things. That's what our servants are for." It seemed for a moment that he was speaking with Zenobia's voice. Then he said, "Take the scissors!" He put the iron scissors into Kalia's limp hands and he now held them in front of Miu.

"These are big scissors," said Kalia. "These are big scissors, big scissors, big..."

"Stop repeating and cut!" Pigras shouted.

Kalia saw that it was all over, everything Menda had told him was over, it was over with the house; Pigras was saying something else, Kalia couldn't recognize the words, just his tone; as he moved the scissors from one hand to the other, it seemed that the wind was howling in his ears. And when the scissors stopped in his left hand, he used his right fist to punch Pigras in the nose with all his might, heard the punch, then watched with surprise as Pigras fell because he couldn't work out when exactly he had decided to hit him. He saw Pigras's nose bleeding as he, looking up as if blind, tried to crawl away from Kalia. He then turned his palms upward as if to defend himself from the next blow.

Kalia stood there for a moment, then squatted, took Miu, cut the leash, put the scissors into his pocket, pressed Miu to his chest. He looked at Pigras crawling.

The wind blew through the windows, down the stairs. Through the yard.

Scatterwind

AS I WAS saying, sometimes—especially when I move suddenly out of a space, such as a cave or a house—I unwittingly drag voices along and they cling to me like burdock. I'll kill you both, Pigras was howling, but only after he'd heard Kalia leave. His master's courage had returned, which I see so often. Courage is rare in slaves, and in animals.

Even in lions.

I once watched a lion nearly kill an antelope, not a fully grown one, but it had horns. It seemed the antelope was already finished, but it came to and stabbed the lion in the leg—and then it went quiet forever. The lion was a loner who was fighting for territory. That day it limped slightly. The next day the wound was a bit worse.

Then it lay in a bush, hiding. Days passed, and it wasn't hunting; the lion suffered hunger, but had to quench its thirst and went to the water, weak, lame. Another lion killed him easily, because that not fully grown antelope had killed him first.

Every cat, even a big one, fears small wounds.

As far as I have noticed, almost nothing in nature shows off with courage. Perhaps sometimes a mating male does, but he withdraws when he comes across a stronger specimen. When an animal confronts a stronger one, you can be sure it's a mother.

The thing with me is that I have no elements for motherhood; but I got involved by entering that stupid bag. And now that little slave had hit a master. Had I lifted his arm or had he done it himself? He ran with the small creature in his arms, the iron scissors in this pocket, like an antelope.

There is little courage, except in mothers.

To Run Like Scissors

DUST ROSE BEHIND Kalia. He held Miu tightly because, if she were to jump out of his embrace, she might go back to the yard. But the yard had been cut off together with the leash, he knew that, and he ran as if he were getting away from a void opening at his heels. Miu, pressed against his chest, heard the thunder of pumping blood; she no longer knew those were his arms, she wanted out, and he gripped her harder. He ran and ran, it seemed that he had to stop otherwise he'd explode. People turned after him and when Kalia saw there were more and more people, remembering that they were awaiting the victors, that Sabas and Zenobia were among them, he changed direction, heading down a shabby street, and then he walked quickly, still holding on hard to Miu, wishing that Miu didn't know where she was: that she didn't know the way back. He looked at her: she seemed lifeless. Had he suffocated her?

"Miu?" he whispered.

She didn't look at him, her tongue hung from her mouth.

His arms frightened him: he put her down and she flopped onto the ground. He stared at her, and then she started to get up slowly, her legs shivering, looking about. She then quickly withdrew from Kalia, as if she were afraid of him and quickly turned a corner. He watched in disbelief the corner behind which she'd disappeared. *Are you going to leave now?*

He ran toward where she had been; she wasn't there. He looked around for her, came out onto a bigger street, saw the heads of the crowd, and turned back. He went back to the place where he'd put Miu down on the ground, sat on a wall. A man waddled down the street and looked at him; Kalia tried to be invisible, transparent, as if neither he nor the man nor the street was there; he felt with his whole being that the search party was coming after him. But this man couldn't know any of it, because he was coming from the direction of the city.

He stopped and asked, "What are you doing here?"

Kalia couldn't think of anything, so he said, "I was running and now I'm taking a rest."

The man laughed into the air and went on his way.

Kalia went into the shade of a bush that grew behind the wall, crawled inside; it was a small yard of a dilapidated house. He sat there curled up with his elbows on his knees, thinking how good it would be if Menda was there, so he could hide behind her body.

"There you go, when you don't know how to play," he said, in the bush, as if talking to Pigras. "There you go," he repeated, full of fear.

He knew what it meant to be a slave.

Then he saw Miu in the little street: she was jumping into the air and rolling around, running in different directions as if chasing a fly, or perhaps it was a dance of sorts; perhaps she had only now understood that she was free, that he'd cut the leash. "Miu! Come here!" he said from the bush, his voice slightly raised. He didn't want to start toward her because he was worried that she might escape before she saw it was him. She raised her head, looked around.

"Come, I'm here!" He stood up.

Then she saw him and ran to him. *She was scared and had to hide*, he thought. She smelled him, made sure it was him, closed her eyes as if in affirmation. He picked her up, started walking slowly, glancing at her—she remained calm. He moved away farther from the sea and Ortigia, the location of the welcoming. He'd go toward the poor market; Sabas never went there.

He took a different turn each time he heard the victors shout and sing. Miu was calm on his left arm, and he rested his right on her lightly in order to keep her down; she looked around the same as he had the first time he went to town with Menda. Miu occasionally looked up to him as if to say: What an adventure! Then he too looked around, as if seeing through her eyes: dusty streets, houses and kitchen windows, the scent of celebration coming from the courtyards populated with slaves—the free people had gone to meet the victors, who must have arrived by now, because distant

ROBERT PERIŠIĆ

shouting came from below, which is where the heroes were, and Sabas and Zenobia. The sun had moved only slightly since they had walked through the yard, but the day had been sliced in half and that was long ago. The scissors swayed in his pocket.

Scatterwind

HUMANS HAD ALREADY domesticated all their animals, were working the land and had settled. Cats were the last to arrive. I wasn't in the business of counting the years—and the ways of tracking time were subject to change—but I know that cats arrived thousands of years after all the others. After the dogs, impersonating wolves, after the sheep, goats, pigs, cows...after they all were tamed. Humans couldn't have tamed any of those without dogs, who liked playing at being wolves. Even the chickens would have gotten away had there not been dogs chasing them back. The trick was always the same: dogs would bring them back to the humans and then the animals would see that humans had power over wolves; that they were powerful and had food.

I have not been to those parts, up in the steppes, so I cannot claim to know how they tamed the horses. It's easy to think that it was a simple case of some brazen person mounting a horse. But it took the Greeks a long time to think of such brazenness, that mounting a horse was even an option. As far as I remember, in the times when a man called Homer lived, they still did not ride horses, although they had them. They just drove fighter chariots.

Then, I remember, there was news of the centaur, a horse with a man's head and torso. I thought it was some kind of a joke, which it turned out to be. Because this happened when some Greeks got lost on their way up north and saw for the first time, in the distance, riders from the steppe, lost on their way south. A man on a horse in the distance, everything melded together in fear. What is this monster, half man, half horse?

A centaur. If you keep in mind that neither Achilles nor Hector had ever mounted a horse, their awe is less surprising. Later, much later, the rider became a common image.

There are large herds of cows today on wide pastures, managed by horse riders who guide them, look after them, direct them. Those cows know only that type of creature, horse and human united, because they never see humans without horses. When a cow from such a herd sees a human being on two legs for the first time, it is petrified. It sees a centaur who is half-missing. It's the opposite from those Greeks who first saw riders from the steppe. This is a halved creature.

There is a valid reason for the cows' fear. When a cow from a pasture herd sees this half centaur, a man on two legs, it's usually because it's about to die. The place it has been brought to is not a pasture.

Kalia, The Poor Market

KALIA STOPPED AT the edge of the poor market. Sabas didn't come here; he could rest. He stopped as if at the end of the road. Miu was wiggling, curious, and he stared at the market like someone who went to get something but forgot what it was that he'd come for. The colors alone hypnotized him, the market changed, shimmered in the sun; he stood with Miu in his arms, far from all things. It was that feeling again. But now, he knew, he was far and he was not going back. *Miu, is this the end of the world?* he thought.

Miu looked around, sniffed the air cautiously, and stayed put in his embrace.

Perhaps he could go toward Alexandros's house? He'd had Alexandros's house at the back of his mind when he headed this way. It was the only house, except Sabas's, which he had ever known. But what could he say to Alexandros when he knocked on his door with Miu in his arms? He couldn't think what he might say. It's best, he thought, to wait for nightfall and then knock on Alexandros's door and say he was lost. *He won't send me home in the dark.*

A woman watched him standing in the sun lost in thought, and the shadows were getting long. He saw her as one of his thoughts, and he didn't see her properly because he was thinking of Alexandros, but then she smiled and he noticed her. He remembered that this same woman had smiled at him before, when he used to come with Menda, a beautiful woman who had her own stand, and perhaps he had smiled back and she waved at him to come closer. He did and she offered him a piece of bread and a fried sardine, which made Miu sit up.

"Wait, I have some for her too. They were giving out food today," the woman said and put a sardine for Miu on the ground.

Kalia bent over to pick up the fish because he didn't want to release Miu. But she squirmed from his gentle grip. Kalia ate quickly and watched Miu; he thought of what the sailor had said, that she had to know where her home was, otherwise she'd run away. But it was impossible for him to hold her constantly. The woman interrupted his thoughts by asking if he was lost. He quickly said he was not. She gave him water. He poured water for Miu in a little hole in a rock. The woman said her name was Zoi. He straightened up and said Kalia, and Zoi asked him where he was headed.

"To Egypt," he said.

"Aha," she said and looked around, then up at the sky.

Kalia thought that she didn't know where Egypt was either, on which side of the sky, and when he looked down again he didn't see Miu near his legs so he started looking around. He then squatted and watched from that height.

Zoi said, "Leave her, she'll find some more food. There were sardines aplenty today, she can eat enough for today and tomorrow."

The word tomorrow startled him, like something unforeseen.

"But she doesn't know how to go home," he said, straining his eyes. "I have to find her."

Zoi pushed some dried figs in his hand and said, "Here, this way I don't have to take them home. I have to go too."

She watched him walking around the market as if sneaking up on things, looking down and trying to find the animal; she thought he walked like someone who'd done something wrong. Kalia walked around straining his eyes while images of the day went through his head; it had been a day bigger than any other. *Will the night be just as big?* he thought. Miu didn't know that they no longer had a home and she was probably looking for it.

He heard a dog barking from a side street and headed that way, looked into the small gardens and yards, but he did not find Miu, so he went back to the market and sat at the spot where Zoi had been. Then he went around again, peeked into other side streets, got close to Alexandros's house, thought about knocking on his door, got frightened by this thought, and went back to the main market square. The day was edging away and he thought that he should after all, while it was still light, go to Sabas's house, to try to sneak into Menda's room, but then in his mind he heard the punch he'd landed on the nose of Pigras, one of many such punches, only this time they would fall on Kalia's nose.

He sat again at the spot from which both Zoi and Miu had left him. Darkness inked up the sky. "Miu, I'm here," he called out softly. The market was empty and everything sounded louder. One could spot a green leaf or a half-rotten fruit on the ground, and he jumped up and stuffed it all in his pocket, ate some. He thought now it was really time to go to the dead-end street and tell Alexandros that he was lost, but he sat back down again at the same spot, the darkness getting thicker, and then he heard a meow behind him and before he saw her, she'd climbed up his tunic and into his lap.

He'd already been feeling cold, and he waited for her to settle in his lap because they had to go somewhere. A silhouette flickered for a second, a male voice was heard from one of the small side streets. Kalia stared ahead, knowing Miu could see better, and everything was probably okay as long as she was quiet in his arms. They walked to Alexandros's house even though he had no idea what he would do when they got there, but it was a place he knew and it was at the end of the street.

He took slow steps, as if balancing on something very thin, thinking about what he would when he arrived at the house.

Knocking might make a lot of noise in the dark silence. Alexandros would get a fright, might even shout and let everyone know Kalia was on the run. As they got closer Kalia thought that Alexandros had never smiled at him. He stopped some twenty steps from the house. Perhaps Alexandros would take him in if he told him he was lost, but he definitely wouldn't take Miu. He imagined leaving her outside the door: where would she go, looking for her way home? If he lost her now his running away would be wasted. But it was getting colder; he moved a bit closer to the house. He embraced Miu with both arms.

"Miu, forgive me," he whispered. "I have to leave you here."

But he held on to her. The moonlight briefly reflected in her glistening eyes, and she meowed. Kalia heard sounds from the barn. *Mikro*, he thought. Mikro could hear them.

Kalia got very close to the house and saw that Mikro had poked his head out of the hole on the stable door.

"Hi, Mikro," he whispered.

Holding Miu with one hand, with the other he took out of his pocket the leftovers he had gathered at the market and gave them to Mikro. The animal chewed, and Kalia had a memory of the first time he'd seen his gray legs and hooves, when Menda told him that donkeys kick with their hind legs. He had always looked at those hooves, thinking how Mikro had a way to defend himself, and he'd been glad. He could see the hooves each time because the door was broken at the bottom.

He watched Mikro's dark outline, heard his breath; Kalia got on his tiptoes to try to see Mikro's eyes, reaching out to him and touching his forehead. He seemed like a good boy, but Menda had told him that he could kill with his hind legs if he got upset.

But it was cold, and he was more afraid of Alexandros than of Mikro, and the door was broken at the bottom and he could crawl in; Miu could too, and Mikro's breath was warm.

"Mikro, you remember me?" he whispered.

Mikro was mysterious in the dark. Kalia stood by the door a bit longer, stroked him once again and Mikro was slightly startled, it seemed that he'd touched his eye. Kalia whispered, "Sorry, I didn't mean to," and decided not to raise his hand like that again. He stood by the door so that Mikro could get used to him a bit more, and he was thinking that it was best if he went in feet first, although it would be a bit awkward. But if Mikro got frightened, he'd kick right as Kalia was crawling in, so it was better if he kicked him in the legs. *But what if I can't walk later, how am I going to go on?* he thought as he lay by the door, holding Miu with one hand. She now wanted to be set free. *Hopefully she won't go far*, he thought.

She was on the ground and he felt her near his face, as if she was trying to peek inside his thoughts. He was considering what might happen if he couldn't walk: Alexandros would see him in the morning and they would come to pick him up. Pigras would beat him, but perhaps not too much if he couldn't walk. If he couldn't walk he'd lie at Menda's side and they wouldn't be able to sell him to anyone, and if he didn't start walking eventually, they wouldn't waste food on him, they'd throw him out into the street to die and he would then beg, and Menda would bring him something to eat from time to time. He'd be cold and maybe he would die, but he would be in some street far from Pigras, and the best place was at the poor market.

Kalia got up and squatted again, because he realized that he had to feel the bottom edge of the door with his hands; the wood was dry and rotting, sharp at the bottom, and he took out the scissors from his pocket and passed them along the door's bottom edge, lightly pressing. The door squealed as if it would fall apart, bits fell off it. He measured the height of the gap with his hands. Miu wandered around near his hands, her fur touching him as he whispered to Mikro, "Don't worry, I have more food for you." Miu was already meowing; it seemed that she was peeking into the shed. The donkey let out a tiny whispering sound.

Kalia looked up again and saw that Mikro's snout was not poking out any longer because he was looking down at Miu. Kalia lay down again and put his head closer to the gap, felt for Miu who was facing in. Were they negotiating? Gently, he whispered, "Mikro, this is Miu. She's small and we are not dangerous." He reached inside his pocket, grabbed all the food he had, and tossed it in. He heard Mikro chew. He touched Miu under the door, slowly took her in his

ROBERT PERIŠIĆ

arms, moved her to the side. He'd stick a bit of one of his legs in first, left foot first, perhaps best keep his heel up in case Mikro thought it a new bite of food. He rolled onto his stomach. Pushed his left foot in. Stayed that way for a while. He thought he felt Mikro's breath on his foot; it tickled. After some time he put both his legs in, up to the knees. He felt Mikro's breath on his calves and stayed that way for a while. Slowly, he rolled onto his back and then sat up. Pressing down with his arms, he drew in his legs. There was no kick. His legs were in, and now he had to lift his knees in order to get his lower back up and push with his elbows, put his shoulders to the ground, drag his heels on the floor, press up with his forearms, wiggle like the fish that look up at the sky from the market stalls. Mikro didn't kick.

His back kept getting stuck, but he pushed along in tiny movements, his spine crackling between his shoulder blades. When his shoulders were through he rested awhile, giving Mikro some more time before he moved his head under. He then felt Miu next to his face, she climbed up against his shoulder, then he felt her tiny weight on his chest, inside the stable.

The sky was scribbled over with tiny holes of the stars; the fish had been separated from its head; he no longer felt cold, he'd warmed up. Except for his head, his body was inside the shed and felt the warmth created by Mikro's body. Kalia felt a sleepy tiredness; it was a long time ago when he woke up in Sabas's house that morning.

Miu was on his chest. He'd planned to duck his head under by turning on his side—because now that his shoulders were in he could turn to his side, and make pulling his head under easier, but he didn't want to move Miu from his body. *She and Mikro are watching each other and talking silently*, he thought. He heard Mikro move, felt his breath next to his knee; Mikro perhaps thought the cat's tiny head had huge legs attached to it. But Mikro hadn't turned his back on them, he was not going to kick. And that's how Kalia fell asleep.

Scatterwind

I WAS INTO all things related to heating and cooling. I saw that living beings could soak up the heat from the sun. A tree did it, a snake did it. The leaves drank in the light, just like snake skin did, which I had at first thought consisted of tiny leaves, like lizard skin: lovely, green tiles set in order as if on a roof. And as for the scales that cover fish, I thought they were tiny leaves, but it was only a similarity, as if the scales were a step between leaves and skin. And maybe they were because I have seen people whose skin starts to turn back into scales and leaves. That must be a memory sickness, I thought, because the human being contains the memory of the lizard and the tree.

Skin is, I thought, in fact a large leaf that covers a being. And only some beings who were well wrapped with the leaf skin were always warm. I could see that this was so with the animals who sucked on their mothers, with humans and birds. Birds have everything: skin and leaves over it, and each feather is like a leaf and feathers make a covering for the skin. Skin, with the leaves of feathers over it, some with colors of flowers—birds are a conglomeration of everything, perhaps because they catch the most light and travel with it. If I would meet any of my family from the higher layers of the atmosphere, and if they asked me what life was like, I would say: life is warm. It's the first thing you notice. That's how nowadays they catch people crossing borders at night. I have always seen this, but there are now machines that detect heat emanating from bodies. I have always seen this, but I didn't quite understand how they produced heat at night too, as if they had been filled with the sun. I saw that the creatures who were wrapped with the leaf of skin eat more than those creatures who are not as warm. A warm body is like a woodstove, and food is the logs. I watched what they ate, what food was. The sun was stored in food, I saw, it had soaked the light. Food had also been alive, until recently. Life was warm with light and the warmer the creatures were, I thought, the more interesting. I had not expected the fact that their bodies were as warm in the winter as they were in the summer. I saw that it was an invention that came together with the mind. Smart animals had clever bodies that stored and imitated the sun. The body of that donkey, who was very smart, made plenty of heat and the boy was saved.

ROBERT PERIŠIĆ

3. To Walk

Kalia, As If Returning Home

TO ANYONE ASKING, on the streets of Syracuse, Kalia answered that he had a mother who was sick and bedridden, and that he had a father who was a soldier and who would be back. He had to say this, although he'd rather have told the truth, it would have been the easiest thing, because he was entirely used to the fact that he had no parents. But he couldn't tell the truth. Still, he couldn't appear as if he was forcing himself to lie, because if he'd said that thing about his parents without much conviction, just to get it over with, some people might be compelled to ask more questions, he noticed, and he'd have to invent more lies. He'd feel fear then, and then he thought he saw them trying to see that fear in his eyes. Perhaps they weren't trying to see it, but he knew that they must not find it. He had to invent everything, and only he knew where he was. He and Miu and Mikro, inside whose stable Kalia was now going in headfirst.

The ideas of mother and father were strange at first, but he knew he should talk about them as if they were real. As he spoke, he tried to forget that they weren't real, and so everything went more smoothly, and he no longer said Mother, but Mama, saw that it worked better. And the made-up images ran more smoothly with time because he realized the following: in order to speak convincingly on a subject, you have to imagine it not only in words, but in space; her lying in a room like Menda's, in tepid light, and him who was fighting distant enemies. She had long light hair, spread around her as she rested; he said her name was Zoi, and his father, whom he had named Diocles, had gone somewhere toward the sun, waving goodbye in the blinding light. Although they did not exist, they were somewhat real too, he'd gotten used to them.

People sometimes asked him if his mother was feeling better and he'd say that she was a little better, and the fact that others cared for his mother, for even a moment, for her who lay with her hair loose on her bed, it felt good, and it was not even that sad. With time it came to seem to him that these parents had, in a way, existed, but that they had lost him somehow.

He said his father had brought Miu from a faraway land, from Egypt. "She's important there," he said. "The goddess Artemis loved her, but she had a different name there. I forgot what it was, but my father knows. I have to ask him when he comes back," he said.

She'd be taken in if she went back, and maybe they would accept him too if he took her there. This was, in fact, a conversation he only had with Miu, and he could talk to her easily because he didn't have to hide anything in front of her, or in front of Mikro who understood everything; the donkey knew that Kalia would come when it got dark, that he'd find something for him at the market, and that he'd even bring him dried figs sometimes. He knew that Kalia was cold and that this was the reason why he was trying to stuff himself between Mikro's body and the wooden wall.

Kalia could pull Mikro to the wall and huddle down under him because Mikro stood as he slept, but he didn't sleep much, it seemed that he was snoozing. He could tell them whatever he wanted, whispering in the night, or just mouthing words.

Kalia woke up with the first rays of light or even earlier—the nights were long—and he'd clean up quietly around Mikro, using the small shovel Alexandros kept in the stable, and he'd repeat this at night, because Alexandros paid little attention to how Mikro lived, though Kalia would leave a bit of dung rolled up in straw in a corner so Alexandros had something to clean up when he remembered, and this heap would be drying up for days. Using the scissors, Kalia slowly whittled the door at the bottom to make the gap wider, and he'd put a board up against it at night which made the space warmer.

Kalia was afraid someone bad might wander down the street and notice how worn out the door was or that the wind might tear the door off its hinges, and he thought about how he might make them more solid. But how to do this without being noticed or making noise? It would take a real miracle, but he couldn't stop thinking about it because everything depended on that door. It must not fall to pieces because then Alexandros would put a new door in. A rope was tied outside the door so that Mikro could not go out if the door fell apart. That's how he understood Alexandros was aware of the door's weakness. Kalia feared a new door every day. Luckily Alexandros was afraid to walk on the ground so he must have been postponing such work. Although Kalia only came when night fell and was completely silent, a different master would have probably noticed him by now. But Alexandros worked with letters, not only teaching them but also writing—he'd once said this to Kalia while he was teaching him to read and write, and he said it in a way that Kalia saw that this was of the highest importance. It is one thing to learn the letters and another to write, Alexandros told him then with a look as if nothing more could be said. Kalia didn't really understand, but the tone had stuck with him. And he would think of how Alexandros was writing up there or at least he wrote in the day—because Kalia didn't hear him much at night—and he imagined how many letters Alexandros had written and what they meant. He already knew that through letters one could get some things that were otherwise invisible. Who knew what Alexandros thought about, but it was definitely not about Mikro or things beneath him. He must have been thinking of something above. That is not fair, he should sometimes also think about Mikro, Kalia thought. But it was also good this way, because otherwise everything would fall through, he thought, and he couldn't decide what was good or bad luck, like that time with Pigras and Miu, and he saw that this wasn't clear, since there are no endings to things.

He often watched Miu and wondered what she thought. When she lay on top of him, purring or snoozing, he didn't think that she was thinking of anything in particular, except: we are friends and this is good. And when she was up and wide awake, he saw that she was alert to everything, watched and thought: *What will be next?* Kalia also thought that was the most important thing. *I'll see later what was lucky and unlucky.*

Kalia would go down to the sea at dawn, and although he was cold, he would wash, because Zoi had told him this on the first day when he went back to look for her at the poor market and asked her if he could be of service to her; she said he could not while he was so filthy, and the second day she brought him a tunic that he'd only use for sleeping. It was an enormous night tunic that had belonged to her deceased father, which Kalia didn't mind since it was so long that he could roll himself up in it twice, once he had curled up into the fetal position for sleeping, and Miu would find room in it too.

When he washed in the sea, he had to run around naked for a while in order to dry before putting on his tunic for the day, and that's why he went a bit farther than the nearest beach, to a small sandy one that he could run around barefoot on, because he didn't want to ruin his sandals. He'd no longer be cold then, would walk with a lightness toward the poor market where he'd find Zoi, and Miu would come and go. He was no longer afraid of losing her because she knew where home was. He was sure she went to see Mikro during the day and slept there in the quiet, while Kalia stayed away from Alexandros's house during the day. This is how he thought about it in the daylight, that it was Alexandros's house. But when night fell, he'd head over there as if heading home, to his house.

Zoi was his daytime family, she always had food for him, which is why he named his invented mother after her. But later he wondered if he should change the name because his imaginary mother was sick, and she did look a bit like Zoi, and perhaps that was not a good thing—this is what woke him up one night, a dream in which the real Zoi was sick and lying down like his imaginary mother. Afraid, he told Mikro about it quietly. He asked Zoi in the morning if she wanted him to change the name of his mother, because she had to be sick and in bed, so that no one would ask him where his mother was. Zoi placed her hands on her chest. She had thought that Kalia had no one, but it was hard for her to hear it, especially since she would gladly take him home with her, she said, if only her husband were less of an idiot. But her husband did not want other people's children, only his own, so he was begging gods for it, and sacrificing his best offerings to them, fertile animals, and she sometimes wished she were not there so that it would all stop. Kalia had a foggy grasp on this, but he saw that Zoi was unhappy, and that it was something like a secret.

       ROBERT PERIŠIĆ

Zoi then told him not to change his mother's name—she wouldn't catch her illness, she said, and it was a beautiful illness that simply made you invisible.

Scatterwind

IT SEEMS TO me that it's easier to imagine things when you have no home. The person who has plenty needs to imagine less, and things that are possessed are no longer mysterious. I saw that when humans stopped walking and settled, they started to consider everything in terms of ownership. While humans were in motion and collecting and hunting their food, ownership wasn't on their mind because wherever they were, they'd be leaving the next day, carrying along with them whatever they had. But when they settled, they became owners of their land. With the help of dogs, they became the owners of their animals too.

People who grew up on the land knew they could never own cats, even after they'd become owners of everything else. The cats came last, came on their own, dogs hadn't brought them. Dogs never liked this fact because they'd domesticated all the other animals. True, they had let humans think that they had done the job of domestication, because dogs are not vain. They didn't mind that humans always spoke about

ROBERT PERIŠIĆ

themselves, and how they had themselves domesticated sheep, goats, donkeys, and the rest. Humans are like that, the most important thing for them is to be the protagonists. Dogs weren't interested in any stories, they had enough to do keeping everything together, they just minded the way that cats had turned up without asking for permission.

At the end of the day, that's how cats came to be domesticated, because they went directly to the humans. Every dog knows that. Everything went counter to the usual procedure and dogs are to this day irritated when they remember how cats came to be friends with humans despite not having done anything, any work or committed to any order whatsoever.

Dogs couldn't believe the way cats behaved. They hadn't gone up to the counter. They went directly to the boss. Humans watched them like: look here, I've tamed another animal. Dogs crossed their paws and said: fine then, you deal with them.

In The Name Of Imagined Things

ZOI SMILED WHENEVER she saw Kalia, so at first he had the impression that she was always happy. But now Kalia knew that she was happy with him, at the market, but not at home, and then Kalia didn't want her to be unhappy because of him. He saw that she thought it was sad the way Kalia lived so he told her it wasn't that bad, really not bad at all, and it wasn't true that he had no one because he had Miu and Mikro and her, Zoi, and he had Menda too, the only bad thing was that he couldn't go and see Menda—the rest was fine.

That's how he told her about Mikro and Menda, because Zoi didn't know them; he told her everything, how he'd cut the leash and run away, and he was glad that he wasn't alone with his own story.

Kalia wanted to help Zoi at the market, and she wanted the same thing, so she could give him food as if he'd earned it. That's why he stood next to her and was always handing things to her, but since she heard the whole story, she became afraid that they might be looking for him. Not only had he run off but he'd also hit a master, stolen a cat and a pair of scissors. So she got him a large cap that covered not only his ears but also half of his face.

Kalia was happy with Zoi at the market and when the time came for her to leave, it always felt too soon. He wanted to walk with her at least halfway, but she didn't want him to. There were streets Zoi didn't like on her way home, streets she'd rather avoid, but she had to go down them when she was in a hurry to get home. Men who met her told her she was beautiful. It's not always good to be told you're beautiful.

"Especially if it's a sailor saying it," she said.

She told this to Kalia so that he wouldn't veer down these streets, and he thought that a sailor might be able to tell him where Egypt was.

"I'll walk you," said Kalia and puffed up his chest as if he were strong.

When she'd walk with Kalia men might leave her alone because they'd think she had a son, Zoi thought, but still she said no.

"I'll come back the long way," Kalia said. "I have the scissors, I'm not afraid."

"You don't walk like that," she said.

Even on the first day she'd noticed a shadow in his gait, and when he later told her he was a runaway, she understood why he was trying to walk as if he were invisible.

And how else might you learn to walk if you were born a slave?

It's not just fear, she thought while she watched him, *it's a world that belongs to others*. And even though he had escaped, he'd not left that world with his whole body; it was all still there, in the air, even on the sunniest of days. Her eyes had gotten used to it, but she now thought she might need to tell him, at least quietly, because sooner or later his gait would give him away.

She told him he walked as if he wanted to be invisible, but that it was clear for everyone to see. He couldn't walk down those streets with her in that way. He shouldn't walk that way—there were people there who watch as you're approaching. And not just there. That's why he should invent a different walk, just like he'd invented his mother.

Kalia was deflated, his arms hung by his body. He had really sometimes thought how good it would be to be invisible, but he wasn't aware that his thoughts could be seen.

Zoi squatted and put her hands on his shoulders. "You see," she said, "some thoughts can be seen, the way a smile can be seen. Some thoughts are visible in the eyes, some in the body. The fact that you want to be invisible is seen through the fact that you look over your shoulder to check if anyone has seen you."

He wanted to tell her that he had to look over his shoulder because he had to see in front of himself and behind himself.

"I'd like to see like Mikro," he said. "He sees all around. That's how his eyes are placed, so that he only has to shift his head a little and he can see me behind him."

ROBERT PERIŠIĆ

"But your eyes aren't like that," Zoi said. "You know why donkeys have such eyes?"

"So that they can see, to see who's coming from the side or from behind."

"That's right. And sheep have eyes like that, and goats," Zoi said. "That's because they were always attacked and hunted."

"I'm also hunted," Kalia said.

"Human eyes face forward, far into the distance. That's how you have to walk, otherwise it'll be clear they're looking for you. They'll track you down easier if it's obvious."

Kalia thought about this. Then he wanted to show her that he could walk differently and pushed his chest out and started walking like a soldier. Miu walked next to him and watched him, slightly surprised.

"That's a bit stiff," said Zoi.

"Look at Miu. Her eyes are also facing forward. Light sometimes reflects in them because she is looking straight ahead."

That could work, she thought.

She said, "Miu is also alert. Sometimes she looks back and is watching everything, but see how she walks. As if no one rules the Earth."

Kalia watched Miu. "You think?"

Zoi thought she was speaking as a mother, the mother Kalia had invented, and the mother spoke in the name of imagined things, as if the world were different from how it was.

"Look at Miu when she walks calmly," she said. "They don't rule if they're not in your head."

Zoi knew Kalia had to think away from people, that he had to walk through Syracuse as if no one ruled the place, and then, walking like a cat, he might actually escape them.

Scatterwind

CATS CAME BECAUSE of mice. Mice came because humans stored food. Mice saw that humans were the only animals that had storage and decided to stick with them. They became so attached to humans that over time a particular variety of mouse came to being, the house mouse. They're not field or bush mice, or some other sort—there are dozens of types of mice—but there is only one breed of house mouse. They live in houses. They are humanity's mice.

While humans moved, they didn't have their own brand of mouse. That's why they didn't have cats either. When humans moved they didn't have cats for another reason, because cats, in fact, are not wanderers. Humans think that cats are wanderers, but humans are much more of a wandering species than cats. Cats don't stray far from their territory. It has happened that when humans moved, they had cat friends if they had found them as kittens. I've seen that. But cats didn't like to roam far with humans.

I've seen, though only occasionally, a cat become so attached to a human—thinking the person was its mother, or that it too was human—that it traveled on their shoulder. I remember a man who carried a cat in this manner, this was some ten thousand years ago, and they traveled together on a small sailing boat. I was studying sailing so I went with them all the way to that island they now call Cyprus. The man was a significant character, and his tomcat had sat on his shoulder and accompanied him to that island where none of its species existed. They were inseparable and I later heard, the one time I went back there, that they had been buried together. Recently, the people who uncover graves found them lying together, ten thousand years underground.

It has always happened that someone tames a member of another species, but that's different from a whole species being tame, which can only happen when many of them, over time, play together.

Kalia, Stones

THAT DAY AT the market Kalia heard people saying they'd conquered something; he wondered where Zoi was, why she was late, he didn't know what had happened, but everything reminded him of the day he ran away with Miu. There was a similar commotion, there was something that resembled joy with a sharp scent. There were smiles on faces, and their eyes shone excessively. He looked to see where Miu was. She sat on the wall surrounding the market. He didn't know how she got up there, but she often sat on that wall. She sat in the sun and watched over everything; this time her ears were tense. She looked at Kalia and he blinked.

Kalia thought how Miu moved up and down, while his world was flat. He had to find a corner, instead of climbing up, because in this joy that was pouring in from Ortigia there was a force, something that brought back Pigras's smile to his thoughts.

Some people came to the market shouting in unison, "Long live Dionysius!"

Then they shouted, "Long live Syracuse! Long live the catapult!"

He looked up. Miu was watching him as if to say, If you're going to run, so am I.

Zoi turned up at this very moment with her younger sister who always gave Kalia a nice smile, but never spoke; she helped Zoi carry goods to the market and then went back home immediately, pushing an empty cart. As he helped sort out the vegetables, Zoi explained to him that Syracusans had conquered the Carthaginian town on the other side of Sicily.

"More people had died there than could fit in at this market," she said.

"That means we won?" Kalia asked.

"Yes. But the Carthaginians will send their ships over all the same."

"So that means we haven't won yet?"

"You stick with Miu," Zoi said. "They send horses to war, yoke donkeys, send dogs wherever they are needed, but they can't send a cat anywhere." Then Zoi added, "But you know, you'll have to find some shelter. You won't be able to hide with Mikro forever."

"But there's no better place."

"We'll think of something. You'll do best to leave Syracuse. To some less famed place. If they tell you they're famed, avoid them and move on."

"And you, Zoi?"

"I'll be here. When they stop telling me I'm beautiful, I'll live in peace. And this sister of mine, who's a little slow, I have to take care of her."

The men who had come to the market were again shouting, "Long live Dionysius! Long live the catapult!"

Kalia knew that Dionysius was the ruler of Syracuse, but he didn't know about the catapult. Zoi explained that the catapult was a device invented by Dionysius's people that could propel rocks far into the distance. That's how they conquered that Carthaginian city, by constantly pummeling it with rocks. Kalia imagined what it looked like to be pummeled by large rocks. He imagined it, but he saw the others at the market didn't imagine it, and he remembered that they, the Syracusans, did the pummeling.

He also wanted to rejoice. Then he imagined what it was like to be the one throwing these big rocks, and it falls over there somewhere, on some people you've never seen. But he then saw the image of these rocks falling from above, as if he was in the enemy town.

He felt that Syracuse was at his heels, that he was and was not in it. He watched everything from a distance again. Menda used to tell him he had to stop this kind of looking at things, that he had to look at something he liked.

He looked around for Miu. She wasn't up there on the wall. She must have gone to Mikro's. Dionysius's people brought a lot of sardines, which they started to grill at the market. The rest started shouting, "Long live Dionysius!

Long live the catapult!" Now the catapult seemed to be something that rains down a lot of fish from above.

Then Kalia saw Menda—she stood at the edge of the market, watching the crowd. For a moment, he thought he was imagining things. He ran toward her. Menda spread her arms and embraced him. He smelled her scent, the scent of the house in which he had slept. It really was her. He couldn't speak, just looked up at Menda. She was so hurried that she hadn't even managed to scold him, which is what he'd expected. She looked around. She told him that they don't let her go to the market, that Zenobia had slapped her when he ran away, that they took in another woman to do the shopping because they thought Menda would be helping him. She couldn't go anywhere, although she'd been telling them that he, Kalia, was a naughty boy whom she'd drag in by his ears if she saw him. She pulled his ear softly, and then stroked his head.

He didn't know they beat Menda because of him and he didn't know how to fix that so he was silent, but he was in fact brimming with words suddenly, without order, in his head. She could sneak out now, Menda said, because the masters had gone to Apollo's Temple to chant for Dionysius, but she had to rush home because a celebration was being prepared there. She had brought him food and a clean tunic.

He told her that Zoi was helping him, and pointed at Zoi. The two women nodded at each other. He said that he slept at Mikro's and that he wasn't cold there. Her face was joyous. She told him to not go back at all, because Pigras's nose was still swollen and was probably bent permanently. If he returned, or was found, Kalia's punishment would be big, to set an example. Menda told him to hide somewhere and put on the clean tunic, and bring her the dirty one.

"Your posture is good," she said when he returned. "Has someone been teaching you gymnastics?"

"No, I just walk."

Chanting came in waves from a distance, for Dionysius, and Menda waddled off quickly toward Ortigia. He watched her leave and when she disappeared, he looked above the houses. The sky was sliced in half and the song celebrating the catapult resounded like thunder.

Scatterwind

CATS CAME WITH houses, wheat, and mice. Humans weren't the first ones to store away food for winter, crows did it too, burying food in a thousand spots, and memorizing each one. Only humans—slowly and accidentally—came up with agriculture, and once they took it seriously, had plenty of food. They stored this food in the houses they'd built, or in storage barns they'd built next to the houses. As opposed to the crows, humans didn't take care of who might be watching them. Because crows, once they notice someone is watching, pretend to bury their food: they dig as if, but leave nothing behind. Humans, since they always thought no one else understood anything, paid no attention to who might be watching. Of course, everyone was watching, especially the mice who lived in the houses anyway. Cats also kept an eye on things since they were keeping an eye on the mice.

People of course had no idea what was going on. They paid no attention to the cats nor did they notice that the cats stole toward the houses at night and went into the barns.

It turned out that they didn't mind, because cats weren't interested in wheat. Cats hated wheat, it made them feel sick; they caught mice and baby rats, and humans saw that they shared a line of interest. Cats befriended humans by doing what came to them naturally. At first they were mere acquaintances, then some children made friends with kittens and the kittens got used to human scent. When they grew up, they stayed close to their friends' homes. They were simply there and no task could be given to them except for the ones they did anyway. No one had a reason to tie a cat on a leash because that would stop them from hunting. No one had a reason to teach cats anything apart from what they were already doing, and they saw that cats didn't want any lessons. There was no reason to stick cats in a cage or close them off in a pen. People didn't pay attention to whether the cats might leave. They were of no use when tied or trapped, so they didn't bother. They could be around and hunt mice, or they could leave. Cats remained free. They were there, but were not part of the property.

I saw that humans had the problem that once they owned something it ceased to have any mystery. Every secret vanishes from things possessed. This didn't happen with cats. Because no one, in fact, owned a cat.

Ships Sail At Dawn

THE NIGHTS WERE getting warmer. Those first days after running away, Kalia thought of the summer as a salvation, because then he'd be able to sleep wherever he liked. But now he didn't feel like leaving Mikro's stable even if it was getting a little stuffy. Zoi had told him several times, in muted tones, that he needed to take advantage of the summer and leave Syracuse, at least to one of the nearby towns, somewhere no one could recognize him. He nodded, but he was no longer looking forward to summer.

Zoi read his palm and told him he'd have a long life, in a beautiful and distant place, and that Miu would travel with him. Kalia was not at all glad to hear this, and Zoi said she was only joking, and that she couldn't read palms.

He later asked, "Zoi, if I were to leave, what would happen to you?" He said it as if he were looking after her.

"I'll be fine, don't worry," she said with a sparkling smile.

"But what happens when you don't see someone again?"

"Perhaps you'll forget me a tiny bit."

One night he woke from a dream. Miu was out wandering around and he whispered the dream to Mikro. He'd gone far and moved with the wind. When he wanted to speak in his dream, he realized that his language no longer existed and he was watching everything from the air, which was what he was made of. He saw Mikro from up above, among the pines, and he saw Miu, who was looking up at the sky as if she was not alive, and then he saw her again walking, except that he, Kalia, was not alive; he had been dead for so long that it seemed impossible to imagine he'd ever walked on the ground. Then he heard a whisper: "Kalia?" That was not part of the dream.

"Kalia?"

Mikro was now looking out of the hole in his door. Kalia looked up from below. He could see, he thought, someone's legs in the darkness.

"It's me, Menda."

Kalia crawled under Mikro's door. Menda was waiting for him down the little street and they went to the poor market, which, now empty, had taken on the color of the moon. They sat on a shaded step. Just like when he set out to bathe in the sea at dawn, Syracuse felt dead in the bleak silence, but this never frightened him. It was when he most felt it belonged to him.

"You can't stay here, you know that," Menda said.

"I don't know," he said.

He'd already heard it from Zoi. But it seemed that this was his home.

"What if you get sick?"

Kalia thought of the nights when he huddled next to Mikro and pulled him closer. Mikro slept standing up, but when Kalia kept pulling him closer, he understood, and for a few nights, when Kalia shivered, Mikro lay down and kept Kalia warm in the corner.

And maybe because he couldn't afford to get sick, this winter he'd had fewer sniffles than ever.

"The nights are warmer now," he said.

"But what will happen next winter? And people get sick in the summer too."

Kalia felt sure he would not fall ill in the summer, and next winter seemed so far it may as well never come.

"The ships sail at dawn," Menda said at the empty market, where everything echoed louder, and then everything fell very silent.

Kalia watched her face as she caught her breath from up above, from the source of the moonlight. Those ships that she had mentioned, it was as if they made a line in her throat and she covered her face with her hands. Kalia saw a cat's silhouette on the other side of the market, it could have been Miu. Better she not come close, he thought, because as far as Menda was concerned, everything that had happened was her fault.

"The ships sail at dawn," Menda said after clearing her throat. "They are going to places where everything related to Syracuse is far away."

ROBERT PERIŠIĆ

"To Egypt?"

Menda was startled. "No. They go north. Master Sabas calls it the Sea of Chronos. Some think it's the end of the world, but I know it isn't."

Kalia was afraid of those words and wanted not to hear them.

"They go to Liburnia."

"Your Liburnia?" He sat up.

Menda gazed toward the sea, which shimmered in the distance, reflecting the moonlight, and she wished to reach farther with her eyes; she lifted her chin as if she wanted to look over a wall that time had built.

"Yes, there," said Menda. "There your slavery will be a distant thing."

Kalia hadn't quite understood and repeated, "Your Liburnia?"

Yes, my Liburnia, thought Menda. It had been shrinking in her mind for decades, cut off; it had become like something imagined. But now Kalia could go back there and everything burst into life again: her bay, loved ones, their names. If they're alive, they'll have changed—time had passed behind the frozen image.

"Up there your slavery will be a thing of the past. Like down here, where my freedom is a thing of the past. When they brought me here and when I said I was not a slave, it didn't matter. So you will return to Liburnia, but it will be the other way around: you'll be free. We'll swap places," she said.

She said she was gifting him her freedom from Liburnia, the life that had been taken from her; may he know in his heart that he was free and may he know to never look back. She said she was glad that the cat had shown up and that he had punched Pigras. Kalia watched her in disbelief.

"They need to take you on board and then everything will fall into place," she said. "Maybe that's why the cat turned up, maybe it was sent."

Kalia was stunned. "You think someone sent Miu to me?" he asked.

"Latra," she said. "Latra could have done it."

He thought something strange was happening to Menda. She had mentioned Latra before, but he'd never seen her. Perhaps the ships will be invisible too?

"Latra is, you know, like Apollo. Only in Liburnia the sky belongs to women."

"You think that Miu came from Liburnia?"

Menda thought about it. Perhaps she ought to tell him that was true and then he wouldn't rush to Egypt. But she knew she'd be lying because there were no cats in Liburnia, or at least she'd never seen any.

"I had prayed to Latra to return me to Liburnia," Menda said. "Then, later, I prayed to her to let me see my family one last time. And years and years have passed, and my mother has never heard from me. I was angry with Latra and the sky became empty for me. But when you ran away, I called her again. And tonight master Sabas came and told me about the ships. I don't know, Kalia, who has been sent from where, but if you go back there free, the circle will be complete."

Kalia looked at her. "Sabas knows about the ships?"

Menda thought maybe she shouldn't have mentioned Sabas, but yes, he'd told her the whole thing because he too wanted Kalia to board one. There were many things that Kalia didn't know, too many things to talk about in a single night sitting in egg-white moonlight. She had thought she'd tell him everything one day in the future, when he could grasp it. *But he ran away with the cat and those ships sail at dawn.* Menda said that Sabas told her this because she was from Liburnia.

"They'll be making an apoikia there. You know what that is? It's a home away from home. You'll build a city. You who sail on those ships. That is a distant home, apoikia."

Kalia looked at her, his eyes and mouth wide open. She'd told him too many unimaginable things, she'd confused him with Latra and other details, and she was gripped by fear that he wouldn't go to the port. Kalia felt a quiet pain in his head, his temples throbbed, he felt something large behind Menda's words that had made his shoulders contract. He'd have to leave at dawn, that's what he had heard.

"Those who first build a colony get first bids on a home," Menda continued. "And their children too. Here, the only thing awaiting you is punishment."

She said she knew how hard it must be for him to leave, said it was difficult for her too, and he could hear it in her strained voice. She said he was her only grandson, and she'd never spoken those words to him before; she mentioned Liburnian words that he learned from her—that he didn't even know were Liburnian—said that other Greeks didn't know such things and that was why he'd have an easier time there. She said he must never tell anyone he was a slave, ever; told him to tell them on the ship that he had come from Gela, that his father died as a soldier, that his mother was dead, that he was sent by a good man who had fed him, that he knows how to read and write, and they'd believe that he was from a good family; she asked him to repeat all this.

She told him to board the largest ship because that was where Oikistes would be; he was the boss and if he took him on board, no one could kick him out. She asked him to repeat: Oikistes.

She had brought him a clean tunic. She told him to wash in the sea at the crack of dawn and dress in a clean tunic.

"Get there as if you're attending a celebration, let that be their first impression of you, then they'll remember you like this."

As Menda spoke Miu turned up. She brushed against Kalia and sniffed Menda.

"You remember me, eh? You've grown nicely," she said and touched Miu with her hand.

"Can animals board the ships?" Kalia asked.

"Please don't not go because of her," Menda said. She then looked at him and understood. She thought awhile and said,

"If they take you, they'll let her on too, she's not heavy. Others will be taking animals, and plants, and all the things they think they won't find there. They'll have to take a lot of food, and there are always mice."

"Okay," said Kalia with a tight throat. He felt that Menda was pushing him away from Syracuse, and from Mikro, and from his home.

Menda said that she would like to go too, but she was old and they wouldn't take her. She stroked his head and then hugged him so that he would not see her face, which was grimacing under the moonlight as if the light was too strong. Then Menda showed him a small canvas bag with a dozen coins in it. She told him to spend this only if he had to.

"If they don't let you on the ship, give a coin to those that stop you."

Once she had given him the coins, Kalia felt that his departure was real.

"When should I come back?" he asked.

Menda watched him murkily. She felt as if she could see in time, and in front of her shone a young man with Kalia's face, up there, by the sea of her memories. The fact she could see him so clearly in the future was a good omen, she thought.

"If you get captured by the Liburnians, tell them you're one of them and that Latra had come in the shape of an animal to bring you back home. Then they will see you're not like the others."

Kalia thought that he might not have to try that hard since he'd like to be like the others, but was not.

"And one more thing: my daughter was called Voltisa," said Menda. "It's a beautiful name, Voltisa, so remember it." Kalia nodded. He'd heard that name before because Menda had spoken it several times in her sleep.

He asked again, "When shall I be back?"

"Not straightaway, Kalia. By the time you build the city, your deeds here should be forgotten."

"Then I'll be able to come back?"

"Yes, when you build the city," she said so that he had this vision.

The more visions of the future he had, the better the chances for him to survive, she felt.

He said, "You know, Zoi will be worried about where we are. Tell Zoi that Miu and I have gone to build a city."

Menda nodded silently. She stood up then, made a circle above him with her hands, and said, "Surround yourself with white light, Kalia." She hugged him again, squeezed him tight, and left, saying, "Safe journey, take care, you and Miu. I will be with you in spirit. Never forget that."

Kalia thought that Menda was already heavy on her feet, as if she carried a burden, and he wished to go after her and help her somehow, but he knew he had to go to Mikro, say goodbye.

ROBERT PERIŠIĆ

Menda, Papyrus

BEFORE GOING HOME, Menda went to Arethusa Spring. Once upon a time, she'd found the bag of coins she gifted to Kalia next to that spring. There had been an outbreak of fighting inside Syracuse, there was a long drought, and a confusing uprising, the wells and food stocks were drying up, and she had come to get water in Ortigia at the crack of dawn, at Arethusa Spring. There was no one there, and the bag sat under a papyrus bush, which grew by the spring. The sight of it filled her with fear. Maybe it was the dirty profit of the slave trade, maybe the pocket money of a rich man's son, or the salary of some poor soldier; it was probably forgotten by a drunk quenching his thirst at Arethusa Spring at night—perhaps one of the two men she'd seen flat out on the street nearby. Or perhaps the person who had not gone back to get their money was dead?

She put the bag in her pocket and delayed going back, waited there in a dead silence because it was already full daylight. She was frightened by the fact that no one else came to get water, as well as by what she had done. Everything seemed to be standing still, and she stood with the money in her pocket and said to herself, "I'll wait a little longer. If someone turns up, I'll see if they are looking for something." No one came to the spring. People had disappeared and only the shrieks of seagulls could be heard. Then a one-armed soldier turned up and she didn't want to look at him, so she listened to his footsteps and watched his shadow as he approached. His shadow paused, it seemed that his shadow was studying her, and then he shouted, "Get out of here!" In the street where the two men had lain, there was nobody.

She was afraid of having taken that bag, until today. Now that was over too.

She had gone off her path home and here she was, washing her face at Arethusa Spring. She could even go back to Mikro's stable again and tell Kalia everything he didn't know. What a burden, she thought, that she should decide who he is through such an act. Because who a person is depends on what they know. This way, his thoughts of himself were unclear, but also weightless. This way, Kalia was a light soul. And if she told him he might turn bitter and rancorous.

Sabas would be watching at dawn, she knew. Sabas would be hidden somewhere, watching to see if Kalia boarded the ship.

"Kalia is my grandson, Latra. He already knows plenty about the violence of the masters, but he isn't bitter. Just let him board, Latra."

Scatterwind

I KNEW NOTHING about Latra. I'd heard plenty about Greek deities but I have never met them. Just like the Carthaginian gods. Neither had I met the gods of the peoples I had known earlier, and everyone had plenty of them.

At first I was a little scared—what if I meet one of the gods, how would they treat me? Even though I'm a totally technical type, I still fall into the category of invisible creatures in the air, which could, I thought, make them angry. Because according to everything I'd heard, I concluded that gods were capricious and did not like competition. I was convinced that it was a question of time when I would, wandering about in the air, bump into one of them who'd shout, "What are you doing here, you idiot? Who gave you permission?" But I was lucky. It never happened. It's like driving without a license for thousands of years and never seeing a police car. I was simply lucky.

It's possible that the gods and I were in parallel worlds. So many people have seen them and spoken to them, some almost every day. Gods understood language, I realized. Had my "I" been a little bigger, I could have thought that I too was a kind of minor god. It's possible that some might have respected me. But I did not feel like a god to myself at all. I also had no desire for people to respect me, particularly not falsely, that would really be a pain. I mean, it's totally clear to me that I have longevity, but I am not at all sure that I am eternal. It seems to me, I might have mentioned it, that I am nearing the end, which is why I have started talking.

To tell the truth, I have seen gods who weren't eternal. When I think about it, there were quite a few of them. Long term, I mean really long term, they had some issues. They were meant to be eternal, but they evaporated, hid, I don't know actually what really happened to them. I noticed that people no longer mentioned them, or saw them, or spoke to them, which I found mysterious, I must admit.

I am actually very glad the Greeks never discovered me, even though I traveled with them so often. Because what if they had, let's say, noticed me and started worshipping me? That would have probably affected me. It's possible I would have become conceited. It's possible that I would have believed I was a god because I too can be naive at times. I really was quite lucky in the whole run of things. Because what would I be doing today as a Greek god and what would be my job? I'd have probably been quite frustrated. I have no idea where Greek gods have disappeared. The Roman ones were, I heard, strewn around the universe, but at least they're rotating around the sun.

And what happened to Latra? I don't know if it's appropriate, but I wanted to believe in her and the female Liburnia sky. It is good for the boy and the cat, I thought, because they'd have to find their own way around there, without me.

Braying At Dawn

KALIA STROKED MIKRO's neck. He then pressed his cheek next to the donkey's. He whispered, "Thank you, my dear. Miu and I are going on a ship. If they take us on, we won't meet again. Be well, my friend."

He wanted to tell Mikro more things, more beautiful and gentle things, but he couldn't think of any. He knew Mikro was glad for them in his solitude; now he'd wait for them in vain, looking through his hole in the door, trying to glance at the moon.

Mikro licked the boy's neck with his large tongue. His breath was, like always, a little rancid. But the boy loved the smell of his fur. He now rested his face next to it and quietly breathed. He fed Mikro some carrots, there were too few for a goodbye.

He touched Miu to wake her up. He took the coins, scissors, and clean tunic and crept out under the door. When he was out, he called Miu and picked her up.

He saw Mikro looking out of the top hole in the door.

ROBERT PERIŠIĆ

"We're leaving, Mikro," he whispered, his throat tight. Mikro watched from the darkness of the barn. He could only push his head out straight ahead but Kalia knew he could see sideways. He wouldn't feel so sad to leave this place if he wasn't leaving Mikro behind. Because Mikro was home, not the stable. Kalia's thoughts were followed by fear. He knew people might forgive him the fact that he liberated a cat, but he'd be called a real thief if he did the same with a donkey.

Miu was in his arms; he sighed and she meowed, then he gripped her tighter and, not looking in Mikro's direction as if ashamed, started toward the sea.

"Mikro belongs to Alexandros," he told himself. "I must not, no, breaking the door would make a noise."

After fifty paces, Kalia heard braying. Mikro normally didn't say goodbye like that. *He's saying goodbye*, Kalia thought while Miu looked back. Miu was meowing, as if chatting. She looked back and glanced inquiringly at the path they were taking. Kalia was heading toward the closest beach and when they came to the pebbly area, he saw blurred shadows of ships in the distance, the flicker of flames at the dock. The only thing left to do was to wash.

He sat down with Miu in his arms and wrapped her carefully into the clean tunic because he'd never taken her to the beach before and he didn't want her to run away now. She watched him in wonder. Only her head was poking out.

"Miu, you must wait," he said in a calming tone.

He took off his sandals and, while removing his dirty tunic, saw that Miu was watching as if in shock. She had never seen him naked before.

"It's all right Miu, it's me," he said.

He wrapped her once more in the dirty tunic, his and her scent mixed in there.

She watched him as if seeing him for the first time. He went into the sea.

Scatterwind

BARE SKIN. THAT always seemed like a mistake to me. I
thought that the monkey without fur was born by accident
one day, but how did he multiply? I saw recently that accidentally a furless cat was born too. Some people liked this.
But it was recently, in a well-heated house, so they let it multiply because they didn't have to clean the hair it left behind.
Some people really don't like hair. But this nude cat couldn't
survive outside a heated house. I wondered for a long time
how naked humans survived on cold nights.

Any slightly sharper twig could scratch them. They had to
be very cautious because every scratch was dangerous. Everything was a threat, which is probably why they had to become
clever. I suppose fear made them think and keep an eye on
everything around them. I have noticed that weaker animals
have to pay more attention to what is going on around them.
A hippo lies down and doesn't care about a thing.

I think humanity was so afraid that they got used to fear.
I still see how afraid people are, but they hold it somewhere

under. Animals don't know how to do this. When they're afraid, they're afraid. Fear overwhelms them, and humans have learned to lie to others and themselves. They're afraid, but they pretend they're not. That's a great advantage, I noticed.

Since I am in the business of ventilation I saw that their skin was bare, and that which appeared to be a mistake gave something too: the best internal ventilation. Because an antelope was always faster than the humans who chased after it, but the people from the savannah ran and ran, as long as necessary, and the antelope had to stop at some point, it overheated under its fur. People carried on running, because of the sweating of their bare skin. Fantastic ventilation, I tell you.

After killing it, people would pray to the mother of antelopes not to hold it against them. They didn't want the spirits of nature to be angry with them. They were humble before nature because they knew they were weak and small. I had not seen such hunters among animals, who were slower but caught up in the end. Yes, they felt cold under their bare skin, unless they were running. But they skinned the antelope and made leather. They wore fur that was not theirs. They took another's skin. Later they wore plants, linen, and cotton. People had two skins, their own and others'— taken from animals and plants—skin they could take off.

I saw that the human body was hidden underneath, like fear, and humans undressed only when they were safe. Every animal is shocked when they first see this. When they see that humans are double beings. When humans undress, when they show themselves, I am always reminded of the running in the savannah.

Kalia, The Door

KALIA STEPPED INTO the sea up to his knees and washed his face, neck, armpits, let his body adjust to the water, then he dunked himself. When he stood up he heard braying again, and saw Miu wrestling out of the tunics with all her might and that she managed to wriggle herself free and went back up the way they came. He called her, but she only paused briefly, glanced at him, and went on. He quickly put on his clean tunic and sandals, collected all his things, all the while knowing where Miu had gone. He could already see himself up there, outside Mikro's door.

Mikro is not mine, drummed in his head as he climbed. *But how is it that he's Alexandros's? He must have paid for him.* As Kalia ran up the same path they had used to come down, the shades of dawn took his breath away and everything sped up with his thoughts. *But whom did Alexandros give money to? Whom did he pay? Did anyone ask Mikro for his opinion? Mikro was Alexandros's slave, like I had been Pigras's. But Miu disregarded all that, and that's why we have to board a ship.*

The farther he climbed, the lighter it got, and he knew they should have already been heading toward the harbor. When he got to the top, he ran down the street and when he finally reached them, gasping for breath and knowing that he had no time, he took a stone from a wall and broke off the rotting wood, cut the rope with the scissors, and all three of them were in the light and he knew again that he had no home.

They ran, leaving the gaping hole behind them and there was no more barn—the only thing remaining was the ship, if they made it.

Scatterwind

LOVE IS THE strangest thing for me. Bodies wanted to be close, that much I noticed long ago. I understood this to be because of heating. I mean, I am an entirely practical spirit and I have followed everything from the beginning. No one can tell me that the whole thing hadn't started because of heating. I remember well that the boy pushed himself into the barn because he was cold. It all started with heating, there's no doubt about it. All that communing on Earth, I saw clearly, started with the heating against the mother's body and carried on thereafter. The person sleeping alone couldn't warm up properly, and used up more food, so they had to commune. I studied this objectively, from the side, because heating is part of my skill set, and I must say that there would have been no communing were it not for heating. The body created heat, I saw, through food made from the sun, the sun was processed multiple times, through other creatures who were food, and at the end the body was heated at night and during winter, which was so fascinating in itself that I had always wanted to meet someone and tell them about it. I didn't talk; not only did I not have any friends, but no one in my family would have believed it either. And also: I saw with time that heat, made out of light, becomes more than a physical phenomenon. I thought that perhaps I was overthinking things. Perhaps I was, but there is always another level to something when you really study it. I watched and there was no doubt, heat had entered the minds of the creatures of skin. It had nothing to do with warming up the body, which I had found fascinating anyway. But this went further, I didn't know what it was, I didn't know how heating could turn into that, I just saw that it had entered the mind. Heat had been in the mind as the boy broke the door at dawn, I saw how the body and the mind were one. Imagine, this is what had become of light over time.

Kalia, Dream

LATER ON HE often dreamed of riding Mikro with Miu in his arms and approaching the ship, which was being untied, and that the people on the ship were watching them. Later on he often dreamed of how the three young men who were untying the ship paused, that he was shouting that he could read and write, that the three men hesitantly looked at someone on the ship, at a strong man with a graying beard. He saw everything stop before him as everyone watched him from the ship—"You're pretty late, boy!"—but without protest, that his arrival served as a delay they were longing for. As if the departure had come too soon. He wanted to give a coin to each of the young men who stood at the entry, he later dreamed often of how he, shouting, repeated that he knew how to read and write, and that he came from Gela. He dreamed that he told them all of his relatives were dead. He was sorry in his dream for his imaginary mother who lay in her room, Zoi, the father who disappeared in the sunlight, Diocles, he was sorry they were dead, even though they had barely existed. He dreamed that he was talking in his sleep, and that he was telling someone, much much later, how it was when he ran from Syracuse.

He had only two coins left—he had left the rest for Alexandros in the stable, because he didn't know how much to pay for Mikro—and three men stood in front of the ship, thinking. All of this came back to Kalia later in his dreams, that he had two coins, and there were three of them in front of the ship. Maybe a different fear returned in that dream, the fear that he never did escape, that he never did board, because in reality those young men didn't ask for money.

The only thing one man did ask another was, "Can a child board alone?"

"He's not alone," said the other man.

The third man asked Kalia, "Where did you get the animals?"

"I don't have anyone else," he responded.

Then the strong man on the boat asked Kalia, "Where have you come from?"

Kalia said he had come from Gela, that the Carthaginians had killed his father, and that his mother had died. And that he knew how to read.

"Is that so? What's written on the ship then?"

Kalia looked at the side of the ship and said, "I-s-s-a. Issa."

"What does that mean?"

Kalia thought for a moment and said, "I don't know."

"It's a good thing you don't lie," said the man who spoke as if he were in charge.

That must be the Oikistes Menda mentioned, thought Kalia.

Then the man asked through crackled laughter, as if he were addressing the others, "Don't they look like a good omen?"

It seemed Oikistes wanted to convince the passengers that this would be a lucky passage. Kalia looked at the ship and had a sensation of lengthened time, as if he saw them all, all the faces, and it seemed that no one was against him. Then he heard a few voices shout "Yes!"

"May they be the last ones to board, open up the lower deck for them!" said Oikistes as if cutting with a blade.

Kalia walked next to Mikro who went down the ramp cautiously; small boards were attached to prevent slipping. He understood that they entered this way because of Mikro—the donkey was to spend the journey in a fenced-off spot, in a space that held sheep and goats, baby cows, piglets, a few other donkeys. Fabric was spread out on the floor, probably in order for the animals not to slide around if seawater got in.

They had to tie up Mikro. He was calm, perhaps even glad to have met other animals. But they tied his body; they had a special way, so that he wouldn't fall over if the sea got rough, they said, and Kalia held Miu with one hand and stroked Mikro with the other to keep him calm.

"Don't worry, my friend. When we get there, life will be easier," said Kalia, stroking his neck.

On each side of the animals, in the front and back, were the oarsmen. The oarsmen were tense. They watched Kalia with Miu in his arms, and then, when signaled, started rowing. One man set the rhythm for them; Kalia felt everything move. Miu looked at Kalia—she sometimes looked for answers on his face. But he had never been on a ship, and perhaps this time she knew more than he did. They told him he had to go up to the top deck with Miu. The donkey watched him leave.

"Mikro, don't worry, don't be afraid, my friend," he said, as if singing a quiet song.

Scatterwind

I WAS ON the ship and getting ready to leave. Once again, after keeping myself on the sidelines for a long time, a renewed feeling for life came over me. Maybe I got it too much. I thought, let them leave so I get back to my peace and quiet. Because ever since I had blown down the zebra's back in the savannah and felt her joy, I'd been filled by a sense of life and, as I already said, have since then recognized life that made me a participant, somewhat alive, because before that my existence was only a technicality. But I always felt that it all happened by accident and that it made me overly sensitive.

I could, perhaps I forgot to point this out, later partially hibernate in a technical state, not exactly go back into my original state, not so that I could forget everything entirely, but I could sustain the technical me, just enough so I could function properly. I didn't do this, I don't think, on purpose but some things I just could not sustain in my crevice because I had become physics and biology too, and there

ROBERT PERIŠIĆ

was, after all, a setting that in moments of crisis, when I had to choose, I could go back to my technical state.

I guess I left physics by accident, the way light had turned into feelings via its many mutations, from bacteria via plants and animals. There is no doubt that this was an accident. But my sense for life was clear. When it happened, though, there was nowhere I could turn to and ask what the procedure was.

I was in some way, as the ship departed, thinking about myself. The thing was that I couldn't think about myself as a self, but only in relation to others since, as far as I could see, that was the only way I had a sense for life. Then I thought perhaps the boy had not gone into the stable because of body heat. I know it had started this way, that he had simply wanted to be warm, but I could see how it developed into the warmth of the mind. And maybe the boy's mind would have frozen if it hadn't been for the donkey and the cat, even if he had been warmly dressed? It seems to me that the creatures underneath the skin had to have warmth of the body and the mind, otherwise they would catch a cold. I saw some whose minds had turned feverish and they were cold within, even in the middle of the summer. I saw how humans and animals could have damaged minds if they didn't have warmth; especially the young minds had to be warm, I saw, because I had time to watch, that a child must not be left alone for long. The cat was like a mother to the boy because she warmed his mind, although I also saw that the cat thought the boy was her mother. The donkey helped, and they helped the donkey and so they floated above the void.

I can't help much there and I had become involved enough, I thought. I am, after all, a technical creature and I must stop here, leave the ship. And I left.

Kalia

MIU WAS CALM in Kalia's arms until she saw that the boat had departed. Then she jumped down and went to the bow. He saw her nervously looking at the shore. Luckily, she was afraid of water, otherwise she might have jumped. Miu hadn't wanted to leave Syracuse, he saw. Whatever it might have been like, her favorite place was the one she had sniffed out and where she knew all the streets and nooks. She started yawling; he'd never heard that voice before.

He went up to her carefully and took her in his arms, afraid she might accidentally fall into the sea or that someone might want to shut her up because everyone was again, he thought, looking at them. Miu looked at the city from Kalia's arms: a long, pained cry. The city, slowly fading into the distance, was quiet under the feeble eastern light, the cool of the sea reflecting under the morning sky. Mikro's broken door flashed before Kalia's eyes: their gaping home. He thought of Zoi heading for the market. Miu cried, it seemed too loud in the silence, and others might have wanted to cry too but were quiet. Mikro's stable, the market, and some surrounding streets blended into Syracuse, which Kalia saw from this perspective for the first time, seeing it whole; he saw, in wonder, parts of the city he'd never visited. Only now could he fathom the city's actual size, as it was shrinking with each strike of an oar; he heard the voice that set the rhythm for the oarsmen, and above him the sails rose and widened. He looked in the direction of Sabas's house, which in his dreams was still his home.

How long does it take to build a city? Now that he was looking at Syracuse from the sea, he thought, *We will never finish it. But perhaps our city will be smaller.*

He had always known that Menda didn't want to tell him certain things because he was a child, even though he was, in fact, not a child. Now he thought, as he watched Syracuse, *Menda didn't want to tell me that we'll never meet again.* It went quickly: Menda and Zoi were there. The ship sliced the water, and Kalia felt a thread that stretched so much it would break. The city became more luminous as the sun rose out of the eastern sea. He looked toward the spot they had sat in the night before. Menda had moved heavily, as if the Earth were tripping her up.

He watched as Syracuse fell farther. He felt the silence of the people around him. He looked around: everyone watched the city, everyone was lost in an internal gaze.

He thought for a moment that a tiny figure was waving from the dock. Perhaps it wasn't waving, he thought, perhaps those were angry movements, as if the person were bouncing off the ground? Was it Alexandros? Was it his imagination? He looked at the others around him. Had anyone else noticed that bouncing dot?

Five other ships followed in their wake and one of them was obscuring his view.

When he could see again, he could no longer spot the figure that might have been Alexandros. The large Syracuse was getting smaller and smaller, more misty. Miu let out long yawls in Kalia's arms. People looked at Miu, people who seemed to have wanted to release such a cry themselves. He had already seen that gaze that envied a cat's freedom. She cried with the voice of those whose pride didn't let them cry. Kalia felt afraid for Miu and gripped her harder. *Maybe this is how she left Egypt too*, he thought. *Maybe everything had blended together*. The blue was enveloping them. He saw tense faces around him, staring at the city that was now a speck on the horizon. They listened to the cat's yawl, and watched their disappearance from the world. They were going to the end of the world, to a city they had to build.

Someone started singing quietly, and the song soon spread around and became louder; the sea reflected and carried it. It was a melancholy song about a promise, about distances that would become home: an anthem to departure. A faraway home. A house far from home. Apoikia.

Kalia also sang. Then Miu jumped out of his arms because the city was no longer visible. She went to the bow. Perhaps she thought the city was on the other side. It was something like a sign and everyone turned around after her. Syracuse was no more.

PART II

4. The Journey

Scatterwind

DECADES HAD PASSED since I arrived in Sicily. Perhaps I have spoken about this already—and that I had arrived from Athens—and perhaps I have skipped a little, since there was something unpleasant, seen now in hindsight, about the fact that I arrived with the navy. I had helped them along with the wind, as it usually happens. I get carried away. I get caught in the sailing game. I like it; it's not work for me, it's also a bit of fun. As far as I could see, things in nature are made so that everyone likes what they do. I don't think that in this respect I am any different from animals: a bird likes to fly, a horse likes to run, a dog likes herding sheep, a mole digging tunnels, and cats like to hunt mice, even after they've been fed. It's easy to get fish into the water, they say. Every animal likes to do what they do, only people are a little different; I noticed that some people didn't like what they did, so I didn't understand why they did it. I had observed this.

Since I had time to observe, I saw that some people were imprisoned and made to do what they didn't like and that those people were slaves. Then again, there were others who I could not tell were imprisoned but they still didn't like what they did and I couldn't work out if they were slaves too. I tried to see how they were imprisoned and I couldn't find anything. But maybe I wasn't seeing right.

Humans are a puzzle. When I see people who like what they do, I think: look, they are working like animals. But there aren't many of those. The rest work like people. Sometimes I hear them envying those who didn't work, saying how they would like not to work at all. I don't understand this and I don't know if they're being honest. Every animal likes to do what it does, unless it's forced. Even then animals don't mind working, except they find it difficult to stand in one spot. A dog on a chain doesn't mind guarding the house, and neither does a chicken mind laying eggs, but they don't like the chain and the coop. Each animal that has space is happy to do what it does. I don't know what's the matter with people. Where has their space disappeared? Why are they feeling bad?

Sometimes I think humans have a chain and a cage inside their heads that take their space away. Physical freedom cannot help them. And it's unclear what humans would like to do. That seems to be the problem—humans don't know what they love. I have seen some who didn't know what to do with their freedom and then they just broke things. I watched them in the aftermath and their faces were not happy. That was not what they had wanted to do. But the damage had been done, which also made me angry, so I sometimes directed a storm toward them so they weren't bored.

I watched people, perhaps more than I did other animals because, as I said, they were an enigma. I guess that is why back then I had gone to Sicily with them from Athens. It's easy to get fish into water, and so it is with me and the sails. I think that's the reason that I, back in those sailing times, traveled a lot more, not even knowing why.

Now I move with the surfers, short distances.

And it's not as if I wasn't interested in where that crowd was going, back then, from Athens. I had seen great exoduses before, of large flocks in the savannah, but never of anything like this: there were only men, going across the sea, with many ships. They were equipped as if they were going hunting and since I had joined suddenly, I thought at first that Syracuse, which they had been mentioning, was some enormous, glorious animal.

Only later did I learn that it was a city, and the Athenians sailed on convinced of their victory. They ended up in their own excrement. In quarries. Then sold into slavery. Syracuse defeated them, which surprised even me a little, since it looked in the beginning as if defeat was not an option. It often looks like that when force first takes off, and I am no longer surprised. Force looks forceful while there is no other force. And then later, there is nothing more miserable than a defeated force.

I was, of course, not enslaved by the Syracusans, although I had at first helped the Athenians simply because I got carried away. It is possible that I also played some role in their defeat because I think the Athenians were too confident about being served by a favorable wind and everything went so well at first. But when I saw the beginning of the battle I decided to go off and explore Sicily. I mean, I am not a military scatterwind, and how would I know on whose side to fight? It's true that I had arrived with the Athenians, and I had gotten to know them so they felt more familiar, but I still thought, It's beautiful, this Sicily place, I will go and have a look around! And why had they come anyway? I hadn't considered this when we were leaving. I heard them too later on, in the quarries, asking, "Why did we come?" Anyway, that's how I stayed in Sicily.

The thing with the Athenians was finished quickly, in a year or two, but then there was the fighting between the Syracusans and the Carthaginians—that dragged on.

There were beautiful Greek towns in the east, and beautiful Carthaginian towns in the west of Sicily. There were many beautiful places, but I couldn't bear witnessing new sieges, retreats, humiliations of the defeated. The victors were also unbearable to watch. Not everyone is horrible in victory but on average there is little that is so repulsive in nature like a victor. And someone always wins, even briefly. Someone always celebrates, even briefly.

As it was all starting to slightly disgust me, I spent my last days in Sicily with Kalia, Mikro, and Miu. I think I rested more than usual. The weather was stable. The cat sometimes stared at me and Kalia thought she was staring at the wall and that she was a bit odd. I wouldn't mind if she could see me, but as far as I can tell, I am invisible.

I didn't plan to board the ship with them, I had made this decision because we had, I think, become a bit too close. I didn't like the fact that they were being followed by military ships; they didn't look like the Athenian expedition, not even close, but they could still flatten some poor village, I thought. That's why I stayed a bit behind the ship, I was merely interested in where they were going. I thought they were unwittingly going to a place I had already seen.

Yes, I had already gone a bit farther up, ran up to the top of the Ionian Sea because there was a place, mysterious and whirling, that attracted me. It was a technically interesting whirling that people had only recently noticed, in these times, and they gave it a name. The Adriatic-Ionian Bimodal Oscillation. A totally technical name. If I were to have a daughter, that would be her name, so that only the one who really falls in love with her would remember it. But there was no name for it at the time and only I could see it from so high up.

I could see that this whirl was incredibly wide and above it an enormous gulf, so large that it could be its own sea, because such a whirl could not come into existence without a massive back force. The whirl pulled the water in from one side, and ejected it from the other, so in that bay, I concluded, water was changing. I had gone to that spot several times and watched it from a distance; I climbed up and watched from above, because the thing was so wide you could only get a view of it from up high, and I was cautious about going closer because it could perhaps throw me out on the other side, and I didn't know what I'd find over there. Up there was a sea that got its name after the city of Adria, the Adriatic, but I didn't know that then. I only knew that this bay had to be enormous.

I went to that spot several times during those months, to the top of the Ionian Sea, because it seemed to me that the whirl was slowly coming to a stop. I thought I was imagining things, that my sight was enchanted, because to see things slowing down is hard when you're constantly watching them. I moved farther and then went back closer.

And then, when they were headed up—I was high above and saw that no, this was not a mirage—I really saw the whirl stop, a tense calm took over, and everything was still and uncertain, as if the sea were about to explode.

Up until that point, the whirl was pulling the Levantine Sea upward from the east, and this sea was warmer and more salty, and if it turned around, it would pull the water from the west, cooler and less salty, with the fragrance of the Atlantic.

I knew I was seeing something special because it does not happen every day that such a force changes directions. And because I could see it stopping, I watched the ship with worry from the great height. There were six ships, three smaller military ones, three large ones like the one Kalia was on, which was quite a bit ahead of the others. I couldn't stop them from going toward the whirl that had stopped, because they were rowing. Then I tried and from above, in a volley, I whooshed past them in the opposite direction, so that I might at least change their direction. I remember their voices, wafting on the waves, scattering sadness. The waves sprinkled the tiny drops that had soaked up their song. They didn't know where they were heading so they sang louder.

Having passed them in a counterdirection, I got farther and heard them in interrupted bursts. When I turned around I could see: they were heading under the fast clouds, which were being met from the side by other clouds, heavier and burdensome.

The stopping of the whirl had made a mess in the sky, it was bouncing back.

And then the whirl went in a different direction. Their ship was moving quite close to the center of the whirl, which had just started to pull from the west where they were coming from, and everything speeded up; it was something like a seaquake.

The sea cracked a little before them and they were on top of an enormous wave that they could not see. Had it not been for that, I wouldn't have come here or stayed this long.

Everything would have been different. I wouldn't be the one telling this whole story.

I'm not complaining or saying it should have been different, I'm just saying I had not planned this or wanted it. Or perhaps I had wanted it, but hadn't planned it?

I must say, despite experience, I never know what will happen next. At the time I was watching this sea and sky storm, which they were caught in quickly, and their voices could no longer be heard although I have, perhaps I've said this before, deep hearing.

I had never seen such a thing before and didn't know what to do not to make things worse; from up above they looked like a speck in the whirl and so, knowing that it could get even worse if I got inside the whirl myself, everything pulled me in closer. I was afraid I wouldn't be able to govern my direction, which could topple them over, but the ships were already like sticks in the whirl, and then I heard the fear of the animals from the belly of the ship, I heard a donkey bray, and I rushed down when I thought it may be too late. So I cut down there with all my silly might, got to the force of the whirling powers, and I broke across, straight, and circled and balanced the pressures as if making a tunnel in the air, and I broke through and circled around this passage, I was already losing my power, but I was persistent in the vapor of the sea; there were masses of drops, I had to stay above, a little above the vapor. I couldn't see the ship, I couldn't see the sea. I don't have massive powers but I circled, wiggled, zigzagged, balanced the pressures, sliced, slid across the tiny foam ahead of them, dug a tunnel in the air, performed acrobatics because I was in now and there was no turning back. I was losing my power and I thought I had disappeared, that only my desire had remained and, to cut

ROBERT PERIŠIĆ

a long story short, because it is hard to describe... In short, I was slicing and calming, I made this little bubble around them, and then everything started to disperse; that's how it goes sometimes, a different center of gravity forms, because that's the way of the air, the main things are the initiating forces, then it turns, and it worked, the wave was getting smaller and they were constantly behind it. They didn't even see it and got past it.

When they came out of the whirl and the sun caressed them again, the boy fell asleep, wet, on the dock, curled up on his side, and the cat crawled in behind his lower back. I was spent and fell on top of them like a cape. I have observed people, as I have said, for a very long time and I don't find them particularly beautiful. There are prettier animals anywhere you look around. But those two were beautiful together.

To The Other Side

KALIA THOUGHT SUCH a faraway journey might last the whole day, perhaps the whole night. He had never taken a trip, and if he had ever heard anything about long journeys, he would think they were shorter. Days and nights passed, and they still sailed. They were served by good weather and favorable wind following the storm. They docked several times, sometimes briefly, sometimes overnight, and the ports in which they docked were getting smaller and smaller. They didn't get off the ships, except for a handful of men who were chosen by Oikistes.

That's how it was when they docked in a small town, and the bay was filled with their ships. Children watched them from the land. Kalia watched from the ship, holding Miu in his arms. She was by then quite comfortable on the ship; for the first few days of the voyage he worried when he couldn't see her, but then she'd come out of a hole that must have taken her to the lower deck, to see Mikro. Kalia wasn't allowed on the lower deck; they didn't want a crowd forming, and they particularly didn't want children down there. He memorized the young man who had tied up Mikro and so Kalia asked him, as soon as they had docked, to go down and relax the ropes.

"There is a timetable for all that," said the young man, who was called Leonidas, and he laughed and said he could tell in advance what Kalia might ask him to do and he had done it. "I let them stretch their legs any time I can, we just need to take care. If the sea starts to get rough, they could break their legs, you know? But your donkey is doing well."

"Liburnia is really far," Kalia said.

"I call it Illiria, but yes, it is far," said Leonidas.

"That's the very reason we are going there," Teogen said, and then added, "A donkey can take a lot."

"After this harbor we will cross to the other side," Leonidas said, as if to indicate they were getting close.

"Only when we cross to the other side will we see where we are headed," Teogen said.

There was something in Teogen's words that created uncertainty, but he spoke as if it was all clear, which made the uncertainty greater. Kalia tried to imagine what the other side of the sea might look like; perhaps everything was upside down over there.

Teogen was often at Kalia's side because Oikistes had told him to look after the boy. Kalia would have preferred it if Leonidas had been charged with the task because Teogen was almost as serious as Alexandros, but maybe this was the very reason Oikistes had entrusted him with the boy's care. It is true that Teogen had held him in the storm even before Oikistes had shouted, "Hold on!" Kalia then held Miu to keep her from flying off the deck; which is why his hands were busy and, before Teogen grabbed him, it seemed that he might fly off together with the cat. Teogen grabbed them hard and held on to them, lying down on his side. Facing Kalia there was Doris. She was holding on to Teogen's neck. Kalia squeezed Miu forcefully so that she wouldn't escape and he was frightened that his and Teogen's grip might suffocate her. Leonidas was holding on to Teogen from the other side, and someone else was gripping Leonidas. They were all holding on to each other, and some of them were gripping the mast and anything they could grab. They must have known what to do because they had traveled on a ship before. Everyone held everyone else and no one flew off the deck. Kalia knew nothing about stormy seas, except that the storm had come suddenly, and after the storm he felt as if he knew them all, although he knew nothing about them, but he felt close to them because they had held on to one another. So even if Teogen was always scowling, Kalia thought that overall, he was good.

In that port the children kept their eyes on them constantly, while some adults tried to disperse the children, as if they thought the people on the ships may be bothered by children watching them. Perhaps the adults were the ones who were afraid, because of the soldiers who stood on the pointy, flat ships, where there were dogs and horses too. Kalia's ship

ROBERT PERIŠIĆ

was taller and rounder, and there were three such ships full of people and animals. Kalia had spotted a cat several times on one of the other ships, perhaps there were even two different ones. Cats were allowed into the food storage areas because of the mice, and dogs and their owners had to stick with soldiers, so that there was no chasing around on the ship.

"That was a cautious rule, even though we only allowed obedient dogs on the ship," Leonidas explained.

There were no dogs or cats on the third ship because that was the place for poultry. Kalia wondered how they had come up with all this, and Leonidas knew it all already because he had once, as he had said himself, chaperoned the settlers going to Ankon.

"Only then, we had ferrets instead of cats," Leonidas said. "I feel a bit sorry for ferrets, the cats have kind of squeezed them out of the picture."

"Same thing," said Teogen.

"Same thing for the mice, that's for sure," Leonidas said.

"I did see a ferret on the ship," Teogen said.

"I think that's the only one," replied Leonidas.

"I heard they took them against their will," Teogen said. "To Ankon."

Leonidas was quiet for a moment and looked at the ships carrying soldiers. "Ha, ha, it can't be said that Dionysius was their fan," he said.

"But it can be said that he is our fan?" Teogen asked as if it was not a question.

"Everyone had a reason to get out of Syracuse, no?" Leonidas and Teogen looked at each other and each closed his eyes silently, the way Kalia and Miu signaled to each other that they had understood. No one looked at Kalia, although he felt for a moment that they might have been talking about him. He'd let Miu go and was pretending to look at her. It was the first time he'd heard such a conversation; no one had so far spoken of Syracuse or Dionysius in this manner. Perhaps it was because they were far enough, thought Kalia. Was it possible that they too had been slaves? They didn't look like slaves. Who knows what they had been, he thought. He knew that Teogen had a donkey below, but he didn't look as if he had liberated it by accident.

"Now we have to wait because of their sales," said Teogen. It was clear he did not like merchants. "That thing they do is not work," he said.

"What do you think, do they have money over there?" Leonidas asked, pointing at the other side—toward Liburnia—with his chin.

"If they don't, they soon will," Teogen said, lowering the corners of his mouth.

"They don't even know they're missing something. It's good to not know you're missing something, no?" Leonidas laughed, as if to himself, and Kalia laughed along without knowing why.

"All I care about is the city," said Teogen.

Teogen had told Kalia he was a stonecutter. Kalia thought it impossible that someone might cut stone, but he was quiet. Later on Teogen told him that he was in fact not only a stonecutter, because he built houses, set down pavements, and he then started to think not only about stone that he worked on, but about an entire house, about houses touching each other, about streets. His teacher had taught him to think this way, a teacher who was now old and sick, whom he had said goodbye to in Syracuse.

"He might not have survived this journey, but he was glad I could leave and he forgave my debt," Teogen said.

At that moment, Kalia saw that Teogen also had someone he loved. Teogen knew he would never see his teacher again; it seemed that this was why he was so gentle with him, because he'd never see him again. If he did see him again, Teogen would have been very serious, Kalia thought. But since he had mentioned debt, Kalia was not sure if that meant Teogen had been a slave too? He didn't want to ask Teogen since he knew that if he had been a slave, Teogen would have to lie; instead, he watched him a little closer. Teogen then said he had the city in his head. Kalia could see his eyes shine as he spoke of houses and pavements, and streets and the flow of water, of the drainage channels. Teogen couldn't wait to see such a place. He said few stonecutters got the chance to build a city from scratch. Kalia then thought this was the reason why Teogen left Syracuse, not to escape slavery. Still, he could not be sure. Perhaps he had been a slave who had dreamed of a city.

Scatterwind

THEY DIDN'T KNOW they were floating on the waters of the Atlantic, which had entered the sea when the whirl twisted around. They were followed in by whales, two whales, perhaps a romantic couple because they were of a similar size. The whales hadn't followed the ship from up close, they had their own route, but I noticed them; I thought I heard them a few times when I got very close to the surface of the silent sea. They too had what people called song, but this sea was quieter than the one surrounding Sicily and it was the first time I heard this language from below, although it was very quiet. And it seemed that whales were creatures of goodwill, as curious about that sea as I was. I am already familiar with the fact that animals love exploring. They look for new knowledge and new food, which comes down to the same thing; cats love exploring, pigs, I saw, take pleasure in nuzzling the ground with their snouts, and humans enjoy seeking. The reward is always ahead and a creature that seeks enters the future. The pleasure sits in the next moment and

ROBERT PERIŠIĆ

that is the current—as far as I could see, the main current—that sucks us in: the time ahead of us.

Is it even necessary to mention this force that sucks us in and takes us forward? It is so deeply seated in everything, perhaps it isn't necessary. But since I had been thinking about timelessness—for which I had a reason—I found it necessary. All of life, as far as I could see, was entirely in tune with time. I was thinking about what life outside of time might look like and how creatures would seek for things then. Would that be life too? That would, I thought, be something else. Perhaps my thoughts were silly, but since I had no body, I considered different ways to ignore time or leave time altogether. I was trying because I had time. I also have a memory I can skip through. Even though it is badly organized, when I finally get hold of it and spiral down it, my memory becomes clear. It's as if I were really there, in another time. And I am there now. But I am also aware that I am resting in the swelter, near the rubbish, where I started.

Those whales left long ago. There is only a tiny cloud in the sky, and it is very slow. I was trying, as I said, to exit time, but I kept going back inside it. I can't say that I have achieved a lot, except this, via language. I could see that I could not move into the future, until the future came naturally, and that my memory was skipping. I wasn't a god and I was in some way, I suppose, alive.

We were at sea, but everything resembled a river.

Destroying In The Mind

WHEN THEY HEADED to the other side, the ships carrying soldiers went first. The barking of dogs was getting quieter and only one boy watched them from the land; Kalia waved at him, the dawn was gray blue, and the boy waved back from the port. Kalia thought of himself in Syracuse, as if that boy were a mirror on this side of the sea, and over there, across, was the place where Menda gave him his freedom. He was already sensing this freedom on the journey, because no one knew who he was, no one could find him on the open sea as the image of the waving boy faded away.

I have gone far, he thought. Now everything was really the way he sometimes saw things: the world was getting farther. It was no longer there, together with Menda's voice and fragrance, her body against which he measured his own growth, around which he orbited.

Is it really true that I have gone away completely? he wondered, not in a way of questioning the thought but rather marveling at himself on that ship, together with Miu and

ROBERT PERIŠIĆ

Mikro on the lower deck. When they were sailing out of Syracuse it all looked like a dream and only at the moment when the boy waved at him, and when he disappeared from vision, Kalia saw that he was no longer there, on that side.

Teogen told Kalia that he had a son, and that he didn't know where he was. "You remind me of the way he was when he was still good," he said.

"He ran away?" asked Kalia.

Teogen sighed darkly and became pensive. He said his son had betrayed him; he had taught him to work the stone and, as the boy grew, he told him about the city and then his son, imagine, instead of becoming a builder turned to words. He loved talking, pretty much. He spoke of the city, which Teogen actually liked. Then he fell in love with a philosopher, a bum from Athens, and started following him around like a dog, started speaking like an Athenian: they spoke of the polis, instead of building it. And now he was *over there*, was supposed to return, and didn't.

"I was teaching him how to build a city, dreamed with him, he had everything in his hands. It's not that he fell in love with a man, that's no new thing in this world, but that he perverted my teaching, you understand? Because I taught him how to really build a city. He was supposed to be here with me, we were supposed to build the polis, and there he is talking about the polis. He could have even brought the guy with him, he could have commented too. But no, they stand in the third row around that scumbag

Plato. And they are commenting there, my son and his lover. They're over there, commenting, and he could have come with me to build a polis! So what if it's as far away as the end of the world? Where else could you build from scratch? You have to go to the edge of the world to build a polis. You definitely won't be building it in Athens. Everything is crooked over there and nothing can be fixed. Every house leans in a different direction. It's all one big mess, believe me, Kalia, I was there. I went to look for them, and I found them. And I told that Plato directly, after I had listened to him from the sides, 'If you want to build the ideal city, come with us and build from zero!' I don't claim, I said to him, that philosophers would rule, but the rest of what you're saying is doable.

"Because what he had been saying is how there should be a division of land and housing in a new polis, and that it should be as equal as possible. Things like that: everyone should be moderate, no one should trade in things. And I've told everyone on the ship what he said and people are mostly in agreement with it, only Oikistes and Kleemporos were looking at me as if it wasn't my business. But they'll have to agree too, they don't want division while the apoikia is being built. There are six hundred of us, and only a few of them. They don't need us to be monitored by the army, because it's an army far from home, far from commanders. But why am I telling you all this, Kalia, I started talking about that boy of mine.... You know, he was uncomfortable when

I came after him and spoke to Plato in this manner. My own son—uncomfortable! And I was calling them all to come, gay or not, to build a polis. And here I am alone with you and a stupid cat. Can you understand?"

"What did the Plato guy say?" said Kalia.

"You know, Kalia, he's not such a fool as he is thought to be. He looked at me for a while, with a smirk, and told me I could come to Syracuse. But he said it as if to say there is plenty of time. I don't know when he was planning to do it because, here we are on the waves, and my useless son is still plotting with his lover in the third row, and neither they nor Plato will be building a polis. But know who will? You and me! Imagine! And they had everything served to them on a plate!"

"Perhaps they will come one day."

"Do you know why I get so upset?" said Teogen. "He's my son. I've invested a lot of time in him. An incredible amount of time. A dumb jenny foals and the little creature starts walking right away. But not him! You teach him to walk, teach him to talk, and you aim everything at slowly teaching him to build a city and the teaching is almost as long as it might actually take to build a city, and then he has all this knowledge in his head and his hands, and then he goes off with some fool and they talk about the polis! In Athens of all places, a city that had no other option but to conquer Syracuse. The only people more rotten than them are merchants."

"Than the Athenians?" Kalia asked, a little absentmindedly.

He had at first thought that Teogen's son had run away from slavery, because that was always his first thought, and now he thought that he had escaped Teogen.

"Philosophers, Athenians, all the same," Teogen said. He was quite upset so he had shouted, unwittingly, and everyone on the ship heard him. "An incredible amount of time! An incredible amount of time to raise a child! And for what? To go to Athens!"

A murmur of negative agreement resounded.

Now Teogen realized that others were listening and he shouted, "Never go to Athens! We will go to the edge of the world, but never to Athens!"

Some people liked his words and clapped.

Kalia found Teogen interesting, and his imagined city, but he didn't like that Teogen saw Miu as a beast on whom food was wasted. Since Kalia had boarded without food, he ate from the communal kitchen and quickly learned to hide from Teogen when he shared his food with Miu. Teogen had seen it and told Kalia that this was a communal kitchen and animals like Miu were not meant to be fed what people ate. Teogen knew that Kalia also had a donkey on the lower deck but Teogen didn't mind Mikro eating common food and drinking lots of water because he said the donkey would be helping to build the apoikia. Teogen also had a jenny, Fisiha, whom he was now going to rename Isiha. Because of Issa.

"Is that a good idea?" he asked Kalia.

Kalia nodded.

ROBERT PERIŠIĆ

"You know, Kalia," Teogen said as if confiding, "if I were to have some bad ideas, I'd push them away."

Kalia thought this impossible and asked him if this had ever happened.

"Hmm." Teogen thought about it. To Kalia's surprise he responded by saying that it had actually happened. "One has to say goodbye to their bad ideas. That's hard. But a builder must do this. Has to learn to do this. If your building is crooked, there's nothing you can do about it later."

Kalia imagined a crooked house and Teogen watching it.

"I used to be stubborn," Teogen said and grimaced and stopped himself.

Kalia wondered what Teogen looked like when he was stubborn. He briefly pictured him with a military helmet on, which he found funny, but Teogen didn't notice.

They were sailing on the open sea, which was like floating in an endless blue.

"When you have to tear it down, it means it's too late," said Teogen. He then looked for some thought, looked around as if blind, and said, "That's why a builder has to see what isn't there. That's the basic thing. He needs to tear down before anything has been built. While it's still in the mind."

Kalia imagined knocking down walls in his mind. It felt good and went well with the sea.

"You'll be my assistant," Teogen said. "I will teach you to build and tear down in the mind."

Scatterwind

VERY FEW WHO had boarded those ships ever went back to Syracuse, but I did. I can move quite quickly above an empty sea. I went, in fact, to observe the whirl at the top of the Ionian Sea, which sucked in the waters of the Adriatic on one end, and spat them out on the other. It took ages to understand what was happening, why the whirl existed and changed directions—this was, after all, connected to my profession. Only the whirl was doing a much bigger job. It balanced out that sea that looked like a gulf, balancing salinity and temperature: because it isn't the same when Levantine waters from the east flow in, with their higher temperature and salinity levels, as when western, Atlantic waters enter, which are colder and less saline, and sometimes bring in whales. Inside that whirl was an enormous ticking clock.

I waited to see when it might twist again. At the time I did not know it would only happen once in a decade. So I would go to Syracuse—once I had reached the whirl, it wasn't much farther. While I was looking for some people, I saw that Plato had really gone to Syracuse.

He was a bit late, but he had gone.

He was an interesting speaker. Back then, I didn't know everything I now know, I was much more stupid. I have gained my knowledge over time, and I cannot say I gained it by myself. I saw things, but I couldn't compose them; I would not be able to say many things if I had not heard them from people, and that also took time for them. I was, as I could later see, missing language, although language too has its drawbacks. It's good to first see and then use language. But if language is used before things are seen, I worry that words might blur your vision.

In any case, I always listened to what scientists said, if I had the opportunity to meet them. Their ideas would then be gone with the wind. That's a bit of a joke.

I remember Plato saying that Socrates thought about the people who had invented language. He had a name for them. Nomothetes, if I remember right. That was the idea, a riddle: Who were they, how did they name things, from what? I thought about this for a long time. It seemed to me that it all led from one signal to the next by itself, bred fast, like a virus. Language was like a contagious disease, only it was meaning that spread. Language was quite a useful virus, I saw. It mutates like every other contagious virus, and people take it in, become immune to it, and use it to kill everything.

That's a bit of a joke. But I saw how things turned dead after being named. I saw how humans, using words, wanted to tame all things, like they did with animals. That was an interesting invention because humanity had tried to describe the world in order to rule over it. All of it had been imagined, a bit of a joke. The world could be made out of words, but it couldn't really be made out of words. That was their map of the world. Yet, they were still traveling on it.

ROBERT PERIŠIĆ

Greeks In The Sky

KALIA SLEPT, BUT he knew they sailed on even as he slept; the waves had crept inside his dreams, the creaking of the wooden boards, bits of conversations carried by the wind, the whole ship slept inside him, and then he heard laughter from above. In his dream, a sky of female laughter opened up, laughter swung in the wind, he felt wings flapping nearby and was gripped by fear.

Was this Latra?

When he opened his eyes he saw flocks of big white birds around the ship, circling around and getting quite close, their shrieks like laughter. He saw Oikistes spreading out his arms as if he'd been expecting them.

"These are Diomedes's friends who have been turned into birds!" he thundered.

He repeated, "These are Diomedes's friends who have been turned into birds!"

It seemed there were others like Kalia who didn't know those birds were Greeks from the sky.

"They are greeting us," Oikistes shouted.

Kalia thought they were simply seagulls, just a bit different and bigger than those in Syracuse; there were hundreds, perhaps thousands of them, and they weren't afraid. Kalia was worried about Miu who had been snoozing by his feet, but she had woken up too; she watched the birds with curiosity. She was sitting tensely, thinking either of hunting or running away. Kalia picked her up because he thought the birds could kill her with a single peck of their large beaks. They were approaching a lone island in the blue. He knew they were near their arrival point, but the island seemed small and he hoped that this was not their Distant Home, because it had already been taken over by the birds.

Perhaps the island will be bigger once we get closer to it?

They got close. There were actually two islands, Kalia now saw. But they didn't look much bigger when they got very close. Kalia looked for Teogen, and saw him staring at the coast. *Perhaps the city Teogen had imagined was made of tiny houses? Perhaps we'd build it very quickly. But that would be like a game*, thought Kalia. He looked at Teogen's serious face and understood that this would be impossible.

"These are the Isles of Diomedes," Teogen said.

"Not ours?"

Teogen said that the Greeks who sail this sea must make a stop here. "This is the last thing we know," he said. "An empty wilderness is ahead."

ROBERT PERIŠIĆ

They lowered a boat from the ship and some men boarded. It seemed that not everyone would have to go down. Kalia felt relieved. The islands were rock cliffs with bits of tufty growth, and there was a tall green tree at the top of the larger island, which gave shade.

"That is Diomedes's grave," said Teogen, "and his friends have been turned into guardian birds, you see."

"I see," Kalia said.

Several men had boarded the boat, Leonidas among them, and Oikistes was still looking around the dock. He saw Kalia and called him too. Kalia first thought that he was calling Teogen.

"Go on, quick," Teogen said, "it's a great honor."

Kalia was surprised because the birds were flying above the ship, landing on the edge of the deck. It's one thing if a small bird isn't afraid of you, but if a big one isn't afraid, even if it's a friend of Diomedes's, that's something else. Kalia ran under the deck carrying Miu because no one was watching.

He found a young woman there—he saw it was Doris when she turned around—and she was squatting next to her goat. The goat stood on three legs, one was up in the air, as if broken. He saw Mikro, staring stiffly. But he stood on all fours. Kalia asked Doris to hold Miu while he was gone and said he'd give her a coin for it. "Stay here with Doris and Mikro," he told Miu. She might have disobeyed him had he not put her on top of Mikro, whom she set about sniffing like a delicacy. He touched Mikro's neck. When Kalia emerged from the lower deck, Oikistes shook his head disapprovingly. The other ships had also dropped anchor; two settler ships set down a boat each. They went toward a bay. They took off their clothes and went naked into the sea. They washed. Kalia couldn't swim and washed in the shallows. Others went in deeper, dove in. Then they climbed the steep hill. Kalia thought about Mikro, who hadn't even looked at him. The birds followed them, some flying so close that he felt the waft of their feathers. Everywhere around them, on the ground, sat their nests with chicks inside them. The seagulls perhaps thought they were being attacked or that their island would be taken over, he thought, as they yelled near his ears.

They climbed up to the tree on the top, got into its shade. Kalia looked at the birds swarming the boat, worried. He saw another man looking over at another ship in the same way and their eyes met. The man was older than the rest and was missing an arm. Kalia saw them dumping something from the ship and the birds flew around in even greater numbers.

They stood in a circle and a bowl with wine reached Kalia. He didn't like the taste of it and drank only a sip.

Oikistes spoke. He was addressing Diomedes. Kalia had heard of him as a great hero, but couldn't remember exactly what it was that he had done. Oikistes asked Diomedes for luck.

He told Diomedes that they were heading farther east, to make the first apoikia on this sea, said they were not scouting like last summer, but were now going to make a city, they had brought their animals, their vines, olives, carob and lavender cuts. He spoke for a while and mentioned the names of the many people who had sent their regards to Diomedes, names Kalia didn't know, except Dionysius, who had sent a lovely ceramic bowl as a gift, filled with wine and inscribed: To Diomedes. Oikistes also left his gift, the bowl they'd drunk from.

Oikistes then told them they could pass on greetings to Diomedes sent by others from Syracuse, and Kalia heard everyone, individually, speak some names, so he also told Diomedes that Menda and Zoi sent their regards.

Oikistes pointed at Kalia and said, "Our children will come in many years and bring their report, powerful Diomedes, that Issa was built in stone. I may not be able to come, Diomedes, because our work will take long, but this boy will, if we are lucky, bring back news."

He watched Kalia ceremoniously and earnestly. "Will you?" Oikistes asked.

"I will," Kalia said.

"Bless us with luck, Diomedes, because we now go into the emptiness. We leave you gifts, we have fed your friends, we leave in awe of you," Oikistes said.

The big white birds flew around them, climbed up in spirals, shot up almost vertically, as if in a wind whirl, laughing.

Scatterwind

THAT WAS MY first time there. I rarely went later, but overall
I visited many times because I had a lot of time. I, Scatterwind, can tell you the place called Pelagos by the Greeks, is
today known as Palagruža. There is no water on those rocks
and no one ever settled there.

I had time to think about this: the Greeks had stopped
at those jutting rocks before, traveling north toward Adria
and Spina. Diomedes died in a great spot, a dry spot, and
they could avoid strangers.

It's true that all water—sweet or salty—looks the same
to me because I don't drink. You don't think about certain
things if you don't have a body. That's in the middle of the
sea, outside of consciousness.

I recently recalled my oblivion. Because I had learned,
by eavesdropping, that the liquid inside donkeys, cats, and
humans is salty. Someone had said it: the internal sea. Those
were scientists, at a symposium at Issa Hotel, but they spoke
like poets. The internal sea, someone said—they didn't see

ROBERT PERIŠIĆ

anything strange in it, because life came out of the sea.When life came out of the sea it brought with it a piece of the sea. Today's symposiums are different. Everyone is sober. I thought: the sea was already inside and that is why they can't drink it. It would be too much. It is impossible to settle in Palagruža and Diomedes had chosen a good spot when he no longer needed water.

The sea produces music from which, I think, the joke started.

Secrets

WHEN KALIA GOT back on the ship, they let him go down and he found Miu huddled on Mikro's back. Doris didn't want to take the coin. She leaned her head against the head of the goat on three legs. Kalia stroked Mikro who looked at him only once, but it was as if he were looking through him. Maybe because there was so little light on the lower deck?

"They say it's just one more day," whispered Kalia.

He wanted for Mikro to see him and recognize him, but it was as if Mikro's eyes were turned within. He thought that Mikro had closed himself inside his circles. Doris was, on the other hand, looking at him as if she had to talk.

"This goat has been with me from the beginning," she said. "We moved around so much. I fed it, but it fed us more. I can't do anything with grass and leaves, it saved my life. Me, my father, and this goat are the only beings left from our home. My brothers died for Dionysius. But he doesn't want to keep the poor he owes so deeply in Syracuse."

She looked at Kalia in the semidarkness, as if searching for someone.

"And he is right, because we hate him so much," she said, wiping sweat off her brow. "Don't tell anyone what I have said."

Kalia nodded. They were far from Syracuse, but Doris spoke as if they were still close.

Doris's eyes smiled sadly as if she believed him. She turned to face the goat again.

Everything is far, Kalia thought, *and everything is here*. He had that feeling again, as if he were here but also far, and he didn't want to feel like this now. He had to suppress it. But still he saw himself, and everything else, floating in what resembled dream time. He clapped three times, remembering how Menda had done this once.

"Chasing away the ghosts of Syracuse?" Doris said as if not asking.

"No," he said, "they're too far away."

Kalia now noticed how everyone was talking about Syracuse differently than when they were there. What Doris had said was a secret, but it could be spoken on the lower deck. Can he tell Doris about Miu and Mikro, the way she had spoken about her goat? He'd not be mentioning Dionysius, but he'd have to mention he was on the run. Menda told him never to say this, not even to those who were his friends because they'd look at him differently. He must never tell anyone because then he will create a shadow that would follow him—that's what she had said. He remembered this "a shadow that will follow you" because he had to repeat it after her that night in the moonlight. "Slavery is a mark," she told him. "It comes back when it is mentioned. Don't ever mention it, even if it means forgetting me too," she said. But what can he tell then? He'd like to tell Doris something. He had things to say about Syracuse. Menda was far, but also near. Everything was like that.

Miu nibbled his hand. Touching Miu in his arms, his cheek against Mikro's neck, brought him back into the present moment. *I'll talk to them*, he thought, *when people go away. I have to pay heed to Menda's words now that I've left her.*

"My beloved friend," Doris spoke softly. "Hold on a little longer, one more day."

She then looked at Kalia as if she were in pain. "I know already," she said. "I know already."

Kalia didn't ask what she knew.

"They will eat my soul, I know."

Scatterwind

I WAS INTERESTED in friendship between the species, having experienced such friendships. That which people call feelings is a blurry thing that exists. While Kalia, Miu, and Mikro were in the stable I observed how everything had started with heat, from light without which there would be no heat. On Earth, it was in the way light was stored inside plants, then inside animals and humans, via eating plants, thus eating light in its raw form. Heat doesn't vanish—it turns into feelings when light is digested. It can even turn into thoughts. People were the best light digesters, and they clearly understood that they had feelings and thoughts. The virus of language helped them with that. But other creatures also had feelings and thoughts, otherwise people would not be able to make friends with them. It would be impossible for them to have mutual understanding and form a friendship if they didn't share the same foundations. Everything stacked up, I noticed, and all of life was a mutation of light. I had arrived there by accident, but I had time to think about this because I had somehow, via a mutation in the virus, caught feelings.

I don't think it would be possible to think without feeling, because there would be no motivation for it. It is really unbelievable that I am alive. I have had this feeling for a long time now, which is why I am here, but I don't want to take it for granted.

Mind you, when I think about it, the fact of others' lives is no less strange. Everything can be explained in language—but how are they, these other lives, possible, I have asked myself from the start, ever since I first saw them.

Humans thought life was an exception. It seems to me that the exception, in itself, as an exception, is less likely than the general rule. It would be more likely to me that the general rule is life.

But, truly, there is also the possibility that there are exceptional things. That would be life among dead things. And the next miracle would be me. I have to admit—so many miracles in the pile—it's a bit suspicious to me.

Apoikia

WHEN THE TOP of the hill floated out of the horizon and Oikistes shouted, "There is Issa!" there was much relieved murmuring, sighing, and some bursting into tears. Everyone looked toward the hill's peak, glimmering in the reflection of the waves; eyes open like fish, palms sweating, they watched this place as if trying to fix it under the sky. The top of the hill danced along with the tip of the bow, as the deck boards quietly whined, and so close to the distant home, the whole ship panted like a dog.

Then, after a flash of joy, many eyes narrowed and many tongues licked their lips, fearing the stories and images from myths filled with surprises. Supposedly everything was as Oikistes claimed and as peaceful as it looked from the ship. But islands always look peaceful from the sea. Hopefully no human power had made a home there already, or Polyphemus, that some said lived in this sea, while others claimed that Odysseus had met him close to the shores of Sicily, which they found a lot less believable.

They were more worried about the people who lived along this sea, some of them had heard of the Liburnians, the fast ships and solid defense of this seafaring people. There were those who knew about Liburnian thalassocracy, their dominion on this sea, but those were the ones who knew more about the world beyond what they had seen, the ones close to Oikistes, and they had been strictly asked not to talk about it. Oikistes had told them with deep conviction that Issa was a safe harbor and here would be no resistance. Even if there was, the army that followed them would suffice. Oikistes knew more, but except for him, Kleemporos, and Arion—who was on a different ship—no one knew anything about it. Because there had been an illness. They had told as much to Dionysius upon returning from their scouting journey to the island the previous summer.

They had stayed on the island longer than planned, and they were ordered to explore the bays, not just their shape and beauty but to look for underwater springs, and if they found them, they were to secretly negotiate with the Liburnian leaders, find one of them who would be willing to sell them land, because Dionysius knew he could not wage war at such a distance. That is how apoikias were built: the Greeks always wanted to come in peace. Not just because they wanted peace but because the building of apoikias was hard to implement while fighting a war far from home. It was too expensive and it was better to find greedy tribal leaders, offer them a good price, and pay for the land. People could

ROBERT PERIŠIĆ

complain about their leaders, which would raise the worth of the Greeks who were coming to replace those leaders. The leaders have sold us, people would say, down with them; and then Greeks turned up like gentlemen and purchased from those gluttons, but at least they might bring order. That was always the plan for the apoikias, and it was the only way for it to work well. And if the people rebelled against the Greeks, especially if there was an uprising straightaway, then the colonialists would die. The grand story would end immediately. It happens.

The previous summer there were ten scouts, seven guards, and three negotiators: Oikistes, Kleemporos, and Arion, and the latter knew many Liburnian words and was in charge of the guards. The guards were soldiers, but none of them could look like a soldier—they were presented as merchants who had lost their way in a storm. Magas was also among Arion's soldiers, and he spoke Liburnian very well. He was probably the son of some Liburnian slave woman, but he always claimed to have learned the language from his nanny who had come from there. Okistes and Kleemporos were Dionysius's commissioners, and Arion and his soldier Magas were a necessary evil, one could not do without them.

Oikistes didn't even tell the whole story to Dionysius, as much as he had wished to complain about Arion—he had to adjust the story a little. Because if Dionysius had wished to probe, Arion could have revealed some compromising details. They were simple things: while they were scouting the island, there was an outbreak of illness. Kleemporos came running one day in the heat and said, "We're getting out, they're sick, some are dying."

Oikistes did not doubt this and they had started toward the harbor when Arion said, "There are certain rules."

"What rules, there's a disease, let's leave," Kleemporos said.

"There are rules for when there is disease," Arion said. "A simple rule: not to return to Syracuse."

Arion wasn't even a soldier, he had left the service, was a veteran of some battles where he had lost an arm. He was the guide who had been recommended to Dionysius from the army, but he had an attitude as if there was a war on and every one of the guards was his people.

"We are not leaving," he said. "We cannot take disease to Syracuse. That is the rule."

"You really love rules, don't you?" Kleemporos asked, also addressing the soldiers who heard everything. Arion had chosen the soldiers, but they might have wanted to avoid getting sick.

Arion looked at them all and said, "Whoever wants to leave may do so. I may manage to kill some of you before you board the ship. Or I may just let you go."

Oikistes watched the old one-armed bastard and wondered at his sudden taking over of leadership.

"You're the grand protector of Syracuse now?" Kleemporos asked, glancing at the soldiers, checking to see if he

ROBERT PERIŠIĆ

could note them changing their minds, because he thought he'd already noticed it.

"I am not a patriot like you, Kleemporos. Not a real patriot. I'm not even from Syracuse. I am from Taranto, the clan of Spartan mercenaries and Pythagoreans," Arion said and started laughing, although it was not clear why. "The thing is, there are many people in Syracuse. Even Dionysius, who is used to death, might hold it against you."

Kleemporos went quiet and Oikistes was lost for words for some time.

"But if it will make it any better," Arion said, "I've already seen this."

"What have you seen?" Oikistes asked.

"In his dreams," murmured Kleemporos.

Oikistes signaled for him to keep quiet.

"I've seen it on another sea, in an isolated village," said Arion. "Nothing happened to me. Me or anyone with me. We waited because we knew the rule. I thought while we waited. We were the disease, I realized at the end. We were fine. And only then we headed back to Syracuse."

"So you think we will be fine?" Oikistes said.

"My dear, I don't know. If we are affected, we must not go back. If nothing happens, it means we are the disease and we can go back. The illness has come now, with us, right? I would say we are safe and that we are the illness."

"You think we are an illness?" Kleemporos asked bitterly. "We, Syracusans?"

"Yes, ambassador."

"So why are we not ill then?"

Arion said, "I am neither a doctor nor a philosopher. But it might be because there are a hundred thousand people in Syracuse and each of them has a different disease. And we are used to it. We have brought a hundred thousand breaths on our breath, that is what I think."

They waited. None of them got sick. The Liburnians nearly all got sick, many died, some recovered. The scouts all went back to Syracuse, except for Magas who had disappeared. That's what happened the previous summer.

The news about the disease will surely reach farther, Dionysius said when they got back. It is unlikely that the Liburnians from other islands would go to defend Issa. The island was on the very edge of their marine territory. It was an opportune moment.

Still, it was better not to mention any of this to the Greeks on the ships, Oikistes knew. The illness was probably over by now, and was brought by them anyway, but people might think all sorts of things. He counted on the idea that the Liburnians wouldn't get too close, at least at first. *Some of them are probably watching us right now, hidden,* he thought. *Others have taken shelter in caves.*

Hearts were beating inside their throats. Kalia gripped Miu in his arms as he pushed ahead and got on his tiptoes to see where it was they were arriving. All the vapor that rose out of hot bodies smelled strangely and Miu nibbled on Kalia and wriggled out of his embrace, jumped onto the deck, and, growling funnily, ran off in a spiraling motion and climbed up the lower part of the mast and jumped down again, clawing the deck, looked around and started, as if playing now, to rub the deck with her back, as if enjoying invisible embraces.

Kalia thought of her funny dance after they had escaped from the house, came up to her, and lay down on his back, his arms behind his head, watching the sky; it was invisible from the light and he looked at Miu, and she at him, her paws in the lazy air, and then Kalia started to laugh as if someone had tickled him.

Kalia saw other laughing faces around him, as if they weren't supposed to, but couldn't help themselves. Since he was the one who had set them off, they looked at him as if he knew why they were laughing, and they agreed.

"Don't do comedy," Teogen said.

The laughter dried up. They sighed and no one acted like a child anymore. Kalia saw Teogen's eyes on him. He thought, for the first time in his life, this might be how a father looks at you.

They went around the island for some time, waiting for a bay in which to anchor. The curiosity in their eyes was mixed with tiredness, the desire to stop, to lay down on the ground, to fall asleep and awaken in the same spot. They looked at the layers of rock on the shore, the sliced body of the island.

"Look at those blocks. This stone has been waiting for us," Teogen said longingly, as if he was fighting his feelings, and that was the way they had sailed, longingly and quietly.

They sailed into the bay that spread around them like an amphitheater with a stage on the surface of the sea. Only the painful bleating of the goat could be heard. Everyone heard it in the silence.

Just before Issa, the goat lost its strength and fell.

Scatterwind

GOATS CAME FROM the Levant. They came from the mountainsides, the rocky landscape of Lebanon, Syria, Jordan, Israel, these are the names of those places today. There was the wild goat, and one of them, pregnant and lost, was looking for help and made friends with a woman. It is a rare species that was tamed by a man. After apes developed hands to grab hold of things and climb trees, men stood up straight in order to have free hands. They needed their hands to be free because when they made weapons out of broken branches, they felt safer, left behind their treetop shelters and walked on the ground more often.

Men stood up straight in order to be able to carry a spear. You can't drag a spear along the ground, it gets stuck; this idea is what made them stand up straight. Men and women straightened up together because the idea of one affects the whole species. But men carried spears, women did not, that made a difference and was clear to any goat.

Whoever has a spear, or something resembling a spear—always a long and straight thing—you don't approach him. Then he goes around saying how lonely he is.

The End Of The World

MIKRO WALKED WELL when they left the boat. But he startled easily, his muscles trembled, and Kalia didn't know if Mikro recognized him. Or was he refusing to look at him because he was cross? Miu sometimes ignored him, he wouldn't have been surprised if she had been doing it, but Mikro wasn't like that. It seemed the journey had made Mikro fence himself off from the world. Kalia knew what this was like, when you fence yourself off.

"Forgive me," Kalia told him and stroked his neck, rubbed his shivering back.

Miu would have rather stayed on the boat because she had gotten used to it. Kalia had to pick her up and carry her off while she protested with brief yawls. They stood on a small plateau by the shore, a little to the side from the rest, and the ground still felt wavy as if the boat had buried itself in the body and had not anchored yet. He watched Miu and Mikro, looked around, took in the almost round bay, the sea that darkened in the hill's shade. The forest above them was still touched by sunlight. He put Miu down, she sniffed the ground and the air, looked around cautiously but quickly; she didn't know where to go first.

The young men were gathering around, sitting in a circle and speaking loudly, as if competing at who felt more excited. He saw families, on the other side, sticking together. He saw the one-armed old man sitting on the side, away from everyone, and next to him was a cat larger than Miu. Leonidas was in a loud circle with other sailors; they drank wine.

The circle around Oikistes was, it seemed to Kalia, wide and too narrow simultaneously, and Teogen was part of it, as if trying to say something to Oikistes, but others spoke over him.

Miu explored the space bit by bit at first, but soon she wandered about. Then she came back to Kalia, meowing as if bringing back news. Everything is new, her eyes said, and Kalia responded, blinking, so she could know he had understood. Even the ship's passengers were new. Something burned inside them. Everything starts anew now, their eyes said.

Miu was soon bouncing around as if playing, as if she had understood that this was the home away from home, she went off and came back and quickly meowed her little speeches, cheered him up.

Kalia replied, "Yes, I understand, everything smells different."

Miu also addressed Mikro who was searching for peace, his mouth agape. Listening to Miu, Mikro's trembling muscles

ROBERT PERIŠIĆ

were settling down, which Kalia felt as he stroked his neck and back. Their eyes met briefly, and then again; Mikro finally looked at him as if recognizing him.

"It's good, Mikro, we are here."

It was getting dark. They lit a fire next to Oikistes. And then they lit another one.

The voices of men were getting louder; they were bringing out more amphoras with wine. Kalia didn't feel cold and did not want to approach the fire, the wine-soaked voices; he gripped the iron scissors in his pocket. He also had two coins in there. He fingered them. They were roasting a goat and Oikistes was speaking, explaining how they would be especially mindful of this sacrifice.

A female figure sat on the pebbles far from everyone; facing the darkness of the sea, she hugged her knees. When Miu next returned, he picked her up and, taking Mikro with him, went up to the woman. It was Doris. He sat next to her. She briefly turned to him and then went back to staring at the sea.

After some time she said, still looking ahead, "Just sit there, friend."

Mikro stood alongside them, and Miu settled next to Kalia's legs as if the exhaustion of the journey had suddenly wrestled her down. The ship inside Kalia slowly stopped swaying.

Doris said, "When I die, I want to be eaten. But not by people. Let my body be eaten by some other animals."

Kalia looked at the sea. Waves of sound wafted at them. *How might I feel if they were eating Miu or Mikro over there?* he thought, but wanted to shake off the thought as soon as he had it.

Doris said, "I want to die in a forest, or in the sea. You know, that's what they're most afraid of. That they might end up being someone's food. They want to be above it. You think that's right? To eat everything, but not give yourself up."

Kalia felt Doris's pain because that can sometimes be heard in someone's voice. They looked at the sea, which was hardly visible.

"Look at them," she said. "This will be their polis."

Kalia turned around: the celebration of men and their song and shadows moved around the fires. He preferred being on the beach with Doris. Next to her was a potted plant.

"You can touch it," said Doris. "That is my vine, or my father's vine, who is over there and has to eat our goat."

"Doris, is this the end of the world?"

"It is," she said.

ROBERT PERIŠIĆ

Scatterwind

GOATS CAME A long time ago. They and the sheep were neighbors with the humans—those who had, after thousands of years of walking, together with their dogs, settled and started working the earth.

Sheep also came from hillsides, only from lower spots than those of the goats. Goats are from farther up, and that's probably why sheep are calmer. Dogs had an easier time with them.

Men took over the herd because human children grow very slowly and women didn't have the time. Job, before troubles took over his life, had some seven thousand sheep and many other things.

The person in charge of sheep became the picture of the shepherd, became a patriarch, and then a heavenly image. The herd of sheep guided by the shepherd became a picture of humanity. That's how far the Asian mouflon has come, the *Ovis orientalis*.

Goats—neighbors from the upper floor of the stone hill—did not become anything, and the male goat became the image of the antigod. That's how far goats have come. Regardless of the nice words about sheep, especially about lambs, sheep don't have it any easier; they are in the same pot.

But they have limits. A goat cannot be entirely imprisoned. It cannot be stuffed into a dairy and food factory, like a cow. Cows are too good. They don't come from the mountains. They come from the valleys, and as large and powerful as they are, they didn't expect all that has happened to them. They did not expect it, did not have it in their genes as knowledge, that it is possible to be imprisoned, to become the foundation of an industry.

Cows, pigs, chickens: good, naive creatures.

Goats lived in rocky landscapes and there was no time to rest; they have to move—it's inside goats. You cannot push a goat into a food and dairy factory. It would sooner die.

Sheep don't go to prison farms either. As good as they are, they still come from the mountains.

You cannot imprison mountain animals. Nothing will come of it. Mountain creatures followed humanity for centuries, up until the entrance into the factories and they stalled there, like a donkey stalls; there's no industry with them.

I'm saying this from the wall, next to the broken chair, close to the rubbish, on the way to Kamenica. I went there once with Doris, which has not happened yet in this story.

ROBERT PERIŠIĆ

5. Miu In Issa

The View From The Coast

TWO MONTHS HAD passed since they arrived in Issa and they were resting at dusk when Leonidas said to Kalia, "Miu has put on weight."

Kalia nodded, tired. At least she was enjoying Issa. He and Mikro had fallen into Teogen's mind city. When someone has something in mind that has not been built yet, it can eat time. He was sleepy with exhaustion.

Leonidas gave him a pointed look, as if he should be more alert. This was the same look Teogen gave him throughout the day, which would make Kalia think, *Are we not done for the day?* Starting at dawn, he walked around after Teogen, carried and pulled ropes. They measured everything: the coastline, sunny fields, they were even going into the meadows, up behind the eastern corner of the bay, where there was a flat valley and a Liburnian village on a plateau.

He took Mikro with him if he managed to spare him a heavier job; because huts were being built quickly, wood was brought from the forest. They had to prepare for the autumn, when they would no longer be able to sleep in tents like soldiers at a siege.

Kalia's head was full of images that did not lose their light with the setting sun, and there was unexpected joy in those images, such as when he would greet the Liburnians in a field in Menda's tongue, and they would greet him back, giving him a different look—as if wondering whom he's related to—a look that was different from those aimed at Teogen and the soldiers who accompanied them.

Kalia wanted to ask Leonidas what he thought of the Liburnians, whom Leonidas called the Illyrians. But he wanted to be out of Teogen's earshot, and he was sitting nearby. Leonidas started to talk about how he was once down below, far south of Syracuse, where the Greeks were darker, and some were completely black.Kalia sat up and asked if that was Egypt, and Leonidas said it was even farther west, where Egypt ends and Carthage doesn't begin yet; it was Libya and the city was called Cyrene. They were in charge of guarding the Greek colony there and Leonidas made friends with a cat that he fed at their seafront base.

"She put weight on like Miu," he said.

Leonidas had other duties, however, and they traveled to the edge of the desert, and when they later returned to Cyrene before leaving, he found the cat in the port. It was on the outskirts of the city because Cyrene was not exactly on the sea, it was a little inland.

The cat still remembered him, she turned up in front of him, walked as if trying to trip him up, wouldn't let him leave. Leonidas picked up the cat, wanted to bring her with him, but as they stepped on the ship she bit him on the hand and ran off the ship. She watched him for a while from the harbor.

"She stood there watching me for a long time and then left," Leonidas said. "But that was not it. The ship had sailed, we were leaving the harbor and I saw the cat following the ship from the bay's edge. She was followed by a little one, and there were two more who wobbled after her. She was explaining to me why she couldn't leave. I told my friend: 'Look, it's the cat.' He said: 'Your cat? No, that's a different one.' You couldn't tell very well from the ship, and there were many other gray-black cats around, but there is something in the moves, in the rhythm of every creature. Over on the coast it stopped, so as not to lose the kittens. It said goodbye with its eyes. I had this unusual feeling then, a kind of attachment, not just to the animal. I felt as if this land was saying goodbye to me. I took that feeling with me. I left that land but it stayed with me. It's different than when people say goodbye, because you know why people are saying goodbye."

Kalia asked, "Was it your cat?"

Leonidas didn't answer right away. Then he asked, "What do you think, Kalia?"

"I think it was."

Leonidas said that the truth could not be clearly seen, and then only a feeling is left—which he could still invoke—and in the end it didn't really matter if it had been his cat.

It doesn't matter if it's that cat or if it's me, he had wanted to tell his friend on the ship, but he held back because he knew it would sound strange. Now as he talked about it, the feeling returned. He said, "The cat was entirely free to say goodbye or not. That is different than when people say goodbye."

He watched Miu who had put on weight and walked around more cautiously than usual.

"Do you understand, Kalia?"

"I do. Your cat had to stay behind because of her kittens. She said goodbye because she loved you."

"But do you get where I started from, do you understand that Miu is going to have kittens?"

Kalia sat up. "You think?"

Kalia had thought he and Miu were the same age, and that he was a kind of an older brother. He no longer considered himself to be a child and he knew he had matured more than was visible, but he was still far from having children. Did Miu go so far ahead of him? He felt it like a slap.

Leonidas laughed and told him that for her time went faster, because she would live shorter. Kalia had not thought about these things, and didn't want to. But he heard everything Leonidas said and couldn't forget, even though he wanted to, but instead of forgetting the thoughts repeated

ROBERT PERIŠIĆ

themselves and went around, drilling holes in his head. He hadn't thought about it, but ever since living in the stable in Syracuse, he considered himself, Mikro, and Miu to be a family. And now she would have her own family?

When Miu walked around his legs later, he didn't reach down to pick her up. She jumped onto his lap anyway. Kalia looked at her with a frown, and she gazed back at him in an ordinary way. Even though Kalia had thought he was something like an older brother to her, it seemed to him that Miu, in fact, considered him to be her mother. She liked to be free and wander about, she walked as if she was the boss and sometimes liked to fight, but she also had the need, especially in the evenings, and sometimes in the day too, for him to pick her up and hold her; she demanded this with special yawls, which came in impatient charges, like speech Kalia understood, and she would stop as soon as he picked her up, close her eyes and softly purr; he heard it only if he pressed his ear against her. The fact that his very being, his hands and scent, made something happy—this in turn made him happy to be alive.

This was important because Kalia didn't always feel happy to be alive, especially back when he lived in Sabas's house. The only reason he felt he ought to exist—before Miu showed up—was Menda, not so much because he felt joyful, but he felt Menda would be unhappy if he told her he did not want to live. True, Menda was always happy to see him, to touch him, but there was misery in her joy, a sadness floating above them. Because people, as he already knew, even though he didn't know how to explain it, always remembered the misery from the day before, from a time before, and it was with them at all times. Memory never left them, knowledge didn't leave them, like knowing they were slaves, and so their joy was overshadowed by what came before. And what might come tomorrow.

He saw the difference memory and knowledge made, and this was the way people were slaves to their knowledge: no one can ever forget things in the way Miu let it all go when she was in his arms. None of them was as happy because of him, and then he couldn't be happy with them only because he was alive. There need not be another reason. Existence was enough. That was why it was better Miu didn't know they had been slaves, that they were on the run, and it was better she didn't know her life was much shorter than his because then she might think happiness lay in the length of life.

But did she know she was pregnant? Kalia wasn't sure. Perhaps she did know because this was inside her belly rather than an external knowledge.

She will be a mother? Will that also make me a mother?

ROBERT PERIŠIĆ

Scatterwind

I THINK THE reason I followed Kalia around was because he didn't know what he should be. He was a creature in process, which is what makes us kin. His feelings reached me somehow, which was normally not the case, and that's why I remember him so well, like one of my own. Most people sounded like something out of a clammed-up shell; I couldn't tell what was inside, maybe because I am not human and I don't see well. His shell was open and that makes it not a shell at all, perhaps because he didn't know who he was, who his father and mother were. Menda had not told him, and I had no means to do it.

Kalia knew that there were many abandoned babies, in the rubbish, on the streets. He thought he had been one of those children, from nowhere. I'm not saying that's what anybody should think, but one must think in this way in order to connect with the wind.

When he understood Miu would become a mother, and he would become a mother, I saw that mother was not a word, but a feeling Kalia could have, and a feeling even I could have. That feeling, I saw, is inside nature. And this feeling was a problem for hunters and they wanted to delete it from the web of language humanity had woven like a spider, but as soon as they'd unwittingly leave the net, even a hunter could be a mother.

I speak with a human tongue because I don't know any other, but human words are as dangerous as time; memory and knowledge in time, yesterday and tomorrow, have taken over words and no one is happy, but no one is petrified either like a panicking animal. Words are softeners, they make everything milder, including joy and misery. Even death can be softened with words. That's why humanity is not panicking, it is constantly wrapping itself up in words.

The whole web of language sits inside a single thread.

Words are, I feel it always when I speak, the tool of the polis. Words are, almost always, on the side of those who rule the polis and only sometimes do words tear away, briefly— those are the most interesting words; you can see them disappear in the wind.

El

IT WASN'T CLEAR who the father was, but there were only
two candidates since no other cats were to be seen on Issa
except for the ones who'd arrived with them. And those on
the other ship, whom Kalia had assumed to be female, were
two tomcats. One was Eno, who belonged to the younger Kleemporos, a boy bigger than Kalia, only Kleemporos had not
traveled alone like Kalia; he was part of a large family said to be
very important in Syracuse, but political reasons had forced
them to leave, although they were Dionysius's family. The
word "politics" was heard more often now, a word that had
not been uttered by anyone on the ship, a word that followed
the word "polis," probably because they were born together.

Eno and Miu were not friends. Kalia had seen Eno trying
to get close to Miu a couple of times and she had boxed him
away with her paws, although they were the same size, and
then Eno had gone off with his tail between his legs. That had
nothing to do with politics.

Kalia was much more suspicious of the other tomcat, the big one. Miu hung around him and performed all kinds of acrobatics in order to draw his attention, because the tomcat looked very lazy.

This was El, who belonged to the white-haired, one-armed Arion, the former soldier. Kalia had heard of him from Teogen; he also left Syracuse because of politics, but Arion was not part of any group because the things he spoke of were of no interest to anyone. "He's not even a philosopher," Teogen said, finding no appropriate description for Arion.

It was not because of Teogen's words, but perhaps simply because Arion was missing an arm, that Kalia stayed out of his way.

The lack of an arm provoked fear in Kalia, a fear that might not have had anything to do with Arion, but everything to do with those observing him. Fear sometimes sits in the very act of fixating at the place that makes one imagine pain. The space where the arm should have been, and was not, was occupied by an image of the arm. Or rather, the mind held the image of the arm, while it also marked the spot of its destruction. The mind held the mutilation and the fear of pain, and the fear of those who brought up the memory of pain.

Arion would sometimes stick a hooked iron extension onto the missing place, below the elbow. He did this when he was in a bad mood or when it seemed—simply because he wore this extension—that he was in a bad mood. The extension included sheepskin and ropes for tightening. The sheepskin

ROBERT PERIŠIĆ

reached his other shoulder, covered the top of Arion's torso, and everything was held together tight with hard rope. It was a complicated piece of attire made for those who waged war with half an arm missing. Wearing it must have been uncomfortable, even painful, which was probably why Arion rarely wore it on Issa. He only wore it on those occasions when he wanted to remind others, or himself, that he was not just some armless loner but, if need be, a walking weapon.

Although he mostly walked around without the extension, the image of the iron hook remained in the mind when gazing at Arion, and one's eyes did not only register the missing arm, but also the missing hook. All that was not there, but had once been, it was all present and absent in Arion's image. And it was not all in the perception of others. Arion himself felt the pain in the arm he did not have because pain, in fact, is never in the limb itself. Pain is in the mind, Arion knew. He did not speak of this pain, not only because he did not need any more glances at his armlessness. He did not speak also because at the beginning, when he was still surprised by this pain, he had asked the disabled beggars in the streets of Syracuse about it—they were mostly former soldiers—and whenever he asked them if they felt something similar, they would look at him darkly and say something incoherent. Not a single one said anything he could understand, except for the one time when an old man who was missing an arm and an ear said, "You're making my ear hurt, you idiot!"

Arion stared at him and said, "Careful how you speak!"

The old man was not in the least bit frightened, which made Arion see that they were alike.

"Not only am I careful about how I speak," the old man said, "I am careful about how I think. But you're just another stupid soldier who is annoying me. Well, I was like you once. Now give me a coin so I can get something to eat."

Arion gave him a coin and meant to leave. Then the old man asked him, "Does it hurt more now?"

"I think so, yes."

"An arm you no longer have? How can that be?"

"I don't know," Arion said.

"Maybe because you talked about it? You have now woken up my ear, because you don't understand anything, but you have paid for my lunch so I will tell you. Your arm wants you to leave it in peace. Don't awaken it. It is only in your mind. You must let it go. It isn't easy because it will sometimes return on its own, especially in your dreams. When its image comes back, that's what hurts. And now leave me alone, my ear hurts because you woke it up."

Because of everything that was in the eyes and in the mind, Kalia would have completely avoided Arion had he not seen Miu go up to him fearlessly several times and walk around him, which was an honor she bestowed on few people. Miu did this when El, Arion's tomcat, wasn't around. Was it because Arion smelled like El? Or was she trying to make family ties in roundabout ways? Maybe she wanted to leave her scent on

Arion and take Arion's scent onto herself? And thus make El consider her one of his own?

And so it happened Kalia also thought maybe he shouldn't fear Arion so much, and they chatted briefly on several occasions. Arion did not use a special way to talk to children, he observed them seriously, as if to say: don't pretend you're a child. He appeared taciturn, but when he started talking, he spoke to everyone, and so when he once orated in the harbor, Kalia listened, among grown-ups, which made him invisible in some way. He didn't expect Arion to turn to him and ask, "Would you liberate the slaves?"

Kalia looked at him in fear and said, "Yes."

"There, a child doesn't need explaining," Arion said to the rest. "Because freedom is natural. Only slavery must be learned."

Arion carried on speaking, but Kalia thought Arion had asked him because he'd detected that he had been a slave. So he quietly left.

As he was leaving he heard Arion say, "Everyone wants the other to be a dog. But a citizen is a dog and a cat in one. That's how one ought to be in the day. If one is just a dog in the day, he'll only be a cat at night."

Scatterwind

CATS CONFUSED PEOPLE. Not just those on the island who had never seen the animals, but also the Greeks who had taken them from the Egyptians—because that was not long ago, they were not used to them yet. They were the first ungovernable animals that made friends with the humans. When humans stood before cats, they did not see their own purpose.

The Greeks thought that this might change with time, if they demonstrated their Greek character. They tied up cats. Pigras wasn't the first one to have this idea. They painted cats tied up, minted coins bearing images of tied-up cats. The Greeks were, as far as I could see, really the first humans who were convinced they ruled the Earth. That was the most important thing with them. I had gotten to know cats before this, so I didn't find their behavior strange. Cats living in the wild did not live in groups and did not have a leader.

Only lions lived in a group where it was clear who was on top; other cats did not live in this way. They did not recognize a leader, did not have this in their genes, and there was no room to create this idea now. They recognized friends, but there was no leader in a cat's mind. That was the entire mystery of cats: they did not have leaders in their genes. I think the Greeks, who invented democracy, could tolerate cats thanks to democracy, despite their confusion. I saw how they proliferated cats across the Mediterranean. In Egypt, cats had been a divinity, because freedom belonged only to the gods, whereas for the Greeks cats were a necessary evil.

The Syracusans were also familiar with democracy. They called Dionysius a tyrant because they understood democracy. He was not an ordinary tyrant either, but one who pleased the people who were familiar with other ways. A citizen is a cat and dog in one. This is how cats arrived together with democracy, scattered via Greek colonies in Europe.

Kalia

KALIA KEPT HIS story secret and would only speak out loud about the past when he was alone with Miu or Mikro. Had he not spoken to them about it, he could have, it seemed to him, forgotten it all.

He felt a sense of oblivion floating over the island.

He told Miu and Mikro about Menda because it seemed as if her image and voice came back when he spoke of her. It was important that he spoke out loud, and didn't keep the words as thoughts in his head, because those words gave him a better sense for everything that surrounded him.

He would sometimes say to Miu, "Tell Menda that we are well," just in case Miu was really connected to Latra. And sometimes he'd say it to the woods, the trees, the sea. He wondered how she was and if she wanted to live longer. "Tell Menda that we are well, tell Latra to pass on the message," he told Miu.

He also mentioned Zoi. He was very sorry they had not said goodbye. It's a strange thing, saying goodbye; there are so many stupid words you say to people, and with her he did not get to say those last words and so it felt incomplete. He had to tell Miu and Mikro these things because he felt that distance made things fade from memory. He saw Syracuse sinking slowly into another world, a world beyond the voyage. Recent events seemed distant in time and space; he saw that it was not only time that created oblivion, but also space. He felt this was the same for other people, that everyone on Issa was forgetting who they used to be; they seemed different than they had been on the ship, as if they were somehow lighter. Perhaps he was imagining things, but it seemed the ship passengers had become livelier on Issa, moved more easily, their faces were different, their eyes brighter. Perhaps everyone had liberated themselves from something although he could not know which of them kept stories that must never be told. But people can't forget everything, just like Kalia wouldn't forget everything. The faces and spaces of Syracuse turned up in his dreams: Sabas's house, the poor market, Mikro's stable. Syracuse hovered above Issa at night; at night the two blended into one mixed-up courtyard.

When the sun would climb up over the bay again, daylight named that which was real and everyone awoke liberated, far from nights full of Sicily. They were building a town that they might one day dream of, a town where their dreams would eventually take place.

Kalia didn't know how this worked for Miu and Mikro and if they needed dreams to leave the world that was spoken of during the day. With people, the things spoken of during the day were both true and false, he knew this from his own experience. And he knew what people spoke of during the day served the purpose of hiding the things of yesterday, and he imagined how it was for Miu and Mikro, who did not cover the world with words.

They didn't have to be something different on Issa. Because he didn't have to hide around town anymore, his hiding place was now only in words. *Maybe they hold everything together in their heads like I do in dreams*, he thought. *Syracuse and Issa are united for them, and the world is one place, even in the daytime.*

Teogen was possibly the only person who did not dream of Syracuse but of Issa. His vision of Issa was clearer than what actually existed and he dragged Kalia along with him.

Kalia thought there were better things than being Teogen's assistant—after working on sheds, Teogen spent all his free time preparing to start working on the real city, even before schedule. He and Kalia were already stretching long ropes along the western side of the bay, measuring, looking for the best direction for the streets, vertical and horizontal, the best positions for houses along the streets, and they dug to see how deep the stone was and how all of this fit in with Teogen's imagined city, which was meant to have drainage canals running down the middle of the vertical streets. "Drainage canals, that's the most important thing," Teogen kept saying. "It's the only thing that makes us different. Drainage canals, not stinking palaces!"

With time Kalia came to see that Oikistes and the rest did not share Teogen's ideas. The hillside that Teogen had decided was the best did not fit the way Greeks usually built because they thought, because of the stench, a city should not be directly exposed to the sun. Only Teogen was sure that this was the right spot.

"The hillside is the best place, the flattest and with a good base," he kept saying. "They believe in the northern wind! Don't they realize we're building a new city! We can connect the sun and the air!" Teogen shouted, mostly in front of Kalia, as if rehearsing saying the same thing to Oikistes, only in a lower tone.

But Teogen wasn't much afraid of the others. Kalia watched as Teogen spoke to Oikistes and the others. Teogen watched them as if they were children asking silly questions. And he considered Kalia to be his assistant, who was more important than the other men. Teogen was so certain that the others could do nothing but frown.

They worked on the sheds only as much as they had to. Teogen was more interested in the stone. Starting at dawn, the pair would walk over to the bay Teogen had spotted from the ship, where the stone was layered like rings in a tree stump, one after another but separate, making it easy to cut the stone into blocks, he said.

"This stone has been waiting for us," he repeated, "because the streets on the hillside have to be built on levels, and with the stone from these white cliffs we can lay a light inclination, and build streets that will remain forever, Kalia. Spread out your arms like that, you see, one block on the left side, and the other on the right, and in between a gap for a drainage canal. A house will look onto the street, and the street behind it will look onto the parallel street but they won't be connected. Between the houses will be another drainage canal because I know what they're like, they love to throw their rubbish out of the window.

"When you're a builder, Kalia, you have to consider the behavior of the laziest fool, who might pollute the whole thing. This will be the first city you've seen that will not stink."

Kalia thought it was better not to mention sleeping in Mikro's stable in Syracuse.

On Issa, Kalia brought Mikro with him whenever he could; when Mikro came with them he carried their water, food, and ropes. But if he had to leave him in others' care, he did not know how Mikro was doing; sometimes he came back and saw pain in Mikro's eyes.

A colony is, they told them, like an army at first, and donkeys were, he could see, the lowest of soldiers. When he wasn't of service to his owner, a donkey had to work on other jobs, which were endless.

Kalia was now Mikro's owner, but Teogen was more in charge—he had become something of a guardian for Kalia. Teogen worked Mikro, and his jenny, Isiha, to the bone. He explained to Kalia that a donkey, above all, drank a lot of water and had to earn that water. Mikro was Kalia's donkey but the water was not Kalia's. It was from the common reservoir of the polis, so the donkey was in fact not his, considering that it would have, were it not for the polis water, died of thirst. And during the voyage to Issa the donkey drank and ate from the common supplies, because Kalia had nothing, and so the donkey was indebted to the polis. Kalia nodded, but it felt to him that Teogen only spoke of debt, and the polis would never write off this debt. It's true, Kalia hadn't brought water to the ship, but the water came from the ground on Issa and Mikro lugged this water on his back.

"It's true that he carries it, but he also drinks it, and that is polis water," Teogen said.

"But the water comes from the ground," Kalia replied.

"If it wasn't for the polis and if we weren't building the city, you'd never have seen this land. There's no land. There is nothing, remember, except for the polis. And everything you see around you, you'd never have laid eyes on it if the polis hadn't brought you here. We have to know what came first, and what was imagined."

Kalia saw that Teogen couldn't wait for Mikro and Isiha to start pulling the heavy stone blocks from the white cliffs of the island, which would be used to build the sloping streets with drainage canals from Teogen's mind. Those blocks were heavy. Kalia also saw that Teogen would never give Mikro his freedom, and neither would the polis.

Mikro was a slave, the polis was human, and Mikro would never be part of the polis. Kalia had liberated himself, Miu was free, but he had cheated Mikro. He could not speak of everything he owed to Mikro in front of Teogen, because then he'd have to tell him he had been a slave. He could only talk to Miu and Mikro in those moments when he would manage to bring him along, as if they had something to do, and then he'd lead Mikro into the woods. Miu, whose belly grew, would find them up there at the top of the hill overlooking Issa, by the leaning cliff, near a holm oak tree. They looked at the sea from above, over at the islands in the distance and the unknown land, huddled away like in the old days. Kalia simply wanted to give Mikro a chance to be free of burdens.

Whenever they returned from their perch above the sea, Teogen would be waiting, cross. Sometimes, Kalia thought he might even hit him. Once, Mikro turned his backside toward Teogen, as if he might kick anyone who approached Kalia because Teogen had met them in a rage, not because he had needed Mikro and Kalia urgently, but because he didn't like their friendship. He was jealous of that which he despised. Teogen laughed at this fighting stance, went around them, grabbed Mikro by the neck, and mounted him. Kalia told him he was a heavy man.

Teogen regarded him in disbelief and said, "So?"

"You are, Teogen, too heavy and so please get off Mikro."

As was his habit when he felt something might be very dangerous, Kalia clutched the iron scissors in his tunic pocket. There were few such beautiful tools on Issa, that everyone knew his scissors.

ROBERT PERIŠIĆ

Teogen got off Mikro and said, "You're a man."

Kalia thought, *I'm Mikro's friend.*

Staring at Kalia, Teogen said, "It's a good thing you don't have a mother."

Kalia didn't understand this.

Teogen added, "You love nature." Then he laughed, but not in a good way.

Kalia said, "What?"

"I don't want anything to get close to me."

"What are you talking about?"

"I'm afraid of mother," Teogen said, as if telling a joke.

Teogen was sometimes quite stupid, Kalia realized. He was smart when he spoke of building, but everything else was lopsided in his head. He'd do well to tear it all down.

Was he really afraid of mother, Kalia wondered.

He asked him the next day, "Teogen, what is it like in your head?"

"The city?"

"No, the rest of it."

"The rest?"

"Everything else you have in your head."

"Eh?" Teogen laughed as if trying to conjure it up for the first time. "I think it is like a fortress."

Scatterwind

I SAW THE loneliness of man. This soul who proclaimed that others didn't have a soul. Then this soul wondered at its loneliness in nature, dove inside itself and sought the truth.

I sometimes thought he really did view nature as a mother. A mother who could swallow him up. This sad little trembling soul. Shivering like a pup in crocodile jaws.

I saw the way a crocodile mother protected her young. Some have houses, others have hands, and others a hole in the ground or in a tree, such as squirrels, and that is where they keep their young. And a crocodile mother has a jaw and a mouth, this is the safest spot, and she hides the young inside, that is their house. She will not swallow them and they know this because this refuge is engraved inside them.

But the human, after proclaiming that others don't have a soul, thinking itself good and alone, became afraid of the body and the mouth; he decided to leave and never return.

He was so maddeningly lonely. A human, a Greek. The offspring of this man grows today.

ROBERT PERIŠIĆ

His loneliness made it clear—there was nothing else other than objects: splints, meat, wood, leather, sandals. I exist and as far as I'm concerned, that is indisputable. He was maddeningly lonely and had to make this statement. Man is the measure of all things. He had to make this statement even if it meant it would anger the gods.

Sooner or later there would be an agreement with the gods about this, he thought.

Man is the measure of all things. Of those who are, and of those who are not. Meat, lunch. Wood, boat. Leather, sandals. He was so lonely that his brain started to work even faster, supernaturally. It was a big day, a supernatural day, when he exclaimed, under the sun, before the sea. As soon as the statement was made, I saw how much he had suffered keeping it in. Because of the gods. But he had to say it. He knew this in fact made him a god. But he had to say it. To the sea, to the gods, he said: "Sorry. Don't get me wrong. It's not what it seems—it's not aimed against the heavens. Be patient and you'll see: this is not aimed against the heavens, but against the Earth. Man is the measure of all things. Of those who are, and of those who are not."

This Greek was called Protagoras. He was a big human hero, laid the foundation for the human-god. He drowned while escaping to Sicily.

The Trace

MIU GAVE BIRTH in a small shelter under the leaning cliff, close to the spot where she, Kalia, and Mikro liked to spend time together. Kalia looked for her, he looked for her all day, and when he found her there, in the grass darkened with blood, he thought she didn't recognize him and she didn't know where she was. Her eyes looked as if she was dreaming a heavy dream. Three tiny creatures lay on top of her, pushing and rolling over as they tried to suckle.

Does she know what's happening? he thought.

She looked terribly surprised. They said she knew what to do and she would do it alone. The men said that. Then he asked the women. They told him she could only know by what was on the inside, but no mother could really know what it was the first time around. He didn't think Miu looked as if she knew what had happened. It looked as if she was expiring.

He had, as he climbed up the hill, heard in a small clearing the voices of people cutting trees and he ran toward them for water. When he returned to Miu and her kittens, El was there too. People had told him that the male cat didn't care about his offspring. But El was often with Miu since her pregnancy. Kalia thought El knew better than Miu what was going on, since he was older. Perhaps El had seen that they were alone on the island and there was no one else who had the knowledge.

El circled, a few steps away from Miu, and growled at Kalia.

"It's okay El, I'm a friend," Kalia said as he set down the borrowed bowl of water under Miu's face.

El quickly bit his hand and Kalia moved away, leaving the bowl.

"It's okay, El," he told him.

The kittens blindly searched for Miu's nipples; one succeeded and the other two wandered. Kalia marveled at Miu as a mother, and she marveled at herself. It seemed her gaze was becoming more aware and she was noticing the kittens on her. She saw the water, drank a little, or just wet her lips.

One kitten was in an uncomfortable position, almost under Miu, but she didn't feel it. Kalia got closer and lifted her a little, so that the kitten could get out. El nearly attacked again, then changed his mind, tensely watching Kalia's movements.

Kalia sat around and watched a little longer, not knowing what he ought to do, and then he went down to the port to look for food. He found Arion coming back from fishing with the gray-haired woman who was helping him out with the rowing. Kalia explained to Arion what was happening, that El was clearly the father. Arion told him not to be silly, tomcats don't behave like that. Kalia told him to come and see. Now he spoke to Arion as if he wasn't afraid of him. Arion brought fish and wine with him.

When they arrived at the spot, El stared at Arion as if wondering how he knew his private business. It was something between joy and protesting—he wove himself around Arion's legs in a way that blocked his path and kept him from approaching Miu. It seemed to Kalia that Miu was recovering. She blinked at him in recognition. Kalia and Arion sat in the shade of the large holm oak, El sat between them and Miu. Arion toasted them with wine, and Kalia with a smile. Kalia told Arion about Miu, how a sailor had brought her from Egypt and how she was supposed to belong to another, but had chosen him. He didn't want to mention everything, but told him how they wandered around the city and she nearly made him late for the ship and that she cried for Syracuse. Arion had been on another ship, but he knew how she had yowled at the departure, many remembered her cries. Kalia showed Arion where El had bitten him, but he said he didn't mind at all.

"You got away lightly," Arion said, serious, the way he spoke to children. "I lost my arm with them."

"With whom?"

"He's a Carthaginian," Arion said, looking at Kalia as if he ought to know what that meant.

ROBERT PERIŠIĆ

Kalia looked at El in surprise as he guarded Miu, who was licking her blind babies.

Arion watched Kalia seriously. "I'll explain," he said. "He surrendered to me when we had conquered a Carthaginian colony in the west of Sicily. He was on their fortress, on the hill above town, and all the other defenders of the fort had already died or run away, there was only the tomcat left. He had climbed up to the top of their citadel all alone. When I got there, because I had reached there first, he looked at me as if I were an enemy, and under him was an abyss. When I saw there were no other defenders apart from him, I held my soldiers back, told them to go down, and I sat there, at the top of that city, waiting for this Carthaginian tomcat to surrender. I sat there for a long time. It was nice to sit there, to rest. He was still standing at the edge of the walls, and as I sat there I had released the rage, at least the rage that would have made me harm this Carthaginian animal.

"I just wanted him as a trophy. Few people had a cat in Syracuse then, it was for me a Carthaginian thing. I don't know how you got yours from Egypt, your father must be rich. I only wanted to bring him to Syracuse, by the neck, and I wanted to say, 'This is a Carthaginian tomcat, their last defender, here he is in my hand!' But he must have seen through my vanity and when I got up on the citadel and wanted to get him, he walked on the edge of the walls, made me walk around in circles. When I sped up, he sped up, and I thought he might fall. I saw that he would rather fall down into the abyss than into enemy hands. I sat back down. I knew I had to address him in a friendly manner, otherwise I'd lose. Then I told him, 'Okay, you have full abolition, you can even have some of my food.' I persuaded him a little longer, and threw him a piece of dried meat. It could be said that he surrendered under his own conditions. When he got off the wall he watched me for a long time. I wondered: What does he see? I had taken off my fighting prosthetic arm, and it seemed he was looking at my missing arm, looking at one arm and thinking: this animal is wounded. If a human being had watched me like that—because it was this very gaze I could not stand—I would have quickly demonstrated I was more dangerous than the rest even with one arm missing. It's probably why I had remained a soldier, to prove it, and they let me stay because of my merits.

"You know, human pity is not a good thing. But with the cat it didn't make me angry, simply because it was not human. It was even unexpected to me when I told the cat, 'Yes, I am missing an arm.' It was the first time I uttered those words. The way the cat watched me made me not feel ashamed, so I carried on, telling him, 'I lost it for Syracuse. For someone. Maybe for a master. Maybe for fame. Maybe for a salary. Perhaps even for the future. But my arm isn't waiting for me in the future.' Maybe I didn't say all that out loud. But the cat got closer to me, sat down, watched me, as if he had nothing better to do than study me. I heard voices from the city. The victory song and the hollering

ROBERT PERIŠIĆ

were getting farther away. I guess I didn't know how tired I was—I fell asleep.

"When I came to, it had been an hour or less, and the cat was lying down in the same spot, sleeping. He had been tired too, from the battle, human rage, the noise. I watched him sleep, and looked up at the sky. It was dusk, a clear silence, and I thought: the war is over.

"It seemed to me then, on top of that citadel, next to the sleeping Carthaginian tomcat, that the war was over. It was an image that showed up for the first time in my life: the end of war. It was not about the world, but my own warfare. Before then, I couldn't think of myself as anything but a soldier, everything was a battle, every day, every man I met, every woman, everything was a battle. I didn't know what I could be but a soldier. I was trapped, armless, I perhaps wanted to be killed. I was no longer an ordinary soldier, I had people to send ahead of me, and I still went first. But I didn't even know how tired I was. And then I woke up on the citadel.

"Some woman told me later: when an animal finds you, it brings a message. I don't believe in such things. I know the cat wasn't bringing me a message, it wasn't there because of me, was not in my service—it had its path, as I had mine. I didn't know its past, and it didn't know mine. Nothing in this world is here because of me, as I am not here because of other things—that's what I think, after everything is said and done. People imagine this sort of thing, thinking they're at the center of everything. We also have gods whom we think are here because of us, because we think we're at the center of everything. But why would we be at the center of everything for the gods, why would we be important for them? Do we think lesser beings are important? How important is a cat to people? How important is an ant to people? We could have mattered to the gods as much as ants mattered to us. You just clear an ant away with your hand when you're sitting down, thinking nothing. There is no center of things. No one is in anyone's service in order to pass on some message. I told that to the woman who was getting on my nerves, although she may have actually been onto something. But it's true, I said, that I learned something from the tomcat. I saw how the tomcat was free: when I saw him sleeping. I saw he was free with me. Because I knew I fell asleep first and he had been watching me, as I watched him sleep. He could have left. He was free to go, but he stayed.

"I was, Kalia, as you might be suspecting, the sort of person who few would remain with if they were free to go. The tomcat didn't have anything to say to me. It was in fact me who had something to say to myself. But when you get to the point where you have something to say to yourself, that means you hadn't said it to yourself before, and you haven't been talking to yourself about it. I had to say it to someone else, someone who was free of me and from whom I was free. That was not another human being. Why, I wondered later. Because they are people, because you're participating with them in a game where it is known in advance who should say what. And you don't trust them. I was perhaps defeated by people. I was an armless loser, as far as they were concerned. And I didn't want to be that. I was a winner. That's how I held myself with people, and that's how I carry on.

"But in hiding my loss, I was further falling into a trap and was ruled by others in a worse way. I was not free from them, not even free inasmuch as I could tell myself the truth, the way I had done it with the cat. I told people the opposite of the truth about myself, so I had completely lost sight of the truth.

"I was mesmerized by the human world, I saw later, human society enchanted me, so I had postured before it the way I would in front of a bronze mirror. I wanted to see something I already knew: to be a soldier—I thought there was no other image possible. But I was finished, war was finished for me. I hadn't won. Even though I had won, there was no victory. Everything looked like victory and this was a good day to retreat.

"All this I told myself, speaking to a sleeping cat. It was an unusual day, this sort of thing happened after battles, when a few hours earlier death had been so close. Climbing to the top of the citadel I had seen several corpses, theirs and ours— the fact that I'd had no time to close their eyes, the fact that I had stepped to the top in the battle delirium that warps the mind intending to kill, and the fact that I had found only El at the top, all of it mattered. As he slept, I felt I too was sleeping. It was as if I were narrating to my sleeping self, which was a very strange feeling. Maybe this is a dream, I thought, maybe I'm still asleep. I may even be dead, perhaps I am one of those down there who had stayed behind with their eyes open, perhaps I only think I have reached the top of the fort. Perhaps death is playing with me and letting me see myself as a sleeping Carthaginian tomcat. Was this cat even alive? Is he breathing? I was not afraid as these thoughts came to me, they were dispassionate, as if I would accept them without a wonder if all of it had turned out to be the case. 'What kind of victory is this?' I asked myself aloud.

"It was not a dream. The cat opened his eyes, yawned and stretched. They had been nothing but thoughts, thoughts in need of an odd way to appear. Why, I wondered later. Because people, and that which I tried to be before them, were in my head. Without the help of the cat I wouldn't have talked to myself up there at the citadel. Maybe I'd have gone to my death the next day because I was prone to danger. Everything in order not to say that I had no victory.

"And so I had fallen asleep at the citadel and woke up. And so I had thought I was sleeping in the body of the animal. But it was actually him sleeping, and I was simply looking on and talking to myself after accepting the fact that perhaps I was no longer alive.

"I named the cat El. It hadn't done it on purpose, it wasn't there for me, but the cat had ended my war and I wanted to give it a meaningful name. El had been their creator, of the Carthaginians, or of their fathers the Phoenicians, over there somewhere, so I'd heard. If I had named it after one of our gods, people would have been resentful of the cat, daring to have such a name, so I took the name of their god, which suited it well.

"I think El and Miu get on so well because they are now both Greek and African. They're Greek after us two, and Africans by themselves. You see, they will form a colony here on Issa. We might be exiled, we might disappear, we will disappear sooner or later because we are at the edge of this world, and there is a huge land before us. We are not the first people here, we are only the first Greeks, but they are the first of their kind. Now that Miu has given birth, we have, Kalia, left our mark. Is that good or bad? What do the lizards make of it? Or mice? What do birds think of it? I will look out for that, Kalia, as can you. These two arrived with us and will remain when we are gone. I will be gone soon. And El is getting on too. If he outlives me, keep an eye on him. Feed him a bite sometimes. Give him water in the summer."

That's how Arion spoke to Kalia. He drank wine, laughed at the sky through the shade of the holm oak and said, "Dear Kalia, you don't think about death. But you see these blind creatures on Miu, look at them. You and I, Kalia, we share time with them, in the distance. Not with my battles. My battles are already forgotten. They seemed great, but they're already incomprehensible. I have won so many times, but I can't remember why."

It was a warm day, a sliver of a breeze moved Arion's long white hair, freshened his face. Kalia watched Arion, who seemed to be wavering between nearby and very far away, and although the whole thing was strange, Kalia wasn't afraid. Were the distances he mentioned the same as what turned up in Kalia's dreams?

"I sometimes see things that are near as if they were far away," Kalia uttered, insecure, as if confessing.

"Near and far, that's time," said Arion. He took another sip of wine and raised his glass to the soft skies over the land. "We Greeks and Africans from Sicily, we are here now and in the distance."

He watched El, Miu, the kittens. "A blind trace," he said to Kalia, smiling.

Kalia imagined time before him, the long time Arion had spoken of; he couldn't do it, it was the empty field of distance.

"I feel dizzy from this story," said Kalia.

"You too?" Arion said, raising his glass again.

He was missing quite a few teeth already, but Kalia thought the light made him look nice as the crickets sped up their rhythm above the newborn city.

Miu and El glanced at them occasionally, the way one does when one is in agreement with what is being said, but has something better to be doing.

ROBERT PERIŠIĆ

6. Mikro In Issa

Kalia

KALIA HAD A sudden growth spurt. Everyone noticed. He
was almost as tall as an adult, although his shape was still
a child's. He had rushed upward like a forest tree whose
path was freed from the shadows and was sprouting thin
branches toward the light.

It was still summer and Teogen and Kalia were working
in the quarry, under the sun. They were cutting marks in the
stone and then with measured hits, so the stone wouldn't
crack in an unwanted spot, broke the blocks into squares
and then shaped them nicely so they were of an equal width.
This was so they could later line them up along the vertical
streets, and so be in harmony with the steep hill, forming
something like lightly inclined steps. There would be white
stone blocks in two rows, a drainage canal bisecting them.
The foundations for the houses were being dug up alongside the blocks, growing in levels. Every new house would
be on a higher spot, so that small islands of houses appeared

between the vertical and horizontal streets, but all of it was still hardly visible, just peeping out of Teogen's mind.

When they finished cutting a dozen blocks, the stone was shipped into the harbor, beneath the town that was slowly sprouting, like a tree that was not yet a tree. The harbor itself was also being built, like a growing root, made from thicker stone blocks because the layers of blocks in the quarry were uneven. The layers had been determined by nature, and they were in turn determining the shape of the blocks. Mikro and Isiha were not needed for this so Teogen had given them over to the public works. But there were other human helpers too, though only Teogen and Kalia were permanently in the quarry, shaping the harbor and the vertical streets, like father and son, only Kalia knew he was not a son, but a stand-in for a son who was talking philosophy in the third row over there at that Plato guy's, in Athens, which he had, just out of fun and together with Teogen, in the rhythm of the hammer, gossiped about.

Because Teogen occasionally shouted under the midday sun, "Plato! Athens! What did I raise him for! Dear god! I may as well have raised a donkey!"

Kalia already saw how to rile up Teogen, which is what Teogen wanted. So Kalia would say, "Don't say that! What's wrong with donkeys?"

Kalia found it interesting how Teogen followed the joke, but would always respond as if it were not a joke. "A donkey is better than him!"

Kalia liked seeing how jokes and truth intersected but Teogen would never admit it if Kalia said something serious. Kalia thought donkeys were better than Teogen too, and himself. It was just a feeling, Kalia knew, and not one to bring up in front of other people. Kalia felt maybe even Teogen thought the same, but it was not what interested Teogen. He often said about his Isiha, "There's not a better creature than her," but this, in some way, didn't matter. Teogen's son, whom he cursed, was still more important than Isiha, as a species, so that their importance couldn't be compared. The difference in species ruins all comparisons in the mind, like the walls of a crooked house, Kalia came to know. Only nothing was crooked in that house. Kalia thought differently of Mikro. This is why Mikro accepted him in his stable when he was cold. He, Miu, and Mikro slept there like a family. It was not the wrong house and he wouldn't be tearing it down in his head. Teogen didn't understand this.

They didn't need Mikro as they worked in stone, and others needed him. There was no sense in the animal resting when it belonged to the polis, and it belonged to the polis by default. That was the law of the apoikia, Teogen said. All forces must be harnessed when the city is being built.

Being beaten by the sun all day, Kalia often dove into the sea, which is how he learned to swim. The smell of the stone was in his nostrils, the dust was in his hair, he had little sores on his hands; the sea cleaned them and they healed. He had arrived on Issa with the smell of stone in his nostrils.

One dusk, Kalia returned and saw Mikro walking slowly as he, along with several other donkeys, was being led by a young man with tiny eyes and a pointy face, by the name of Linos.

Linos left Mikro and Isiha and asked, "Where is Teogen?"

Kalia saw, by the way Linos looked at him, that he was asking for Teogen because he considered Kalia unworthy of a conversation. Kalia answered him without words, by glancing at the port. Then Linos walked off in silence.

Kalia shouted, "Why is the donkey looking so unwell?"

Without turning around Linos shouted, "Because it's weak and small, that's why!"

Kalia thought of picking up a stone and throwing it at him, but didn't want to miss and hit one of the donkeys that Linos was taking ahead.

Kalia lifted the leather cover on Mikro's back and saw sores and other spots where the fur was peeling. Isiha also looked exhausted, but went to eat in the little barn. Isiha was larger and stronger than Mikro and she still had an appetite. Mikro remained at Kalia's side.

He stroked Mikro's neck. Then Kalia sat on the ground, put his elbows on his knees, hung his face in his hands. He saw himself in Sabas's house and Miu tied up by Pigras—he was suddenly back there. He and Miu had left, but he couldn't think of a way out for Mikro.

The Liburnians didn't use donkeys for very heavy loads and they worked them a little, in the fields, because the

Liburnians were not building a city. Kalia had thought he should sell Mikro to some good Liburnian woman who was not building a house. He asked Ceuna, the white-haired Liburnian who helped Arion with the rowing when he went fishing on his little boat; he asked her if she might want to buy a donkey, she wouldn't have to pay anything for it, just say she'd bought it. It could be her donkey, if she was going to treat it well. Kalia would feed him. It was up to her.

But when Kalia mentioned selling the donkey, Teogen ruined his plan with a wave of his hand, saying Kalia needed his permission, because the polis had entrusted him with Kalia's care, and he wouldn't allow it. He added that it wasn't just up to him, because even if he agreed, Kalia would need permission from the polis, because no able-bodied animal could simply leave the polis. The building of the polis is like a war, Teogen said, and everyone is enlisted. Him, Kalia, Mikro, Isiha, everyone. None of them had paid for the trip to Issa, Teogen said. And why would they travel for free? To build the apoikia. Why had Mikro traveled, drank, and eaten at the expense of the polis? To build Issa. Kalia couldn't sell the animal as he pleased. The polis wouldn't allow it.

Kalia had already understood that Mikro's fate was to be a slave and that Mikro was not his own master, but had to be someone's property—that's why he had left the coins for Alexandros—but he now saw that Mikro wasn't even his property; he belonged to the polis.

"How is it possible that Mikro's debt is always increasing?" he asked Teogen. "No one asked Mikro for his opinion."
"I've already explained everything. Are you stupid, Kalia?" said Teogen. "Are you too going to become a philosopher?"
"I am stupid for bringing Mikro along," Kalia said. "Your son isn't stupid."

"Why are you mentioning him?" Teogen snapped.

"Because you love no one," Kalia told him. He wanted to say something harsher, so he added, "You have no one. Only the city lives in your head."

Teogen raised a hand, as if to hit Kalia.

Kalia still had his scissors. If he hadn't, he might have worried, but like this he said, "You want to hit me? And then what?"

Teogen looked at him in disbelief. He thought maybe he did love this boy a little. His mood changed as a result of these thoughts. He thought again that he would like it if Kalia were his son. "What do you fear, Kalia?"

Surprised by Teogen's shift in tone, Kalia said, "The polis."

"Oh yes," Teogen said as this was a matter of fact. "You're not as dumb as you seem."

Kalia laughed. Those were Menda's words, and it seemed again that Teogen was his friend, which made him happy. He and Teogen were getting to be the way he had been with Menda. Teogen looked out for him. He'd sometimes glance at Teogen and think, *That's my Teogen.*

But now when he saw Mikro's sores, he wished he'd not laid eyes on them. He knew what Teogen thought: a donkey can take a lot. He wanted to agree with Teogen, but he could see Mikro's back. He sat on the ground, put his elbows on his knees, hid his face in his hands. When he looked up, Mikro was watching him. *Maybe this is the way I looked at him*, Kalia thought. *Back when I was looking for a place to sleep, when I asked: Do you recognize me?* Kalia averted his eyes, and Mikro did the same. He looked to the side. Soon after, Miu walked in from the same direction.

"Hey, Miu," Kalia said.

Mikro greeted her with a quiet sound. She rubbed the side of her body against Kalia's legs and Mikro's lowered snout. She sat between them. Nothing was happening. Nothing was happening but Kalia was thinking, *What's happening here? Why is it so hard to sit here? I am a citizen of the polis. I am a citizen, and he is a donkey.*

Scatterwind

I SAW, LONG ago now, that friendship with a human was risky business. It would start as a friendship, but would mostly end in slavery. If it hadn't been the wish of the friend of a donkey, it was the wish of the others; that's what the polis wanted, those were human politics. True, each animal humanity domesticated had a friend in the beginning and I thought friendship with a human was a trap. The only animal not to have fallen into this trap and made a human friend was a cat. Cats didn't have leaders in their genes, there was nothing that could be done about it, and they were small enough not to present a threat to humanity. They have remained alongside humans as a reminder of nature that cannot be governed. Cats are therefore thought of by humans in the same way as nature: beautiful and dangerously mysterious. But cats are no more mysterious to humans than donkeys are, except they cannot be ruled. That's the whole of their mystery. Cats are as mystical as the wind. And a donkey, male or female, made friends with someone in Nubia, or somewhere along the Ethiopian plateaus. Of all the creatures that ended up in the polis, only donkeys, cats, and humans were from Africa. A donkey, always on the side, zebra's cousin—I saw it even down below, when I left the savannah and climbed up into the hills, I saw free donkeys with several zebra-like stripes on their legs. Mikro too had two stripes lined up above his hooves, which can still be seen in the donkeys on Issa and the land they later called Dalmatia.

And there was, seven centuries after Mikro and Kalia, a Dalmatian man, a distant relative of those who came to Issa from Syracuse, whom I remember since he, the only one of the emperors, gave out an edict in the year 301, where he ruled that a donkey cannot be burdened with more than two hundred Roman pounds, and that is, I calculated later, 65.49 kilograms. That was the Roman emperor Diocletian. Every emperor, I saw, defends some boundaries. That's how I remember the emperor, the Dalmatian: 65.49 kilograms.

Kalia

ARION WAS GETTING ready for bed when Kalia arrived. He was out of breath and Arion told him to sit down. He sat down, but he was still out of breath. He was catching his breath as if he was running from somewhere and Arion saw that it was not because of running, but because of the words struggling to get out.

Then Kalia said, "I was a slave and I ran away."

Arion looked around and hissed, "Quiet!"

Kalia knew he mustn't say it to anyone ever, which is why he said it so quickly, in case he changed his mind. Had Arion even understood?

After what seemed like a long pause, Arion asked, "Why are you saying this? Those words could get you killed and then burnt!"

He'd understood, there it was—he'd broken his promise to Menda.

"Arion, I will run away with Mikro. Please, feed Miu and her kittens sometimes."

Arion took him by the shoulder, and it was clear he would have grabbed both shoulders with his hands if he'd had two. "What are you talking about?"

"I saw Mikro's sores," Kalia said. "We have to run."

"You're an idiot. Do you know what an idiot is?"

"I do. But he is a slave."

"Mikro?"

"He's the slave of the polis. He will die before repaying his debt."

"You think it's your fault? Because you brought him here?"

"Yes."

Arion thought about it. There weren't many Greeks who saw anything strange in slavery. He had told them they should find it strange, but instead, they always thought that he, Arion, was strange. Now he thought Kalia a little strange. Where did he get this idea of liberating animals? From some philosopher? He was surprised by the fact that Kalia wasn't simply *thinking* about it, but was planning to do it. That was because he, although having grown suddenly, was not a fully grown man. Should he even be made to grow up? Arion watched him: on the one hand, no—he was better the way he was—and on the other hand, if he did not become a man, he would be punished. He didn't stand a chance. The donkey's slavery was so ordinary that it wasn't even called slavery. In any case, an animal without an owner was immediately categorized as a wild animal. And the only thing you could do with such an animal is kill it, because it didn't belong to anyone. *That which is no one's, that is wild,* Arion thought. *That is the essence of wild, and not actually being wild. Things are wild by default if they don't belong to man; it's a question of property.*

Arion was silent for a long time, long enough for Kalia to be breathing normally again. Finally, Arion said, "You know what I'm going to do to the polis? I will suggest to the polis to become the owner of the forest. They will like that, they'll vote for it. And in this way I will protect the forest because the polis is so stupid that they protect only that which is their property. How did I not think of this before?"

"Why are you talking about the forest?"

"Someone cut down the oak next to the leaning rock. I saw it yesterday."

"Our oak?" asked Kalia. He wanted to talk about Mikro, but this distracted him.

"Yes," Arion said. "Our oak, Miu and El's... But it wasn't ours. It was no one's, you understand? That's the problem."

"But the oak is no one's. It's... the oak's," Kalia said, staring at Arion and thinking, *Why is he so stupid?*

"Kalia, the law doesn't accept this, the law says it's wild. Then it is better if it is someone's."

"An oak is not a slave," Kalia said. "Why does it have to have an owner?"

"Human law is like that, that's what I'm talking about."

"I'm against the law," Kalia said.

"That's good, but it isn't smart," Arion said. "Whatever is outside of the law, it is outside property, and then it is wild and can be killed. If you're against the law then you're wild. You're not human."

"I'm not interested in being human," Kalia said. "I can't bear to see Mikro's sores."

Arion thought, *Should Kalia grow up, become a man?* He still believed he was better off as he was and it wouldn't work this way. He'd be punished, and lose everything. He wouldn't have any rights, he'd be a slave, an animal.

Arion said, "It's like this with or without you. Mikro won't be better off anywhere else. You feel bad for having brought him, but it's not your fault."

"Who cares if it's my fault," Kalia said. "The main thing is to run away."

"Hey, you silly fool, you have rights here."

"I have also been a slave and I escaped."

"Why are you repeating this, you idiot? I'll pretend I haven't heard it."

"Because. You don't know. Mikro took me in. When I escaped with Miu."

"You escaped with Miu?"

"Yes, and Mikro took us in."

"You owe Mikro?" Arion looked at Kalia with respect, as if the boy had grown up.

"I owe him, yes," Kalia said. He wanted to add: but it's not just that, he is also my friend. He paused. He saw that Arion was thinking.

"You owe the donkey? And that's why you want to escape with him?"

"I'm doing it tonight. You keep an eye on Miu, please."

Arion sighed as if catching air from up above and said, "You're really already a man, Kalia. But do you know one day you have to go to Diomedes and..."

"I'm not a man," Kalia said.

"No?" Arion laughed unwittingly.

"Mikro and I have to run," Kalia said, standing to leave.

"Stop!" Arion shouted. He knew how to give orders and it worked. "I won't feed Miu and the kittens. I'll kill them all!"

Kalia took a few steps back and muttered, "I shouldn't have said anything to you."

"You shouldn't have," Arion said. "Sit down and shut up, you idiot."

Kalia sat down. *So what if I am an idiot?* he thought. *Does that change things?*

Arion said, "Someone will steal the donkey from you. And then you'll both be slaves. I'd rather kill you both myself."

Kalia thought that maybe Arion was right, and there was nowhere to run to. It would be hard to hide on the island.

"I'll kill Miu and her kittens, and then I'll set everything on fire," said Arion. Then he narrowed his eyes and added, "You know, Kalia, only living things can burn. Or those that had been alive, like wood. Stone doesn't burn. Only living things, connected to the sun. And if I think about it, I was always keen on a large fire!"

"You're not like that," Kalia said.

"I am and I'm not," Arion said. "True, I haven't killed many animals, except fish. I am not good, Kalia. But your debt to Mikro makes me a better person."

Kalia didn't really know what to do with this. He felt like everything was closed to him; he had no options. Back in Syracuse, he'd managed to escape, with Miu. Perhaps that had been a great exception.

"I will give you an ointment for the sores," Arion said. "Put it on his back until we come up with something, otherwise I'll kill you all right now."

Kalia didn't actually trust him, but he thought maybe it was better to do so.

Scatterwind

I THINK THAT people, because they domesticated animals that served them, thought the whole of the Earth could be their servant, and even found among their own species those whom they could own. As far as I recall, that hadn't happened while they just had dogs. I later heard about those people who in ancient times populated America and Australia: they went there in the times when humans only had dogs and carried on living in the old way. They never domesticated animals for service. They looked at nature—at everything— differently. Everything I heard about them was familiar to me from old times. I wasn't surprised they weren't able to be slaves; when they were enslaved, they died quickly. They were the remains of the old human kind.

Maybe donkeys had been the catalyst; they weren't kept for milk and meat, they were the true first laborers. When the peasants domesticated them down deep by the Nile, in the Nubia, the first pharaohs soon appeared. The donkeys later built the pyramids, together with the slaves. Sheep, goats,

ROBERT PERIŠIĆ

and cows had been domesticated before donkeys, but none of them were just workers. Was it donkeys that first gave the idea of a slave? No, not them, but the straw broke their backs, so to speak, and thus man got his idea of a worker. I saw people, those who worked the most, who knew donkeys were their brothers. But slavery, that comes from above. It is the organization from above.

Sometimes it seemed to me that ants had prisoners, slaves or something similar, I wasn't sure, but I saw that people and insects have similarities in how they organize. Ants, bees, spiders, all of it, I saw, in some way made its reappearance in humans. I didn't at first see what the difference was between free men and slaves, which confused me. Was it a matter of luck? Kalia and Pigras looked almost the same, because they had the same father, but Greek slaves and masters looked the same in any case. I saw later how people, whenever they could, wanted to take slaves whose skin was a different color, to better mask their own evil, which was even more repulsive. In those times the Greeks didn't even have skin color to believe in, but they still believed in difference. Do you find it perhaps strange that I kept them on the side a bit and spent my time with cats and donkeys? That's what I do to this day.

Aristotle said: "Again, thus it is between man and animals: domesticated animals are better in their nature to wild ones, and it is better for all of the tame ones to be ruled by man, for in this way they are kept safe. Still the same applies to the natures of men and women: the one is better, the other worse; the one the ruler, the other the subject. And the same pattern is necessarily the case for the whole of mankind too, for in the same way as the soul differs from the body, thus men differ from animals (and this is the way for those who are given to use their bodies for work, and who are at their best this way), they are slaves by nature, and it is best for them to be ruled by this principle, just as was the case with the things we mentioned. For a slave is someone who by nature is subject to someone else (and because of this he is the property of another), and who takes part in logos such that he can perceive it but not possess it."

I read this on the beach once. I was peeking over the shoulder of some bearded student. The book was called *Politics*. It was quite clear to me that *Politics* was from the polis, and not from the air, forest, and water. You could see it later in the air too, in the forest, and in the waters. I tried to whisper to the student—imagine politics from the air, forest, and water—but he didn't hear me.

I had expected more from Aristotle. But I have to give it to him, he lined it out neatly. First it was the animals, and then the idea of slavery was developed. All the way to the difference between body and soul. As a spirit, I felt a little uncomfortable because of it. But I could see that Aristotle was really an influencer.

I watched it all, unfortunately, a little from the sides. I had a spirit, but not a body. I was sometimes sorry about that. But if I'd had a body, they would have probably told me I didn't have a soul.

Escape With Mikro

ARION HAD MADE a big catch and was grilling fish. Even Teogen and Oikistes were there, along with some Liburnians whom Arion introduced as Turus and Volsuna, because the Liburnians, as opposed to the Greeks who left their wives at home, came as couples. And not only that, Turus and Volsuna brought their children along too, three daughters and two sons. Miu and El hung around also; their kittens had already found a new home, which was not hard for Issa's first litter. Kalia brought Mikro because it was a holiday.

When they had eaten well, Arion took Kalia aside and said, "You can now save Mikro."

Kalia's eyes shone for a moment and then he frowned. "How?"

"Give him to Turus and Volsuna."

"But we can't give him away," Kalia said. "I already checked."

Arion put his hand on Kalia's shoulder and said, "You were ready to run away with Mikro and lose all your rights. Am I correct?"

Kalia nodded.

"We will give Mikro to Turus and Volsuna as their dowry. I've thought it through. No one in the polis is allowed to stop an engagement. That is the first rule of the apoikia: we must multiply. And in every colony the Greeks have married the people who were native. There are few Greek women here and if we don't marry the Liburnians, there will be no apoikia. You understand?"

"No," Kalia said.

"With the Liburnians, it's the man who brings the dowry. It is their custom. You will give Mikro as your dowry."

"What's dowry?"

"What you give when you like a girl. That's how it goes with Liburnians. Go on, take a look at their three daughters. Maybe you'll like one of them?"

It was a strange question, but Kalia had found the one with the black curly hair nice, although he wasn't intending to admit it. Earlier, she'd come up to stroke Mikro. Then Kalia told her the Liburnian words he knew and she laughed because he must have had funny pronunciation, or perhaps the Liburnians on Issa found Menda's way of speaking funny. But she had understood him, so she told him the Greek words she'd heard. Then Kalia laughed because her Greek was funny.

ROBERT PERIŠIĆ

"We could announce it today, or another time," Arion said. "We will announce the engagement and give them Mikro. Teogen and Oikistes won't have anything to say, they'll have to drink to it, and that's it. I've already spoken to Turus and Volsuna. They respect their daughters' will. If none of them likes you, they'll give the donkey back. That's what the Liburnians are like, their women have rights. So, now it's up to you. I mean, think of Mikro."

Kalia was flabbergasted. "Am I getting married?"

"We can say today that it can be any one of the daughters. As if Oikistes and Teogen will remember who is who. We announce the engagement, Mikro goes as dowry, and the polis can't touch him. You understand?"

"You really want me to get married?" Kalia asked.

"I don't, but Mikro does," Arion said. "And it's not a wedding yet.... Just a thing."

Kalia blushed, dumbstruck.

"Do you want to save Mikro or not?"

Kalia was silent.

"Miu brought you here. Mikro will find you a wife."

Kalia's eyes darted and he said, "I'm off."

"Where to?"

"I'm off."

"Think it over," said Arion, "but please don't run away now."

Kalia went to the shore, sat on the beach. Miu followed him. Kalia looked at her as if to say, "Miu, can you believe this?" Miu blinked for a moment and looked at him again, as if to say, "Carry on."

"It's better if we run away," Kalia said.

Miu looked up at him.

"What is this, Miu? I wanted to free Mikro but now I have to get married. I am not grown up yet," he said and thought a little because he had been holding himself as if he were grown up for a while now. He wouldn't have admitted this to anyone but Miu.

Miu sat by his thigh and watched the sea.

"Miu, is this freedom?"

Miu looked at him as if to say, "Don't be a pain," and rested her head on her front paws and continued to watch the sea.

Kalia was thinking about Mikro again. Could Mikro hold on a little longer? Then he wondered if Menda would have liked Arion's words.

"And you, Miu? You also started early."

Miu blinked as if in approval.

Then Arion appeared. He trampled the beach as if charging uphill. "We don't have to make the decision today, Kalia. I thought you were in a rush, because of Mikro. But there is time. And, as I said, they can give the donkey back."

Kalia sat up and said, "You know, Arion, your gait is bad."

"It's my age."

"Like you're some sort of an army."

"Ah yes, that stays inbuilt."

"Never mind," Kalia said, "but please keep an eye on Miu."

Arion frowned. "You're really still thinking of escaping?"

Kalia nudged Miu and she rose sulkily. "Watch the way Miu walks."

Kalia got up and started walking on the small pebbles. He said to Arion, "Does it look like I'm walking on water?"

Miu walked behind him, a step away from the sea, watching Kalia with interest. He walked softly, carefully, like someone with a mask who acted effortlessly.

Arion laughed and shook his head. "You want to teach me to walk at my age, is that it?"

Kalia was also laughing. "I'm getting married for Mikro and you're going to complain about walking?"

Then Arion started behind him, acting like an armless cat. He chortled. Since he didn't often laugh, it came out a little horsey.

Teogen had come to see where Kalia had gone off to and he watched them from a distance. And then the girl who had pet Mikro turned up beside him.

Teogen said to her, "You see, this is unbearable!"

As if she had and had not heard him, she began mimicking Arion from a few steps behind.

Teogen watched them and wondered again, *Why are they doing this and what for?* He sat on the beach and thought about going to Athens again, to bring his son back. But he'd resist him, for sure.

When they got back to the party, Kalia was afraid to look in the direction of Turus and Volsuna. He was also afraid to look at Avita, who sat beside them, the one who had walked behind them on the beach, and then ran off. Finally, he looked at her. She glanced back at him as if to jokingly say he was a fool. She was lanky and skinny, with black, curly hair.

Kalia thought of Menda in Syracuse, saw her sitting in the yard looking over the walls. *I will learn Liburnian well,* he thought as he spoke to Menda's image in his mind. *They will learn Greek from me. All for Mikro. You know how you said you had no use from being loved by an animal, but that you were happy anyway? Now you might say there was some use.*

He went up to Mikro, resting in the shade. He didn't have the cover on his back, the sores were healing. He stroked Mikro's head and neck. He put his head on the donkey's, pressed his ear against the animal's. When he turned around, she was there, the daughter of Turus and Volsuna, and she was watching them.

"Why are you crying?" she asked.

He understood. "Me?"

She stroked Mikro's neck.

Kalia said, "Even if I do sometimes cry, I am not spoiled." Then he added, not knowing where it came from, because it sounded a little silly, "I'm actually very strong."

"Avita," she said. She touched her chest with her fingers. "Avita."

He made the same movement and said, "Kalia."

"You would look after Mikro?" he asked.

She stroked Mikro's neck and confirmed with her eyes.

"There's no one to look after him?" she asked.

"No," he said.

Arion came up to them later, gave them a handful of dry figs.

"I'll give mine to Mikro," Kalia said.

"There are some for Mikro, but you have to eat some, and Avita too, because these are figs I brought back from my hometown, Taranto, from Simon's garden. One day I'll tell you about Simon. Come on, try and see if they're any good still, I've brought them from far away."

The figs were very dry, but they were still good.

"You know, figs are all made out of seeds," Arion said. "Now be careful where you shit tomorrow. Choose the most beautiful spots."

The Phantom Arm

ARION WATCHED THE Issa hillside from the other side of the bay, watched the sunset above the vertical streets, which gleamed white with the stone carved from the side of the island. It was as if the streets were climbing up toward the sunset. That was how he bid farewell to the end of every day, watching the sundown. Sometimes, El would follow him to the end of the bay, which had been left untouched by the Greeks, and lie down next to Arion when he sat down by the sea on the flat rock that was still warm from the light. He liked the sunset; it helped quiet the pains in the missing arm.

That evening, El settled in Arion's lap and snoozed. The sun sank above the rising city. Arion closed his eyes, following El's example. They imitated one another like that sometimes, which is what creatures who live together always do. There is something like a shared blood flow, a nervous system, and common dreams in creatures whose bodies touch. Arion felt his phantom arm: pain in the place where there was nothing. On rare occasions, he'd feel his nonexistent arm without

ROBERT PERIŠIĆ

the pain. He liked those moments. If he focused, it seemed to him he could even move his imaginary fingers. It felt as if he'd spent a long time lying on his arm and the blood was starting to flow back in. That's how it was that evening and Arion didn't want to open his eyes. Then, his eyes still closed, something unexpected happened. He felt El licking his missing arm, the cat was licking his fingers with its rough tongue, and he was stroking El's ears with the palm of his hand. He knew the arm was not there and he didn't want to open his eyes.

Later, when the feeling passed, when under his eyelids he could tell that the sun had set, he opened his eyes and saw El snoozing on top of him, not entirely peacefully, but as if he were having a dream. Arion stroked his ears with the existing hand, and El opened his eyes, looked at Arion, slipped out of his lap, and walked the way of return.

Arion was slow and lost sight of El. He spotted him later, on a small plateau where there was a well that, despite sitting a mere twenty steps from the bay, gave drinking water. The plateau was now empty because of the Dionysian celebrations and yesterday the ships launched back to the sea with a cheer. A new sailing season had begun on Issa. Arion walked slowly, and El watched him from his spot by the well.

Arion thought he had already seen this, in a moment the memory came back. This was how El had watched him when he was leaving him in Syracuse in the care of the old woman. El had stayed in Syracuse on a small square, watching Arion leave. Arion had looked back and saw him sitting up straight and watching, having given up following him further. That image remained in his mind, and he didn't know why it returned at this moment. Then everything seemed normal again. He came up to El, the cat followed him another ten steps, and then a little later Arion looked back and El was gone. There was nothing strange in this. But Arion hadn't seen him since then.

Arion walked around Issa the following day, walked everywhere, waited for the sunset, watching the vertical streets alone, waited and walked in the dusk, his non-arm hurt, and three nights passed and then in the morning he climbed up the hill with the help of a stick, walked over the hill, went down toward the bay, came to the Issean village, which was called Komissa—because three nights on Issa were longer than three nights in Syracuse; there was room to get lost in Syracuse, but not on Issa. So, Arion thought, El might have been, through some strange coincidence, in Komissa.

Some Isseans were sent to the shipping bay to help control the island, to be among the Liburnians. They had sent the very people who were on good terms with Arion, who were perhaps Pythagoreans in spirit, or simply happened to be in the way. They hadn't sent him, maybe so he wouldn't be giving speeches, though those came less frequently now since he was increasingly short of breath. Because it wasn't only the non-arm that hurt, the pain was spreading. He didn't know what his sickness was and how long he ought to wait for it to pass.

Arion had put on his prosthetic arm, walked over there, over the hill to Komissa, because he thought there had been a theft. He suspected Leonidas, who had been moved there, and who had taken a male kitten from Miu and El's litter because Leonidas wanted to have a firstborn on Issa. He called him Protogen. Now Arion thought Leonidas had also taken El because Leonidas had said he'd never seen such a tomcat in Syracuse, or Cyrene, or Massalia. This is what Arion was thinking, *El has been kidnapped.*

When he barged in at Leonidas's, Leonidas eyed up the hook several times as if wondering if someone had sent Arion to kill him. Arion's eyes were strange, without light. Since being sent to Komissa, Leonidas had thought Oikistes had caught wind of what he'd been saying about him. Because once in Issa, after having too much wine, Leonidas had said that compared to him, Oikistes had no military knowledge, and that he was also a sellout because he was in the service of gamoroi, who wanted to rule over everyone also on Issa. Since he had been sent to Komissa, he had repeated it several times to those like himself, or those whom he at least thought were like him. But, Leonidas thought as he brought out the food to the table, even if Oikistes had heard this and they wanted to kill him, it was impossible that Arion would carry out such orders. Then he thought, *Maybe the very fact that I think it is impossible for Arion to be the one makes him the best executor.*

They ate, drank, drank a lot, and Arion kept on drinking; Leonidas kept up. Arion didn't want to ask Leonidas anything about El while Leonidas was sober. He wanted to get very drunk with him, so he could see his bare mind. Leonidas was thinking the same thing: he started talking about Oikistes and carefully watched Arion's face. Leonidas thought he had to clarify why Arion had shown up with the hook—with that weapon he pretended was an arm—before one of them snoozed off with the drink, because then it might be too late.

"Do you know, Arion, why he came to Issa in the first place?"

"No," Arion said.

"He is, in fact, from Croton, he came for the Olympics from there. When it was clear he was going to win, then our people, from Syracuse, approached him. We didn't have a single Olympic winner and couldn't return empty-handed to Dionysius. They made nice plans at his expense. They must have chosen our contestants on looks. And then they bought him. When he won, he didn't say he was from Croton, but repeated three times that he was a Syracusan."

"Really?" Arion said.

"I'm a bit surprised you don't know this, but okay, maybe you spent more time warring for Syracuse than living in it. But that's how it was with our Oikistes. Dionysius accepted this. He forgave everyone's losses. The important thing was to have a winner. You know, that was Dionysius when he was still gentle, the Dionysius before they raped his wife, the Dionysius before he returned. I still put up with that

Dionysius, and then when he came back bitter, everything was different."

"What are you telling me, Leonidas? And why?"

"We are free, Arion, no? Aren't you interested?"

"Not particularly, but go on."

"Oikistes couldn't go back to Croton. They celebrated him in Syracuse. It was like—he's one of us! Hurray! At the time you couldn't say he wasn't one of us. And so he came to believe it. He married quickly, to a gamoroi with a pedigree. That was a clever thing to do. Because after some time, other gamoroi saw him as a bought Olympian. So he was never at home in Syracuse, except for those first days. Dionysius knew this of course, so when someone suggested he should get the honor of founding a colony, everyone thought it was a good idea."

Arion interrupted him. "I know all that."

"I was a bit surprised that you didn't," Leonidas said, looking at him with as much sobriety as he could muster.

"I know," said Arion, "but he came here voluntarily, I have no doubt. This was the place where he found a home, and even if he was a cheat, or just another sly fool, after all he may have, in his own way, gained some wisdom."

"Come on!" Leonidas said. "I thought you despised him."

"I do despise him. He was so dependent on Dionysius. He was so miserable because he knew no one really respected him. But to be honest, when we announced Kalia's engagement, he smiled and said he knew such plotting—because, you know, we legally cheated the polis for Mikro. I figured he'd expose himself, which he did in a roundabout way, because later on in our conversation he said privately, as if he wasn't a ruler, that he hadn't wanted to return to Croton because of some political matters. I have some idea what sort of matters those could be because they exiled Pythagoreans there too, even without knowing they were Pythagoreans. They might have just not publicly renounced their beliefs, or perhaps they were too proud to renounce anything. And the persecution was important because the polis is sometimes all about persecution. Sometimes it's all of its politics, those are the shadows, the polis in the night. And, you see, I then thought he had used the Olympics to run away. If that was the case, he was sly enough not to tell it to those Syracusans who had negotiated with him. Because if they had known that he wanted to get out of Croton, they wouldn't have offered him the money he later used to live well in Syracuse. Perhaps it was why he later said nothing about it—because instead of asking the Syracusans for citizenship, he cheated them instead. I can imagine him too: the Syracusans meant nothing to him then, he didn't think he'd have to spend the rest of his life with them. He just wanted to get out of the shadows of his polis. You see, maybe that was the secret he brought to Issa: he had tricked the Syracusans and robbed Dionysius.

"It is therefore possible that he was a runaway who couldn't say it, and that he was no sellout, which is what they were saying in Syracuse behind his back as soon as the excitement died down. And the Olympian excitement does die down over the years. And a cape of shame mixed with glory always followed behind him, and as the glory faded, the shame became more prominent on his cape. You know, he really did wear a cape, a Liburnian cape, I saw him with it back in Syracuse. Isn't it strange that he wore it before he ever came here? It must have been a coincidence. I knew even then, I mean not about the cape, but about Oikistes because I had wrestled sometimes myself, and he had been an Olympian. Now, imagine, Leonidas, if this is a story that he can never make public? In the end, that he was a sellout, no one said it in front of him anyway. Maybe he thinks it's been forgotten?"

"Well, it has been, to a degree," Leonidas said with a frown. "People on Issa rarely mention it."

"Nothing has been forgotten, you can be sure of that, Leonidas. Everything is still known, but it doesn't matter anymore."

"So a cheat will be known to our children as a founding father?" Leonidas said, getting drunker, but his eyes turning sharper all the while, because he was now thinking it was possible that Arion was indeed on Oikistes's side.

"We are all founding fathers, me, you, El, that's how I see it," Arion said and stared at Leonidas after mentioning El. Then Arion asked hoarsely, "Do you, Leonidas, perhaps know El's whereabouts?"

"Your cat?" Leonidas said, startled, for he found it difficult to change the flow of his thoughts when drunk, and he had just been considering attacking Arion. Were Arion not so old, and if he didn't appear slower after each drink, he'd have gone for him by now, but he kept delaying it, wondering if Arion was pretending, which, drunk as he was, turned out to be difficult to discern. "I don't know, Arion, how would I know where El is?"

"It's been a few days since I last saw him," Arion said.

Seeing that Arion's eyes were full of death, Leonidas gave up on the idea of attacking him. "You're here because of the cat?"

"I'm here because of El, Leonidas. Where is El? Do you know, my friend?" As he was saying this, Arion casually made a slow loop in the air with his hook.

He has been pretending to be drunker than he is, Leonidas thought, and he felt again that Arion had come to murder him. "Is this what this is about? You don't know where El is?"

"I don't know!" Arion searched for signs of fear on Leonidas's face.

"I know nothing about El, I swear, Arion. Only Protogen is here, he should turn up any minute now."

"You took Protogen. And then El?" Arion shouted, as if hoping he still had a reason to attack.

"That's a very strange thought, Arion. I would never take El from you. This would, in fact, never occur to anyone. I'd kill anyone who even thought of it."

Arion watched Leonidas carefully.

"I'd kill anyone who thought of it."

Arion thought, *Yes, Leonidas has other things on his mind.*

This was the worst outcome. It had been Arion's hope that Leonidas had stolen El. Of all his ideas about El's whereabouts, this one seemed the best.

"Forgive me, Leonidas. It is not right of me to turn up like this."

Leonidas watched him, thinking that Arion's image was diluting.

"Forgive me," Arion said quietly.

When Leonidas looked at him again, he thought he looked like a ruined man, a shadow.

"You're just tired, Arion," he said.

"Forgive me, friend," Arion mumbled, as if all of the weight of the wine fell on him.

Leonidas got a second wind of energy from all this, and started talking again. About the polis, the gamoroi who had been the bosses of all his people. He hadn't wanted to work for them so he went into the army, he said, but then he still felt like he was working for them. He wanted to talk, even if Arion wasn't listening, which was maybe better. He said he wasn't only a Greek, but his mother's side was Siculian, real Sicilians.

"The gamoroi were considered to be gods because they were there first, but my people were there before them, like the Liburnians are here. We don't need the gamoroi rulers here, and least of all those who were plotting around the court in Syracuse, Kleemporos and his kind, and here they are, miserably ending up on Issa. And now they're carrying on here. That's why they've sent me away, to watch over the edge of the polis, to get me out of the way."

As Leonidas spoke in the garden, Protogen turned up and approached the dozing Arion and sniffed him. He lay down by his legs. He was similar to El, but he wasn't tired enough to be the same.

Arion suddenly got up to go back to Issa, but Leonidas held him back. He pitied him.

This old madman, he'll fall somewhere on the hill, Leonidas thought. *He was once a man. Now he's a shadow, but he used to be one of us.*

Scatterwind

WITH TIME I got that feeling too. Everyone else had appendages, but sadness is alone, has nothing. I saw it in animals and people. None of them could stand it for long. No one is bad in sadness. Humans and animals are both light and dark then, like a light burning out. Sadness does not go with anything except for clarity of knowledge.

I couldn't be sad for long. Sooner or later, I'd be captured by the other thing, a consequence or reason, because I was sinking—somewhere into myself, and I know that this means nowhere—and I had to fly higher and farther, even in a rage.

Above The City

RETURNING TO ISSA the following day, Arion went to bed, fell asleep, and dreamed that he was a child. As a child he thought of himself not being a child. He couldn't wait to embody his real shape. He woke up, quickly got ready, and learned to walk. The spring sun was warming up the island; Arion walked uphill. Looking down over the water, he saw a boat entering the port, deep in the sea, heavy with burden. *Those are the stone blocks from the side of the island, Kalia must be with them*, he thought.

Kalia was no longer a child. Everything went on. The paving of the vertical streets. Everything went on. The vertical streets stretched upward, cut across by the horizontal ones, and in between the foundations of houses slowly sprouted. Everything went on.

Arion climbed and saw Miu going up the hill. He went after her and found her at the top, lying next to the leaning rock, close to the spot where she gave birth, in the shadow of the oak that had been felled. She watched him approach, not moving. He sat near her, on the oak stump. She then looked ahead of herself, glancing at him occasionally, her eyes in a squint. He thought that El must be around. Then he found him in a hole under the rock; it was him, his fur, he felt him with his hands. He left him there and sat with Miu. He sat there, without his hook, and without his arm. They watched the sunset sink into the sea, from up above, a small sun. He sat and thought, *Death*. He delayed covering El. Miu lay near the hole. The sky above Issa was quiet.

What had been my wishes? What did I want? Arion thought. *In the center of my being I always felt I could become divine. But I am El's friend, and he lies in a hole.*

He threw earth on El's fur. Miu disturbed him, meowing.

"Rest in peace on this sea, my Carthaginian brother," he said several times.

Then the wind started. It hit the town, banged, took everything with it.

Scatterwind

FIRST CAME THE image and then the city. I wouldn't have known this had I not seen the image first, from up high, when I watched them at the beginning, Teogen and Kalia, measuring, pulling and tightening long ropes, marking directions. It was all drawn as if someone from a height were watching. They imagined my vision and I thought at the beginning it all had something to do with me, that they were telling me something, because one could not see this image from the ground. I didn't even know then they were planning an image of a city, that it was a plan, and I saw with time that one of them had this image as if seeing it from above, even though he couldn't have climbed up so high. They surprised me there, like that time with the sails. They couldn't fly, but they could have a bird's-eye view. And of all people it was Teogen who really didn't resemble either a spirit or a bird. This was one of the things that kept me here, the image that emerged on the ground, which at first I thought was drawn for me.

ROBERT PERIŠIĆ

Now I saw that it was an image for them, being filled out slowly by rock. It would not be a big city like Syracuse, I saw, but it would be the first one I'd see being created from an image.

Now death was also already inscribed in it. I thought about leaving, like I did back then in the savannah. Death made me angry, and I didn't know at whom. Then I started to look at things differently, and it slowly came to me that death was part of the floor plan—and this is why I settled down here.

Naked Without The Polis

TEOGEN NEVER SAID he was the founder of the city, he just looked at the city as if it were his child, watched it grow like a mother who watches over every step—when the city was planned and founded, when the streets and drainage were laid out, when it was all being filled in and the first contours of houses grew, blocks that would be copied.

Oikistes told Teogen one day at the agora, "You know the vision of a child is unclear."

Teogen didn't understand.

"I mean, Teogen, that those who look at their own child never have a clear vision. A different person can better see the nature of the child."

"What child?"

"A child. A small one. Then growing. Is the child spoiled? Does the child need as much care, since it's not so small anymore?"

Teogen looked at Oikistes for a little while and said, "But in any case a parent raises his child, no one can take it away from him."

"Yes they can," Oikistes said. "The polis can."

Teogen waved his hand as if to say he had no time for such talk, and with a hard step walked to the work that awaited; he didn't even bother to look at the faces around Oikistes, who were approving. As he got farther, Teogen called Kalia, shouting, "Come on, we have work to do!"

Teogen was much too focused on the building to listen to opinions. Because there was always work, something was always out of place, threatening harmony, and there was no one but Teogen who could put it in order.

Even Arion had heard that Teogen's expulsion was being prepared and he asked Kalia what was going on.

"He is still driving me and Isiha as hard as he always has," Kalia said.

"Maybe it's just rumors," Arion said.

"They can't kick out Teogen!" Kalia said.

"Sometimes they get rid of those who get too attached to the polis," Arion said.

When it was announced at the agora that Teogen was moving to Komissa, to spend his old age there in peace, Kalia was with Teogen. The polis gave him some land on a hill-side close to the sea, that was stated: close to a pebble shore with a freshwater spring. Teogen was confused and was speechless for some time. It had been planned smoothly, the decision fast; Oikistes withdrew first and the gathering was breaking up. Teogen hadn't thought of asking for favors before he started scolding them. "You, ignorants!

Asses! You!" Everyone left the agora fast, no one wanted to look Teogen in the eyes.

Later on, when they were alone, Teogen asked Kalia, "Where do they get the right?"

"I don't know, Teogen."

"They really voted like that?"

Kalia had already noticed that Teogen wasn't aware of the fact that he didn't have many friends. That wasn't his concern—all he cared about was the city in his mind. Perhaps he thought working for the polis was how one made friends.

Then Kalia followed Teogen and Isiha. He saw them a little differently now, as if at the end of a story. She had a crooked back, as did Teogen, who was silent and looked straight ahead. He couldn't talk to Kalia. Teogen understood now that everything he'd said so far was from the polis. He had no words left. A void opened up on the road outside of the polis. He wanted to remain strong, at least in front of Kalia, but he felt as if he were losing shape, dissolving.

They were at some distance from Issa when Teogen wanted to speak. "They took my city away. I am now just a bare body, like her," he said looking at Isiha. "I have nothing left to say. This is the end. You can forget me."

Kalia watched him. He remembered himself when he ran away with Miu. It was not the same thing, he knew, but when he ran, he had also thought it was the end of the world. Now it looked like the beginning.

"I know that," Kalia said.

"You're young and you don't know," Teogen snapped.

"I knew it even when I was a child," Kalia said.

Teogen thought for a moment that he might turn into a child too, but then he swatted away this thought. "I have nothing to do with any of you now. Leave!"

Kalia had put up with Teogen's guardianship for years, but still, he could easily think of worse.

Kalia said, "There are things outside the polis too."

"Leave me alone, Kalia, I can't talk. I'll hit you if you don't leave!"

Kalia left.

Teogen stood there with Isiha. They climbed farther up the hill.

Teogen said, "We're the same now."

Isiha looked at him, which she didn't often do.

"Now we are just bodies," he said. "Without the polis, without a language."

Isiha looked at him calmly.

"I pestered and worked you so hard."

And then it occurred to him, out of the blue on the road to Komissa, to set Isiha free even though she was carrying his things. He untied her and watched. She stood still. He took his things off her.

"Isiha, leave me!"

The jenny looked at him, happy. But she didn't move.

"Isiha, this has happened to me, but who am I? It cannot even be spoken of outside of the polis."

Teogen lay on the ground, didn't want to go on, wanted to end his path. He wanted this to be the end. But death didn't come. Isiha watched him curiously.

"What did I want?" Teogen asked Isiha. "Did I want to be a man? Or a god? For you I was definitely a god, Isiha."

She walked around, inspecting the bushes, looking to see where they were.

"Isiha, it is you that has to kill me!" Teogen screamed.

He sat behind her and punched her in the thigh, so that she would kick him and kill him. But Isiha didn't kick. He hit her again. Isiha stood there, frozen.

"Why don't you kill me, you stubborn animal?" Teogen rolled around on the ground. "I am naked and I have no language."

Maybe he had gone mad, that's what they said later. Isiha waited for him all the same. Teogen might have lost his mind, but she had, in fact, always known him. He was always the same to her.

"Isiha, please, kill me so that I don't have to do it myself."

Isiha now looked at him with slight concern. He was rubbing his head like a confused child. He started speaking with a different voice. Nasal, as if mocking his own voice. "Aaaa, I've been exiled, Teogen, the only Greek... Me, of all Greeks, Isiha, can you see, aaa, I'm eating my own shit..."

He said some more such things and then he asked Isiha, "Why doesn't death come? Why am I not here, Isiha? I'm not even here enough to call death... but you, you exist?"

He watched her, sat up straight, and watched her as if seeing her for the first time. "You still, still, still... exist? I don't." After rolling around on the ground a little longer, Teogen spent a long time with his head in his hands. Then, some hours later, dusty and drained, he said, "Take me away, Isiha, from this emptiness."

He tied himself to the donkey. "Let's go to Komissa, I'll wait for death to take notice of me, and you will rest."

Isiha looked as if she was thinking, then she farted and started walking.

Teogen was remembered in Komissa as the one who said that no one must burden his donkey and that she would inherit everything. The stonecutter set it all in stone, which was never found.

Scatterwind

WHEN THEY STOPPED believing anything had a soul except
for them, an emptiness enveloped the polis. There was just
the polis, its words, and the words had become so incredibly important, as if they could fill the void. They did to a
certain extent, as far as I could see. They started writing
everything down because it seemed that words might be
magic and would last for an eternity. But the words of the
polis made no sense outside of the polis. Whoever might
find them, and didn't know of the polis, would regard them
as if they were hollow bones.

Oblivion is massive, I saw. I remember when they were
worried about getting on the wrong side of the forest spirits. I remember when they caught the antelope, and bowed
to the mother of all antelopes, so that she wouldn't hold it
against them. They respected everything when they were
weak and they didn't dare to deny the soul in anything. Until
they felt powerful.

When they stopped believing trees had a soul, they soon stopped believing anything around them was truly alive. It was just matter. I saw that it wasn't about the existence of spirits, like me, but that it was about life. When human words deny the spirit of something, then it really ceases to be alive. The spirit is true life, and not the body. A body without a spirit is matter: meat, wood. They wanted to handle matter freely, so matter couldn't have a soul, and that was why matter was dead. Enter the void.

There is physics and metaphysics. The Greek language set this difference. Physics is mere matter. Anyplace where there is matter, there is a void. It gapes and produces fear in creatures who are lonely in spirit, convinced it is they alone who exist. This conviction is the reason for the void, which otherwise isn't there. I mean, it is there in some higher parts of the atmosphere and where I come from, and there might be some, according to my judgment, the farther one goes into the cosmos, but there is none on Earth. It is dense here, every nook is alive and each death instantly decomposes to life. There is really no void on Earth.

Layering Time

KALIA SAW ARION slowly climbing up the steep street. He must have seen, from his hut, that someone was at the site of their stone house.

While Issa still resembled a bare hill striped with vertical and horizontal lines, the houses waited on the edges of the streets to give them a framing. Where the streets had been laid, houses could grow, the stone hill gave them a terraced rhythm.

From the side of the house that entered the hill, the ground floor largely had to be cut into the rock. The ground floor with three rooms and a floor—that's a house, and whoever didn't think it was enough could build a villa in a field.

The polis built streets through communal work, the drainage canals, walls, wells, and the rest, and the citizens finished building their own houses. Since they'd arrived as lone old men, Arion and Teogen were given a unit within the city walls, each had a half of a house, and the polis would later decide on the rest in case any of them built a family, and this was Kalia's case too; this is what had been said. This common house was delayed because Teogen had worried about the city as a whole rather than his own house, and Kalia had done the same with him, while Arion couldn't help much with one arm. Arion had also been the only colonist who had not thought he'd live to see a house within Issa's walls. That's what they must have thought in the polis too—that everything would be inherited by Kalia when those two died, unless something odd happened. When Teogen was exiled to Komissa, it was thought that his part already belonged to Kalia.

The city was palpable, could already be seen nicely from the sea: a square grid on a hillside. There was nothing like it on this side of the Adriatic, is what those who sailed past it said. Such order. The old Liburnian Virno, who knew the coast and traveled the land, said he'd seen a town that looked as if it had been built by a spider, spreading to the walls from the middle, but like this, everything with straight angles like in Issa, he'd never seen such a thing.

"That's completely Greek," Turus said. "I think it came from dividing land. It came from the rope. Didn't you and Teogen stretch ropes at the beginning?" he asked Kalia.

"We did."

"I remember you greeting me in Liburnian then," Turus said.

Kalia could tell Turus was joking about the rope. The picture of Issa wasn't so unfamiliar to the Liburnians because they drew and replicated geometrical shapes on their ornaments—rectangles, circles, triangles—they hardly drew anything but geometrical shapes. They liked Issa, it looked like a large Liburnian ornament built by the Greeks. They respected Kalia because he had been Teogen's assistant—he who had sown a shape on a hill, as if it were a shepherd's bag. After Teogen's departure, the polis didn't give Kalia much to do. At first, he thought they were giving him time to rest after years of unrelenting work following Teogen every day. Then he went by himself and turned up at the community works, where he had the impression that his presence made other builders remember Teogen—both those who had respected Teogen and the gamoroi too, of old Syracusan heritage, who no longer mentioned Teogen's name and who had, after his departure, taken upon themselves all the organization. They walked around as if they had always been in charge, as if they were the ones who'd carried the city in their minds, as if Teogen had never been there. Kleemporos walked like that, and along with him the younger Kleemporos. Oikistes had, they said, fallen ill and was hardly around.

One day, the elder Kleemporos approached Kalia and said, "Feel free to rest. We know you've worked hard."

It was kindly said, because Kleemporos was a politician; it was as if he was showering you with tranquility. Kalia felt a bit out of step, with a stone he was holding in his hands. It was as if his whole mind had become occupied with the question of where he could put that stone. Kleemporos had already walked away, and his son stayed behind a little longer, staring at Kalia. Then he turned away too.

Holding the stone in his hands, Kalia knew something strange had taken place; few people in the polis were told to rest. He knew it had to do with Teogen, whose shadow continued to drag itself behind him. Kalia didn't think about the fact that people loved him, a lot more than the young Kleemporos. He didn't even think about the fact that he had been called to Diomedes as a child and charged to return bearing the news of Issa.

He wasn't aware the gamoroi saw this as a future problem and Kleemporos had long wondered why Oikistes had done it. He probably hadn't thought of the power he gave to this little nobody. Because Kalia having been chosen to take the news of the finishing of Issa to Diomedes was such a massive honor that some might get confused, could think that he was Oikistes's heir, marked by Diomedes himself.

So let Kalia rest, let him spend as much time with Liburnians as he liked, let him participate as little as possible, even become a Liburnian himself.

As Arion climbed the steep street, Kalia again held the flat stone in his hands. He put in on the wall of their house, the prepared space, laid with thick, sticky red mud mixed with pine amber. And another flat stone on the inside. The mud was in the middle. Then he sat, mixed water and wine in the black skifos, dipped barley bread into the drink.

When he arrived, Arion said, "Our house will be beautiful. I'm here to help."

Kalia said he'd just sat down to rest.

Arion took out a pot of fried mackerel. "This is from Ceuna, for you."

"You do some good fishing together. Send her my thanks," Kalia said with a smile.

Ceuna had helped Arion with rowing at first, and then with everything else. Now she was almost living with him in his shed. Arion called her his friend and Kalia thought that was exactly what it meant. Ceuna had a limp, and gray hair like Arion; although she didn't look like Menda, Kalia would still think of Menda when he saw her. Perhaps there was something in how she moved, the way she turned to say something: in her lip, her hand. Kalia never found out anything about Menda. He'd waited for a message, but there was none. He recently found out from a merchant and ship owner who'd arrived in Issa to buy wine, one hundred and twenty-five amphora, that Sabas had died, and that his son was a drunkard, but still an important man in Syracuse because there was always a party at his andron. But he couldn't find out anything about his Liburnian cook—the very question seemed strange. "You mean, his slave?" There were things like that, which reminded him.

They ate mackerel, sprinkled with oil, chopped garlic, and parsley, because the Liburnians didn't spoil their fish with cheese like in Syracuse, which Arion would never fail to mention. Menda had always prepared food in the Liburnian way and Kalia knew nothing else. Perhaps that was why, he thought, being around Ceuna reminded him so much of Menda.

"Miu came to me two nights ago, meowing, nosing around as if looking for someone. Last night, again. I fed her, but that wasn't what she wanted," Arion said, as if casually.

Kalia said he'd spent a bit more time with the Liburnians and had come back this morning.

"Ah, she was looking for you then," Arion said.

Kalia felt calmer with the Liburnians. The only thing that made him restless was knowing that Miu looked for him on Issa. But everyone on Issa knew Miu, she got fed, Kalia wanted to say. Then he thought Arion knew this already.

Instead Kalia said, "Maybe she was looking for El since it was at your place." He knew Arion would have liked to think that Miu still remembered El.

Arion thought and ate for a while before he said, "A lot of time has passed. Maybe she was looking for a friend who was no longer there. Or the one who is neglecting her."

"I can't be in two places at once," Kalia said.

Arion sat on the sloping street and watched the islet before them, which was turning into a peninsula; Greek and Liburnian young men, who had joined in on the construction, were pouring the extra stone that had been formed with the city foundations. The islet, on which they planned to build an amphitheater, had almost joined the agora on the seafront.

"Imagine, they have no words, they don't remember names, they don't tell stories," Arion said. "We tell stories and therefore organize things."

"Who is this 'we'?" asked Kalia.

"We, humans. If you think about it, language creates time when we tell what happened. We organized things, this is what happened, that's what came before. They don't. So perhaps time doesn't exist for them. Miu probably never thinks of Syracuse the way we do, but if you brought her back there, she'd know every street."

"I think so," Kalia said.

"You see, she doesn't tell stories, perhaps doesn't even know when it happened—yesterday or ten years ago—but she hasn't forgotten. It is beyond time. And then, if she was looking for you... She looked for a friend who was gone. Perhaps she was looking for you and El both, perhaps you became one feeling."

They ate slowly, drank the diluted wine, the day was clear, and they could see far.

Kalia thought about Arion's idea of El and him turning into one. If he blended the feelings for those whom he missed, or gathered them in one place... Where would he go to wait?

"Thank you, Arion, for placing me alongside El. You think I deserve it?" Kalia asked, slightly joking.

Arion nodded. "I'm thinking about what is thought, and what is feeling."

"What does your thought about feeling say, Arion?" Kalia asked with a curious smile. He was already, without thinking about it, addressing Arion as if he were an old man, almost as if he were a child.

Arion pretended not to notice. "Say, when I am gone, and when you remember me, will you first have a thought or a feeling?"

Kalia thought about it a little before saying, "A feeling. I'll always feel for those I care about. And for the others, I'll have a thought."

"I'm imagining this," Arion said. "A feeling for Arion." He laughed. "But you'll remember my name, and Miu will remember my smell. I smelled like El. I think that's a good feeling, the smell of me and El together. And the thought that goes with me, it can even exist longer if it's retold. Only, what's a thought without feeling? Those are the ones you don't care about."

Kalia felt as if he were looking at Arion from a farther spot. As if Arion had mixed too many things together. But still, it moved him to see things from a distance. He thought what it might be like if no one ever talked about what came before. How would he remember anything? The past wouldn't be the past, but as if it were the oncoming present. They would be only images and feelings, which would sometimes surface. All of it together, as if space were surfacing; memory would be like a wordless dream.

Dreams too are memories, mixed up, he thought. *Maybe Miu walks around Issa like that, but she still sees every fly passing by. Or perhaps she only walks around in her own night like that, when she's looking for someone. Perhaps El and I have blended together. I was gone for too long and she didn't know if I'd abandoned her. Or if I were dead.*

"If she remembers El, then it makes no difference to her when it was. He is still alive for her, but she can't find him," Arion said.

"Who knows, maybe someone will remember us like that. A bit mixed up," Kalia said.

"That would also be good," Arion said. "But I doubt they'll have a feeling."

Arion watched the Issa bay, then looked at the growing walls. If they hadn't been sitting there, at their end of the world, he might not have had such thoughts. It seemed to him he might not have such thoughts in Syracuse, in a large polis, with many voices, where you think you're in the center and everything around you was known. But this little protrusion, at the edge, made for different thoughts. *If anyone were to remember us, how would they get the feeling*, he thought.

Miu was already there, lying down near them on a warm rock, on her belly, her paws straight. Kalia stroked her; she merely gave him a glance. She resented his having been gone, he saw. The cat demanded presence. He sometimes thought it would have been better if he'd had a dog. A dog waits differently. The Liburnians had several dogs, black and white. They were village dogs, and he had come to love them. *But no dog would have liberated me from slavery*, he thought.

"Miu, it's me," Kalia said. "You know, I have to be with the Liburnians, I have a family there, and you don't want to move an inch off your territory."

He had tried, had attempted to carry her over several times, but each time she wriggled out of his arms when he started to leave Issa. She would then stand and watch him: Where are you going?

"Miu, it's me," he told her.

"You're not the Kalia I know," Arion said with a weird voice, as if answering for Miu in jest.

"You think I'm not?" Kalia asked, accepting the game and looking at Miu.

"You're now a man, a citizen," Arion said, imitating Miu's voice. "And who am I? Yes, I brought you here, but I'm still nobody."

It was a game, but something in it stung Kalia. He looked at Arion to see how serious the joke was, and said, "Arion, I have to, I can't be in two places..."

"I know," Arion said. "You're a man, a father. Your eyes will survive."

"So what? Is that wrong?"

"No, Kalia. I was a man, and you've become one."

When Kalia averted his eyes, Arion felt he shouldn't have spoken those words. He didn't want to remind Kalia that he had been a slave, he had wanted to say something else. But Kalia had heard what he had always feared hearing. Menda had said: even your friend will remember your shadow.

Arion said, "When one becomes something, he loses something too."

"And what's that?"

"I don't know, Kalia. Probably it's the thing that gets forgotten. Ask Miu."

Kalia then felt rage. "You were a soldier! Just a soldier! You're telling me about a man, a family. You don't know! I have to! You're old, and you don't know!"

"A man, a soldier, it's all the same thing," Arion said, smiling and showing the gaps in his teeth.

Kalia watched him with confusion and Arion said, "A man is the same as a soldier. That is the most beautifully described part of the empire."

"I don't get it," Kalia said.

"Ask Miu."

"She won't tell me anything."

"Yes, she won't tell you anything else."

Kalia looked at Miu, who was still horizontal, and then at Arion. He was enraged. "I became a citizen, so what? What have you become?"

"Nothing," Arion said. "Now go to your children and disappear from my mind."

Kalia left, his face twisted.

He shouted back at Arion, "It's only one child! Darmo! You haven't even asked about him!"

Arion had partially heard him and said into the air, "A little Greek. I will leave him my part in the city walls. Since I can't leave it to a donkey."

Scatterwind

I SOMETIMES FOLLOWED Kalia to the Liburnian village, hidden near the coast, close to the caves where they could take deep shelter. They hadn't been safe on the island before, I saw. It was the edge of the world for the Liburnians too, since their people were not on the land ahead, but quite a bit farther to the north. They had occupied several islands to the south and had not so much territory on the mainland, since they were a sea people. They lost battles on land, from those who came from the interior. But the Liburnians won at sea; they therefore shrunk on land, and the fan of islands made their territory wider and spotted.

I saw Darmo, the son. Yes, I saw him. He looked like Avita; he looked like Kalia, but also like Pigras. No one knew that; Kalia didn't want to know it. The memory of the faces was in the feeling, there was no print of light. Kalia would sometimes get startled when he saw Darmo, but he'd tell himself he was imagining things.

I thought Avita looked pregnant again. But I didn't spend much time there, I left quickly. I wasn't drawn to his family in the same way I had been to the stable in Syracuse. Perhaps the human family is too much for me. It was all in language, and I didn't understand the language even though I knew the words.

I suppose I was really interested in friendship between different species. It wasn't hidden in language so I saw it clearly. Or was it because I, ever since I came to love my zebra, knew that feeling? I didn't know much about regular families, perhaps because I was blown out by my family a long time ago. And my folks were cold, up there in the heights. I saw it was where people put their gods, not knowing how cold it was up there. I don't recall the feelings from up there.

It's hard to tell today how I existed up there, since I had no feeling. It sometimes seems to me I had made it all up later since I didn't know how it was possible to remember what I had no feeling for. Sometimes I think I am entirely made up because I don't know how it is possible that I came to exist. I console myself with the fact that other things that exist are no less mysterious. In truth, everything is pretty incredible. If there had ever been a betting shop, up there among us windy spirits, I never would have placed a bet on all this being possible. Especially the creatures who have a body.

I saw that people found my disembodied existence unusual—I also find it somewhat so—but the formation of a body is even more unusual. It's easy to imagine a spirit, but: Where

ROBERT PERIŠIĆ

does the body come from? All of it from the sun, from light. And some water and earth.

And Miu runs.

Kalia walks.

Arion sits.

Incredible.

The Newcomers

THE RAGE KALIA walked out of Issa with made it hard to breathe. He had to stop on the way up toward the Liburnian village, before the path leading into the valley. The exchange with Arion had taken the air out of his lungs. Arion was getting thinner, wrinkles were crowding around his eyes, and painful grimaces pinched the corners of his mouth. That was on his mind, but something was off in his field of vision and then he suddenly saw: there were ships waiting to enter the bay. He looked at the port and saw the anchored Issean boats. The ones entering the bay were someone else's. He ran down. He wondered who the newcomers might be.

Getting down, he saw Miu flash through the bushes. He stopped. "You followed me?"

Miu came out of the bush onto the path and he wanted to pick her up, for them to run together like they used to. He took a step toward her and she edged away. But she carried on following him.

Kalia found Arion outside his seafront shack. He was still out of breath from walking, all shrunk and bent, but his face unwittingly brightened up.

Kalia spread out his arms. "Arion..."

"It's okay, Kalia. I was also quite hard."

"Arion, there are lots of ships coming in."

Arion looked at the sea, closing one eye. Kalia looked in the same direction, saw the ships that were edging into the bay.

"I see," said Arion.

Ceuna watched it all too.

"Best we move from the coast, and we'd better hurry," Kalia said, because Arion was weak and Ceuna lame.

How am I going to drag them uphill? he thought. *We had better start moving right away.*

"Find his hook, find some blade for yourself," Kalia told Ceuna. He had his scissors and a Liburnian *sica*, a short blade that he used to clear forest paths.

Arion was putting on his hook, Ceuna tied the ropes for him, and while she was doing that he was aiming at the ships with one eye. He turned to Kalia. "They are Greeks!"

"Greeks?" Kalia exhaled with audible relief. "How do you know?"

"Take a look, doesn't it remind you of something?"

Kalia watched: three round-bellied ships and three flat ones.

This is how we came too, he thought. *It's us.*

The image of an empty bay flashed before him as if he were watching from the ship, the braying of goats, the broken stable door, the moonlight above the poor market.

"They must be the Parans," Arion said.

It is very strange that I am here, Kalia thought.

He looked for Miu: she lay ten meters away in the shade of a bush. Next to her was a young cat.

"They must be the Parans," Arion repeated because he had thought Kalia had not heard.

"Yes, it reminds me."

The Parans were supposed to arrive two summers before, and it was talked about a lot. The Greeks were coming, from the island of Paros—not from Sicily, but from Greece itself. They would settle on the neighboring island toward the mainland and the Isseans would no longer be alone on this coast. They had to dock in Issa first, to rest. Then the previous summer the Parans were meant to arrive again, it was still a topic of conversation. But they hadn't come, and then no one believed it anymore.

"Look at how they've huddled together, they could crash into each other," Arion said. "We stopped expecting them, and they think we are made up."

"They think this is the end of the world," Kalia said.

"The end of the world, why not," Arion laughed.

"Fuck their end of the world," Ceuna said seriously. "What? They've been at the beginning of the world up until now?"

Arion really started to laugh then, neighing a bit like a horse, and he held his ribs with his arm, as if the laughter hurt. He squeezed out words. "Yes, yes... they were... at the beginning..."

Kalia also found it funny, although he didn't exactly know why, while Miu, attracted by the snorting humans, hopped around his feet, and he picked her up. She didn't resist, and he whispered to her, "Miu, look at this, they are at the end."

When the laughter ceased, Arion took a breath and as if asking for permission to speak, said, "This is how I want to die."

It sounded serious and Kalia gave him a somber look, but Ceuna said, "Then you should have done it now!"

Arion doubled over again and said through laughter, "Can't be done... Everything can't be done... cannot be according to plan... And where is... Where is Teogen... cannot be according to plan... I have to take the poison... where is it..."

"Poison?" Kalia asked, looking at Ceuna.

Ceuna clicked her tongue and told Arion, "I know where the flute is... But... Let's have our mead. The Parans don't arrive every day!"

They drank as the Parans docked, and as they watched, with Miu in his arms, Kalia said, "I am amazed at how brave I was, although I was constantly afraid. Zoi taught me to walk like a cat. A cat is afraid and not afraid. But one thing is sure: it goes its own way. There was no other way for me apart from that ship. And when there is no other way, the fear is weaker. Because I think the fear comes from options. You go one way, you think it's dangerous, and then you consider returning. But, if there is no other way, fear cannot go back, and there is no fear."

"You've progressed in your speech with the Liburnians," Arion said. "You talk more there?"

Kalia thought about it. "Yes. I speak more. I teach them Greek."

"It's a good day today," Arion said. "Look at them approaching. Can you hear them?"

Kalia strained his ears. The sea sang a hymn to a faraway home.

They listened through memory.

"We were not attacked from the mainland," Arion said. "And they will go closer. You think they'll attack them?"

"How should I know?" Kalia said.

"You live with the Liburnians," Arion said. "Someone else might ask you the same question."

Kalia looked at him darkly, and Arion said, "I'm telling you as a friend."

Those who might attack the new colony would probably be the Liburnians, up from Iadera, Kalia knew. They were the only ones with a navy.

Arion asked, "Does anyone ever mention Magas? Does he show up?"

"No," Kalia said. "Who is Magas?"

"He was with us on the first expedition. I thought I saw him recently in the port, but he turned away immediately. He didn't walk with a slouch, as if running away, but he straightened out his shoulders and his cape flowed behind him."

Kalia and Arion watched the Parans docking. If the mainland Liburnians attacked the Parans, it would not be a good thing for the Liburnians on Issa, they knew.

"If Magas should turn up in the village of yours and start talking to them about the law and rights, stop him," Arion said.

"But what should I tell them about the law and rights?"

"That which you already know. The law is from the polis. The seagulls too have the right to this island, but they're not members of the polis council," Arion said. He then grimaced as if a stabbing pain went through him.

Kalia thought it would be hard to stop Magas if he started talking about the law and rights. But he saw that Arion wanted to prepare him for something.

He watched the Parans' ships, their tired sails.

It would be better if they had never come, he thought.

Then he looked at it all again. Whoever entered the world, in its end or beginning, even if he was just born, he had no idea what he was getting into.

They walked toward the docks in the port. Arion walked between Ceuna and Kalia, holding on to her shoulder with his hand, and touching Kalia carefully with his hook.

Scatterwind

THERE WERE MORE than half a million Greeks scattered across the Mediterranean, mostly in Sicily and the south of the Italian boot, where they settled long before they did on the Adriatic islands. They arrived in Marseille long before they did in Issa. Issa was closer to them, but as they entered the Adriatic the Greeks actually realized they were heading north, whereas as they neared Marseille they did not know that, bit by bit, they were going farther north than ever.

Those who left always had a reason to leave, and if they didn't, they found one along the way. I heard many times that the founders of colonies were refugees, and that the founders of Ancona were exiled from Syracuse, which didn't surprise me because Dionysius had exiled his opponents across Sicily before, displacing entire towns. No one really wanted to go north, into what was a great void for them, and I only later heard the word "gulag" and wondered: How many of them really went voluntarily on those ships? Was Issa too, without it having been explicitly stated, a gulag at the northern edge of the world? True, they were lucky with the climate here, to which I did contribute somewhat. It's odd, but once they did settle, few wanted to admit that they had been forced to leave. They were afraid or embarrassed at first, but later on they created an identity there, and they found it difficult to admit that they had been forced to be what they are. That's how it was, I saw, with humans: if you force them into something for long enough and they take to it by force, they won't want to remember the beginning. Except for those from Taranto, because they were a particularly difficult case—they hadn't completely forgotten that they were unwanted children, although they did try.

Later on, they divided the land into equal parts, both on Issa and Pharos. If they had been exiled, it must have been because they were democratic. And this division of the land is still visible from the air. I see it always, and recently, when people started flying in machines, they noticed it too: the boundaries in the fields of Pharos had somehow remained, after all, no one had changed them, they are perfectly visible from up high. I heard them holding lectures about it. One said that it was a reflection of philosophical ideas about the ideal city, where justice was founded on equality, and starting out equally. I listened to this from the third row, alone, thinking of Teogen's son who never did reach this sea. A shame, because it was an incredible voyage.

They carried everything with them, planted vines and olives immediately. And soon vineyards and olive orchards looked as if they had always been there, but then, I have to mention this too, those who watched as the Greeks brought their world to the Mediterranean, they didn't think this was such a natural thing. Many refused to drink wine, out of resistance—it was a Greek thing, it was their globalization.

The Gauls drank beer, as did the Illyrians, and those on the Iberian Peninsula, and the Thracians on the Black Sea, the Armenians, Egyptians, the Celts and Germans. Beer is an ancient drink, everyone made it, mostly from barley, only the Hellenic and the Italic peoples did not drink beer; they had completely forgotten about it and entirely replaced it with wine. The Greeks, and then the Romans, considered beer drinkers barbarians, which meant pretty much everyone but themselves. It was a culture of wine, then an empire of wine. So if they called you a barbarian because you didn't drink wine, then you won't drink it out of spite.

Later on, the Romans took wine, donkeys, and cats across the Alps. The Greeks brought a cat to Marseilles; the Romans brought a donkey to Paris.

The Greeks are only the coast, the Romans are the mainland.

It actually went on for a while, their globalization was a success and the Mediterranean became one world. And it remains one and the same coast to this day—in its tamed nature, in the fields and on the plates, in the visible and invisible, when speech dies down and only gestures remain.

Some say its boundary is as far as an olive grows, others claim it's the fig tree that marks its frontier. Few of the polis philosophers, and even fewer of its politicians, thought that when the Greeks disappeared the polis would spread out via nature.

And at that time, over where the boundaries of the polis lay, toward the wilderness or the void, there the Greeks established Artemis, a woman of nature, mistress of animals, who exists between two worlds. Her celebrations were led by women, men could not participate, and I thought then that she could gain the respect of Liburnian women on Issa, and join their goddesses. And I saw that, with time, it happened.

There was a shrine to Artemis on the edge of the town of Issa and there was one in Komissa, on the edge of the polis, where today sits a meaningless void, and where I rest.

They found Artemis's head on Issa.

It is beautiful.

Spiros

THEY WERE DIZZY from the sea, exhausted, but their eyes shone. The passengers from Paros were glad to see that the Isseans really existed, and that they spoke the same language, because they had not been sure at all that they were real.

The Isseans were glad to see other Greeks, to know they were not all alone on this sea any longer, though the Isseans found it odd to hear their language, the same but still different. These were their people, actual Greeks from Greece, but the melody they played in language was a bit off-key, sounding as if they were singing unwittingly. There were also some funny words spoken by youngsters that belonged to the old people. They saw them as foreigners who must not be seen that way.

Kalia watched to see if any of the arrivals stood aside, and walking among the people who were hugging the Isseans through tears, he noticed a boy who was observing the whole scene cautiously, his head tilted. *I must have looked like this when I arrived, and I must have been even smaller,* Kalia thought as he approached the boy.

The boy said his name was Spiros.

"You're alone?" Kalia asked.

"I'm with my father. My mother died."

Kalia thought he might even have invented the father.

"Do you have an animal with you?"

"Why do you say that?" Spiros asked, as if disturbed.

"I don't know, I'm just asking."

"I had a chicken," Spiros said.

"A chicken?"

"Yes, a chicken!" said Spiros. "And they... they ate it."

"An ordinary chicken?"

"Yes, an ordinary one, and so what? You're also ordinary!" Spiros said.

"I mean... I wanted to ask... was she a friend of yours?"

"You know how a chicken runs away? But I could hold this one, and she'd settle down. I fed her from when she was a chick."

Kalia thought for a while about what to say next. What Spiros had said required a response, but Kalia had none. He saw, in his thoughts, in Spiros's arms, a chicken that confused him, watched him with her tiny eyes. Finally, he said, "I'm sorry."

Spiros looked up at him, appearing to have a beak, and said, "They also said sorry. That's not sorry."

What a strange boy, Kalia thought. *Was I like this?*

"Where is your father?" Kalia said.

"He's over there with the guys who are roasting a goat," Spiros said and pointed.

Why did I ask about his father? So I could get rid of him? Kalia was thinking as he sought better words inside himself. Because as soon as he saw Spiros, he had felt like embracing him, as if he were a little Kalia. And now, after Spiros told him he was being a fake with his "sorry," he still felt close to him. But Spiros supposedly had a father, which meant they were different, and they had killed his friend on the voyage; nothing was actually the same.

"Why do you care?" Spiros asked.

"I care, but I don't know how to explain it," Kalia mumbled. Then he said more clearly. "I'm sorry, Spiros. I also traveled with animals, but not of the edible kind. I was lucky."

As soon as he'd spoken, he realized how stupid it sounded.

"I will never ever cry in front of any of you again," Spiros said, and as he walked over toward his father he shouted, "What a horrible place!"

What could I say to this boy? Kalia wondered, watching Spiros.

"Yes, I am as ordinary as your chicken," Kalia said, loud enough for the boy to hear him.

Spiros looked back, saw Kalia watching him, and went to his father and there was nothing to be done. Kalia wondered if it had been easier for him when he was coming here. *Probably it is easier for Spiros because he has a father. Maybe living with his father will obscure his memories. Maybe he'll become like his father.* Kalia had seen this happen.

A young man touched Kalia's shoulder at that moment. He said, gravely, "Oikistes wants you."

Kalia turned and saw Oikistes, under a mulberry tree, in a high chair with handles on each side; he might have been carried over. Kalia approached him, and Oikistes motioned with his hand for Kalia to sit by his side, on a small three-legged stool. He then signaled for the young men, who had carried him over, to move away.

Oikistes looked as if a wall had collapsed inside him, but words came from his stretched-out face. "I came to greet the Parans, but I saw you talking to that boy. I don't know what you were saying to him, but... It was as if time had doubled, and gone back. I remembered you from back then, and I thought: I could drop dead, and I've never told you. And I'm forgetting, by the day." Oikistes looked at Kalia as if expecting a question in order to carry on.

"What have you never told me, Oikistes?"

"You know Kalia, I knew. I knew your father."

These words resounded with a crack for Kalia, he even thought he'd heard someone crack open a log, over by where they were roasting the goat.

Kalia said, "You knew Diocles?"

Oikistes looked at him with dim but calm eyes and said, "Diocles, or whatever you want to call him. You know, when we boarded you on the ship, I told everyone I knew Diocles.

You had, I think, gone down to the lower deck with the donkey. And I told everyone on the upper deck, so that they could hear me—I knew Diocles, from Gela, who had died for Syracuse. I confirmed Diocles, and called you over to Diomedes later on. Because I know your father. We drank in his andron. And you know, he wasn't like those gamoroi who only invite you over when you're famous. Your father is a good man. He was my friend. He told me to protect you, as much as I could. And I protected you, as much as I could, Kalia. That's what I wanted to tell you, while I can still speak, so I don't forget."

Kalia watched him.

"No one else knows this from me, and I see you didn't know about it either."

Kalia considered whether he had known about it or not. He said, "Thank you, Oikistes. You kept your word."

Oikistes could tell that Kalia was thinking about saying something more.

Kalia had found out about Sabas from the wine merchant, and he was thinking whether to pass on the news to Oikistes. *But*, he thought, *what will it serve Oikistes, who is about to die himself, to know that Diocles has died, when he was already dead.*

Scatterwind

I WOULDN'T BE quite fair to the Greeks, or to their philosophers, if I made it look like everyone thought like Aristotle. In fact, it was only later that everyone thought like Aristotle. Because this way of thinking was, I saw, in the people's practical governing of the land. It was practically in man's governing over women, it was practically in the rule over slaves. Everything was, actually, a slave, except the citizens with logos.

Aristotle's way of thinking won because it gave humans all of the rights of rulership over the Earth, it created a huge void. There was no logos in anything—reason and language, spirit—except in humans.

That void was the human empire. Humanity only could create its empire on Earth if animals and forests were free of spirit. But I wouldn't be fair if I did not remember those Greeks who did not share in this way of thinking. Which is why I remember Kalia. I remember those who were known in their time, and what they said was later forgotten. They weren't practical, and some are just remembered for their names.

There was Pythagoras, remembered via mathematics, who thought a dog might carry the soul of his friend. There were those who followed Pythagoras, especially in the Italic south, such as Empedocles from Sicily, who thought all life—human and animal life—came from the same source, and that animals had thought. That is also what Porphyry from Syria thought, and he propagated vegetarianism. There were many mindsets among the Greeks that could hardly be heard of later, which I remembered through my windy memory, because I guess I carry one such mindset. At that time the debate was about what is a man and how far his rights extend on the Earth. Does reason stem from language and does spirit stem from reason and language, and is this the evidence for the entitlement to govern everything? That was the debate then, and later the debate was closed.

I think the Stoics closed it, who came after Aristotle; they thought that animals could in no way be compared to humans, that they had no reason or soul—and no need to speak of forests—and so the void in nature was created, and humanity has been ruling over it, in a world entirely human, never doubting their rule, until the glaciers started to melt.

But still, sometimes I see the loneliness of man, his gaze into the void, into the dead things that were killed long ago. Sometimes I think I see him looking back at himself as if in a mirror and that he is looking at an empty animal. There is

ROBERT PERIŠIĆ

the sadness of the void in man, which is patched over by language, and that is why he has to constantly speak as if he's on the run, through the void.

At El's

KALIA AND MIKRO had come to Issa to visit Arion. He wanted
to go to the leaning rock, but couldn't walk uphill without
help. "I'm not even sure I'd remember the way," he admitted. Paths from Taranto came back in his memory, streets
and shortcuts, sand packed by bare feet, small stone walls,
all of that space came back to him, but what was the point
of it, he wondered.

After Arion threw a fistful of wheat into the air, they started
uphill. Kalia didn't ride Mikro, he only allowed children to do
this; he had no doubt that Mikro could get a sore back, and
whoever thought it impossible, Kalia told them to touch the
donkey's spine, and then compare it to their own. But Arion
was very light now, probably from the pain that was visible
around his eyes. This was probably why paths from his child-
hood came back, because he was as light as a boy.

Issa was celebrating; it was the annual commemoration
of their journey—the day they left Syracuse and the day they
arrived in Issa. These were the holidays of remembering

and recounting, and if he hadn't known it back then, Kalia had found out over time who had traveled with whom, who brought what animal, who carried which plant and where they had planted it, who had held on to whom in that storm, and who had wanted to throw Miu off the ship when she had cried for Syracuse—her cries over time had reached a supernatural pitch. With all those stories, the voyage had become a full picture, more detailed every year, larger, branching out, clearer and less clear. This year there would also be a special celebration of the day they had arrived in Pelagos, at Diomedes's.

Normally it was the fishermen from Komissa who carried Issean greetings over to Pelagos. Komissa faced in the direction of Pelagos and those who wanted to demonstrate their courage went all the way to the island. This year they would sail from Issa and Kalia had to get on board the ship at dawn. He had been told that things in heaven stood in the same order as they did back then. The city walls, streets, and drainage canals had been finished, together with the temples to Apollo and Artemis.

Arion, on the other hand, wanted to go to El's. As they went uphill, Arion threw several handfuls of wheat in his wake. Kalia watched this silently, and saw sparrows gather behind them.

Arion asked about Teogen. "How did he die?"

"Doris was with him."

Kalia said he had asked her some time ago to go to Komissa because a Liburnian fisherman had told him Teogen was walking around aimlessly in rags and that he had fallen over and was going around with a hole in his forehead. He'd said those very words: a hole in his forehead. Kalia had explained this to Doris, who was also spending more time with the Liburnians than with the Greeks; the women had taken her in, she was teaching them how to cook Greek food, and they taught her to bake on the embers under the baking bell. Since Doris never married, she had a better time with the Liburnian women, rather than in the polis where there was no place for her unless she opted to be a hetaira, which was out of the question.

"When I told Doris about Teogen," Kalia said, "she understood. She knew I found it hard to visit Teogen in this state. I found it difficult to visit Teogen anyway, I don't know why. Not that he ever invited me over. When he left, he had chased me away and never sent a different message. If Komissa had been on the way, I'd have visited him. But I had no business there, so I neglected him. Even though Komissa isn't far, you still have to make your way there." Kalia was silent for a while before saying, "I'm making excuses. There was a part of me that wanted to visit Teogen, but another part of me always overruled the idea, and that part wanted to forget him; he belonged to those whom I had liberated myself from. You know the polis had made him my guardian, he was almost like a father, but I didn't need such a father, if I had needed one at all. I wish we had become friends, like you and I, Arion, have become friends. But this was impossible since he had been assigned to me as a father. That is why I didn't go to Komissa

ROBERT PERIŠIĆ

to visit the man the polis had designated to be my father, and then the polis also renounced him. I was sorry for him, but I was free when he left. He must have known this too; maybe that's why he was rough with me in the end. That makes me think he was a good person: he chased me away to give me my freedom. He wasn't interested in me, and that was good. Now that he is dead, I can say we have become friends.

"But Doris was with him until the end. She had gone there and sent word with that fisherman that she would stay to look after him. I felt relieved. Some women are so good, it's incredible. No man would have sent such a message, not me or you, Arion. And they say Doris is not a real woman. Imagine what the polis would consider a real woman? She was with him until the end and told me he didn't suffer, or at least not consciously. He was in pain, but it was fading away by the end. She couldn't name his disease, but she said he was telling her he was better every day because she was there."

"Did he really have a hole in his forehead?" Arion asked.

"He'd fallen over and chipped off some of his bone. It was not a large hole, Doris said, but there was one. A scab would form, but since there isn't much blood on the forehead it had nothing to stick to, so it would fall off with frowning and the hole would be visible again. It was a small hole, just above where the eyebrows met. He had lived like that for some time already, Doris said, because it seems one can live like that too. But perhaps a disease entered his head through the hole, or came out of it, she wasn't sure. Because Teogen remembered his exile in a strange way. He told Doris he had exiled the city from his head, that the city had colonized his head, that the Greeks colonized his head, that he had barely liberated himself from them. They had thought he was a slave, he said, and he had been one, he said, because he feared the void outside of the polis. Are you from the polis, he often asked Doris, because he kept forgetting who she was. She eventually learned to reply: No, I'm not from the polis, I am of Liburni. That would calm him down."

"So, he was insane," Arion said. "But maybe less so than before." Arion threw seeds behind him, the sparrows followed them, together with colorful forest birds.

"He died like that, with a hole in his forehead, but without pain, Doris said. When she sent for me, I went over toward Komissa. Teogen's land wasn't small," Kalia said. "The polis had at least considered that he built Issa, and there was plenty of space. The land was a little farther than the port and other houses, on a hillside, going down to a pebble beach with a freshwater spring. He had built a small shrine to Artemis on the path to the beach, without permission—he couldn't have known anything about it, but he'd built it anyway."

Kalia paused a bit before talking about how when he'd arrived there, he saw the man who died in Komissa had been a different man from the Teogen from whom he'd rescued Mikro. "I would have visited him more often if I had known this," he said. "But maybe he was embarrassed of the new

Teogen, or the old one, most definitely one of them, since he never invited me over."

Kalia said he was surprised when he found donkeys of all kinds on Teogen's land, aging, limping, with crooked backs. There were many of them. "There was a jenny with a foal too. The old donkeys protected them, gathering around them. Because they didn't know who I was. There were quite a few cats too, and I couldn't work out whether they belonged to Teogen and his land or if they had come by themselves. One never knows this with cats anyway. There were a couple of goats as well, and now that Doris is there, there will be more for sure. This is what I inherited. Teogen left everything to me."

"You'll end up with quite a lot of land, bit by bit," said Arion. He thought of telling him he too would leave him something but remained quiet.

"Doris will stay there," Kalia said. "Someone has to take care of the animals, and she has come to love them."

"You can get rid of those old donkeys, they serve no purpose," Arion said in order to see to what extent Kalia had become a citizen. He feigned surprise as he asked, "Are you actually keeping them?"

"He didn't leave me the land without debts. Those donkeys are his debt," Kalia said. "I think he actually kept some of the ones used to build Issa, I think I recognized some of them."

"And his mule, whom he called a jenny, is she among them?" Arion asked.

"Isiha is no longer alive. I also thought she was a jenny. But I did always wonder at how she could be so much stronger than Mikro."

"Workers without offspring are a special phenomenon in nature," Arion said.

"I remember wondering why Isiha never had a foal."

One of them then said that it was a good thing Miu stopped having kittens.

She'd had three litters and stopped. Kalia and Arion had talked about it before: perhaps she had injured herself, had suffered some kind of disease, they couldn't know. But they knew it was the reason she was still alive, otherwise she'd have been depleted.

They continued uphill. Arion was silent, threw wheat behind him.

Arriving at the leaning rock, Kalia helped Arion off Mikro. Mikro snorted mildly, as if to say, okay then. It seemed Mikro knew where they were. He went to El's hiding place, stopped there and lowered his head, breathed in the silence. It wasn't a big hole, but it must have been deep. El's remains were not visible.

"El, my friend, wake up, you have visitors," Arion said.

When he said this his breathing faltered. Kalia watched Arion's face. He was surprised. He then thought of Miu. She was with her daughters; they had created a colony at the necropolis. As if they recognized each other through a mist.

Arion watched the sea. He sat down on the oak stump. "You know, the night before last, I dreamt I was coming down this path and shouting about a birth in Issa. Some laughed because I was drunk in my dream. But I didn't pay enough attention and the wind blew me off to Pharos and the mainland, carried.... I dreamt I was on ships, scattered, as if I didn't have one body, or one time. It was a sea of ships, Kalia. I dispersed into many tiny beings on those ships. Then, Kalia, I dreamt that I had returned and there was nothing that we knew. There was none of us, none of our languages, none of our species. And it was quite ordinary, I didn't feel surprise. It seemed stranger that we had ever existed. I was in the wind and everything I was became incomprehensible. I spoke and my voice echoed back to me via overgrown streets. Because there was no one who didn't look like a stranger, except for El and Miu's descendants, who walked around, hungry. Only they. I marveled in the dream: out of all the buildings, all the gods, the polis? The Greeks, Liburnians—is there no one left?

"That was my dream, Kalia."

Kalia thought Arion had sensed his impending death. Then Arion threw another fistful of seeds behind him, attracting more colorful forest birds.

"Is this some custom?" Kalia asked. He had thought it was related to Arion's departure from this world and had only dared ask now.

"It's about El and my debt. You know, I have asked a lot. I found out from the Liburnians that there were mice and black rats on the island before we arrived. I asked the fishermen who go out farther. I realized man had brought mice to the large islands, and still there are islets without mice and rats. Fishermen know this is the case when birds nest on the ground. Where there are rats, they attack eggs and chicks. Rats easily climb up trees, they're lighter than cats. I was, Kalia, interested in our debt, and the sky, because I don't want birds to resent me. So I asked and watched. I wanted to know how much damage we have done to birds. I saw it, there was no doubt—cats attack birds. And I watched to see how much I owed because cats also killed rats who attacked chicks. I wondered how it was when there were no cats. And where there were no cats, but there were rats, birds were attacked just as much."

Kalia had only seen cats attack birds. Because of it, he didn't want to think about it any further.

"When people arrive and bring rats unwittingly, they need to bring cats too, that's what I have come to conclude," Arion said. "It made no difference to the birds, but it was better for people."

"That's what you'd like to think," Kalia said.

"True," Arion said. "That's why I'm chucking this wheat."

"I'll do the same from now on," Kalia said.

A small branch had sprouted from the side of the oak stump Arion was sitting on, which Kalia might have never even noticed had a lizard not gone past it and attracted his gaze.

Avita's mother, Volsuna, had told him that a stump is not dead as long as there is a forest around it. She said the other trees feed the stump because they don't know it has been cut. They hear the call for food in the roots, which are intertwined, so they feed it. And so the stump doesn't die, because they don't know that the rest of the tree isn't there. Its own roots don't know either. It doesn't have leaves, gets nothing out of the sun, but it's still not dead because nothing in the forest is aware of the tree's absence. Kalia had been learning about the woods from the Liburnians. He thought Volsuna's stories were just Liburnian stories, but now, as he watched this little sprouting twig growing out of the side of the stump, he said, "Look."

Arion looked down, saw it, and laughed. "El's stump is strong." He said it as if talking about himself and then added, "You know to whom we are definitely indebted? The lizard."

"I don't think we will ever return these debts, Arion," Kalia said, a little tired. "Let's go down."

And they went.

Arion was silent for a while, but then said, "You think my concern about debt is because I feel my time is running out?"

Kalia didn't know how to respond truthfully. He had to soften his response, so he said, "It's not that, Arion."

Arion didn't want to bore Kalia, but he thought, *We are returning from this hill I doubt I'll ever climb again. Why should we be silent?*

"I have one thing to say, Kalia. People think they have to pay a debt. And if the debt is large they prefer to forget it.

That's how I used to live too. But now I see no one had ever paid their debt, or will do, especially to those they owe it to. I now see that the most important thing about a debt is not to forget it. It's not a burden. Whoever thinks of debt as a burden, rejects it and becomes free in the void. That's death without feeling."

"You think feelings are in debt?"

"I don't know. But those who refuse debt are in the void. As I said, it's not about paying it back. Let it be."

"And all this is about the lizard?" Kalia asked with a smile as they went down, and the sea shone at them from below.

"Because of the lizard," Arion said and laughed.

"Will you go to Diomedes in the morning?" Kalia asked when they had descended.

"I can't, Kalia, the wind will blow me off the ship."

Scatterwind

THE SOUND OF birds in the forest stayed inside my ear, dragging itself behind me like a snail. Music existed before people, this is clear to anyone who has listened to a forest. I had thought people were imitating birds from the start and at first they had tried to sing, but then, since not everyone is a talented singer, they invented talking. I had seen, back in Africa, that not all monkeys had a sense for music, there aren't many who sing songs, so I think humans learned it bit by bit from birds, because I saw how humans learned from other animals. Humans are great imitators. They don't have an essence of their own, they are subject to great change, really obvious change. Basically, since my arrival, nothing has changed on the Earth apart from humans.

I don't know what else could have caused this except the language virus they had grown in their brains by imitating birds. It mutates from one generation to another, I saw, and every generation has its own language, inside of which it has its shivers and fevers, and every generation thinks there is nothing more important than its own language, which is a new variant of the virus. And when the new variant stops being new and cannot infect anyone, there are already new types of the virus spoken by those who are coming, and the virus that speaks goes farther, from one mouth to another, wiping out the old forms of the disease.

This was the case in the polis. And as far as I could tell, all of it was accelerating.

Although they spoke, constantly spoke of values and heroics, rot was starting to set inside language. Matters of the polis were the quickest to turn, and they threw off a certain stench, although they were the hottest topics. Perhaps this was exactly why. I saw how this was the way with the language of the polis and that after a certain time not a single story was clear, no matter how much they repeated it—actually it was with each repetition that the immunity strengthened.

All this came from music. Birds had no idea what they had done.

I, Scatterwind, attempt to crack a joke here and there, but I never know if it's part of the virus too.

The Port Necropolis

KALIA SLEPT AT Arion's and rose before dawn. He went out
and watched the stars, because they said the stars were in
the same positions as when they'd left Syracuse. He couldn't
tell if this was true, and just watched them.

*The same? Is this the same heavenly moment as when I broke
Mikro's door?*

He had spoken to Menda at the poor market for several
hours; the feeling of that night came back to him, the fragrance of Menda's embrace, the white light.

"They say everything's the same, Menda," he said to the
sky. "Where are you?"

He watched the moon now, the same. Everything was mute.

I'll never pay back my debt, he thought. *It's not a burden,
Arion is right, but I would like to tell you I'm alive, Menda.*

He got ready, wearing the same kind of tunic as back then.
And then said to Mikro, "So you know, they also invited you
to Diomedes. I said you didn't feel like traveling. But you'll

be in the front when we get back. It will be a big celebration, so I ask you to be polite and not bray too much."

Mikro bared his teeth and moved his head, touching Kalia's chest. He began walking toward the port, wearing the same kind of tunic as back then. Yes, they had wanted him to bring Mikro, and Miu, so that everything was the same, as much as possible, but he knew Mikro had suffered on the journey and Miu didn't like moving. They told him it was young Kleemporos's idea, as if that made any difference, and they were a bit surprised when he refused.

Since Oikistes fell in bed last winter, it was being said that the young Kleemporos was meddling with everything. Not everyone liked this and whenever Kalia came to the city, he felt that something was afoot, like a dim fire, which he dared not touch. He was happy to be with the Liburnians, and he had a good reason: they had a second child, Voltisa.

They told Kalia that Oikistes wanted to take the news to Diomedes now—supposedly while he was still alive—so that he could die. He couldn't travel, but he'd finish Issa in his lifetime.

He went toward the port; he might find Miu along the way, now that everything was the same in the sky. She was with her daughters and granddaughters; they had formed a colony over time, near the walls, on the necropolis. No one shooed them off the graves. They chased off animals who were less clean, who did not bury their excrement; it was not for a pig to hang around the necropolis, or a dog. And those animals only might

ROBERT PERIŠIĆ

have attacked the kittens—there were no other threats, apart from the sea hawk. The necropolis, not far from the port and the fish market, was a quiet central location, the cats knew.

Arriving there before dawn, Kalia called out to Miu in a quiet and undulating tone, "Come-come, come-come..." That was their simple song.

He sat on the ground on the edge of the necropolis, called her for some time, and Miu turned up. She stood right in front of him, half seated herself down in an expecting pose, as if watching a bird. He knew she also took this position when she listened to something, and sometimes if she was in pain, because when she was in pain, she'd sit looking straight ahead, not exposing her side.

"Are you okay, Miu?"

Even if she were in pain, she wouldn't show it. He couldn't do anything except feed her.

"I brought you some nice sardines, here, they've been cleaned too."

Miu set about eating, and several other cats turned up, which he'd expected, so he fed them too. Kalia felt he'd been neglecting her even though he knew it wasn't his fault. He had children, she didn't want to leave Issa, and there was nothing to be done about it. But without her, he knew, he would have grown up as a slave and never become a citizen. How could he pay her back? Seeing how she lived at the necropolis, even though she might be fine, he felt a sadness of alienation, as if nature had left him.

"Mikro says hi, you know, he's over at Arion's."

He was a little surprised she hadn't sniffed them out yet, although it wasn't that close, it was on the other side of the bay. And yesterday, when they had climbed up to El's, he'd expected her to be there, as if she'd sense their whereabouts in the wind.

"You're old, my dear," he said and slowly reached out a hand to her.

She blinked, he saw under the moonlight. She didn't eat much. She left the food for the others. Maybe she was in pain. But he knew she wouldn't yowl with pain like she had cried for Syracuse. She'd cry out because of something she had in her head, not because of pain in her body. She would one day disappear quietly, he knew. And he couldn't do anything about it. There was no doctor, or herbalist, at least not on Issa, who could cure a cat better than the cat would cure itself.

She watched him, sitting, straightening her front legs, as if she was preparing to hold a speech. There was a Greek on Issa, who was in fact from Syria, and he had a jug painted with a cat in that very position. "He says the jug is from Egypt," Kalia said to her. He remembered when he was a boy and thought he'd return her to Egypt; he had imagined that they'd both enjoy it there.

"Miu, what should I say to Diomedes for you?"

She stood as before.

"Nothing, eh?"

She put her head in his hand, into the sleeve of his tunic, leaving her scent with her whiskers. It was dawning already, the same as the time they were leaving Syracuse, back in the time that remained on the other side of the sea.

"I have to go, Miu. The ship is down there. And just so you know, I didn't mean to bother you, but they also invited you to come along."

She wove herself around his legs, as if blocking his way, and he avoided her, laughing.

Scatterwind

THERE IS ALWAYS a trace of what happened before, a feeling that can no longer be connected to its source. There is no heat of the light under which things take place. But the feeling is still there, although it isn't lit. Perhaps it is fed by the roots from before, like El's oak stump.

Language eats everything, on the outside, like a speedy crawling plant weaves itself around a being: yesterday was yesterday, it's been digested, what's new today? Language invented time, and bygone days.

For Miu, Syracuse happened yesterday, or perhaps today. She understood he was departing, got under his feet, and he made that sound, which was hardly part of language, when words can't be formed, because a person purrs hurriedly, when something is funny.

He purred like that, stepped over her and boarded the ship.

Miu watched him walking away. She didn't know his name, or the name of the place they had met, but she could always tell him apart from the others, and he was hers. But he had left.

Pelagos, Over Komissa

THEY STARTED FROM Issa and sailed around the island toward Komissa. Sailors boarded there, led by Leonidas, because those from Komissa knew the way to Pelagos better. Several smaller boats joined them, in case something happened to the main ship.

Leonidas's beard was already graying, but he was still strong. He embraced Kalia powerfully. "You're not a child, and I'm not a young man."

"You're stronger by the day," Kalia said. *He's a bit rougher too*, he thought.

Leonidas laughed. "I still have some things to do."

"Is Protogen alive?" Kalia asked.

"He's alive," Leonidas said. "But you know, every species has its own time. He's older than me now."

"It's good of them to invite you," Kalia said because he hadn't forgotten Leonidas's exile to Komissa, but probably enough time had passed since then.

"They had to invite you because it was promised that you'd speak, and we had to come from Komissa because we have already sailed there. The gamoroi wouldn't have invited us if they didn't have to." Leonidas laughed more.

Kalia thought Leonidas watched for his reaction after making that joke.

"We are all Isseans," Kalia said.

"That's what I think too. But tell them that," Leonidas responded. "How is it they are ruling again? This isn't the Syracuse they founded. If even that is true."

Kalia wasn't sure if Leonidas was surprised by all of this. If you had once been a slave, it becomes difficult to be surprised by the lesser vices of the polis, but since this wasn't something that could be spoken, he thought about what to say.

Leonidas spoke first. "Ah, forget it. I know, this is the kind of day when you have to speak about unity."

Kalia saw the younger Kleemporos watching them. When he approached them Leonidas moved away. Kleemporos came, not entirely close, but as if he was casually leaning against the railing and looking at the distance. Kalia tried to remember when they last spoke. Probably when they were kids. Kleemporos was followed by several others, as if they were his gang.

They sailed in silence. Kalia thought of the boy who'd waved goodbye to him as they crossed over to the other side, and how tall that boy must now be. So tall that this was no longer the other side, but the main one.

Diomedes's island was in the middle. They got close and here the flow of time was not visible at all. He thought the wind seemed exactly the same too.

ROBERT PERIŠIĆ

The Earth ages so slowly, and the sea not at all. Kalia thought that one day, even when everything he knew was gone, someone would come here, to Pelagos, not knowing anything, and everything would still look the same. There was no water on Diomedes's island, everyone would come and go accompanied by the laughing seagulls.

"Diomedes chose well, even if he falls into oblivion himself," Kalia said as they got closer, to which no one responded, but just looked at each other, because it was insulting to talk about oblivion.

Kalia saw Kleemporos frown and asked, "What happened to your Eno? I haven't seen him in a long while."

Kleemporos looked at him as if the question was offensive. Perhaps the question wasn't appropriate for the occasion or his status.

He snapped, "Doesn't matter."

"Doesn't matter? But he was one of the first. Even if he was the second, he's as important as the first. They'd have fallen sick otherwise."

"And what about the third?" asked Kleemporos.

"Thirds are also important," Kalia said, although he saw it was not a real question.

"I don't know what you're talking about, Kallias," Kleemporos said.

"I was only asking for Eno," Kalia said.

Kleemporos's face was pale with rage. "The second, you say? Were you the first? Is that how you know?"

Kalia laughed. "I came with a female cat. A female. You got it mixed up."

"Is that some Liburnian philosophy?"

"No," Kalia said. "Well, it could be. A Liburnian philosophy, yes. Have you studied it?"

Kleemporos's face was incredulous.

"There are several ladies in the village who could teach it to you," Kalia said.

It's incredible what can be spoken. It is in fact, limitless. This is why Kalia had started writing his speech several times, but never finished it.

"You're lucky you were chosen to speak a long time ago," Kleemporos said.

Kalia sensed a veiled threat, but decided to ignore it because they were docking at Diomedes's.

"It's good you're following my obligations, I nearly forgot," Kalia said.

Scatterwind

NO ONE HAD studied Liburnian philosophy. The Greeks said the Liburnians were governed by their women, whom they thought of as loose. As far as I could see, they looked after each other well, more than the men did, because a woman knows she cannot escape after mating. And if the husband had been unfaithful, the Liburnian woman would say nothing, she would simply stop doing his laundry. And if the husband became too rough, she would tell him he was free to go to war. There was always a battle to be fought somewhere; he could try out his force elsewhere. If a Liburnian told her husband this, she'd tell him quietly at first. If he feigned not having heard it or that he forgot, she'd say it more loudly, so others heard it. You're free, as far as I'm concerned, to try out your strength in a war.

True, the husband could stick around after such words, but then his right to show off would be cut. If he were to try again, by any chance, which almost no one dared to do, then the women would embarrass him on holidays, dancing around him in a circle, singing: "Why have you stayed here, when you're oh so strong!" The whole village would laugh. It would be retold for a long time because it rarely happened. Yes, Liburnian women could get rid of their husbands, from their own homes. This is why the Greeks said that their women were loose.

Kalia

THEY CAME OFF these ships in the same way as back then, when they came from Syracuse. Some swam; Kalia did not. He saw flashes of that distant journey upon the waves. Something far and familiar came back to him: the way he saw things then.

He thought about how he'd forgotten it all. Then he thought, *No, I didn't forget.* Both were true.

The birds were laughing, that's what he had heard back then. But later on he had heard, from other Greeks, that the birds were crying, because this was, after all, Diomedes's island. The first time Kalia heard them, he thought they were laughing, which is what he heard today. No one had brought rats to Diomedes's grave and the birds still lay their nests on the ground, dug them into the ground, layered with twigs and soil, and the chicks opened their beaks.

He remembered the birds as seagulls; back then, arriving here, having lived at Sabas's, and then in the stable next to the poor market, he knew only that a sparrow wasn't a seagull.

Now he was no longer sure that they were seagulls, although they were similar white birds. He didn't know any other name for them except Diomedes's birds, with flaming eyes and long, sharp beaks. Some of them had feathers wet from the sea and they shook off their wings and sprayed around. And again they flew up vertically in one place, into the sky. *There must be a particular air current*, he thought, marveling as he did when he was a child.

They climbed up the hill in the same numbers as back then, toward the shade of the great plane tree next to Diomedes's grave, and Kalia spoke the words for which he had been invited.

"I have come, Diomedes, to bring news of Issa. This is what was promised—although I am of no importance in the polis. Keep this in mind, Diomedes: there are those who would say things that are of more importance to the polis. Even I won't miss the most important things. Many years have passed and many of our elders are no longer with us. Oikistes sends his greetings, as does Arion. Teogen the builder is gone, as is the elder Kleemporos, and many other important people are gone too. But their intentions are completed. We passed this way together a long time ago, we were rushing ahead of ourselves then. We wanted to enlarge the world, Diomedes. And we built a city, by rope and measure. Our distant home is no longer distant. Issa is now where our dreams take place. Over there, where we once thought was the end of the world, now Isseans are. All of us who were on those ships became Isseans, we and the Liburnians who received us, us and our plants and animals— we are people and donkeys, and goats and vines, carob and samphire.

"I sometimes thought, Diomedes, about how your sailors, after your death, could turn into birds. Now I understand, Diomedes. Because we too, the Isseans, are many species. That is how we will survive on this sea. And the vine that Doris carried with her will survive, as will the lavender and the capers from our ships, the daughters of Miu and El will remain, and the bay leaf and Apollo's cypress, the myrtle and fig from Taranto, all those things we brought and those seeds that we and our animals brought in our bowels. The seeds we also carried in our minds will survive too, like Teogen had brought the angled streets and drainage canals. We carried also in our minds the city that is above physics, we carried the polis in our minds, and the polis council elected by the demos, or at least it had been promised this way, in the seeds.

"We brought a world, Diomedes. It is blooming. We brought a world of plants, our animals and language, together with the skies and stories. It is the world in which you exist, you and other Trojan heroes, in which Greek gods live, and there is, on the other side, Latra, who was on Issa before us. We brought our world and mixed it with what was already there, because there was a world where we thought was the end of the world. There was the olive and the vine there, which we enriched and ordered. There were oak barrels, which I first saw at the Liburnians'. There was a baking bell, and bread under it. There was carob and holm oak, which we had thought was ours, Zeus's. Zeus must have passed this way before us, you would know this better. I don't know, Diomedes, if anyone has kept track of it—what we brought, and what was already there, because all of it blends together so fast and looks eternally united, like Miu's daughters who look as if they have always belonged on Issa.

"Issa is the name of the city and the island, what we brought and what awaited us. Issa is the city and the island, we are Greeks, and the Liburnians and the Illyrians, we are people, and the animals and plants too, we are the fish, we are the Isseans.

"I would like to add something else, Diomedes, which is only mine. I was sent on the voyage by women, women I haven't seen since. I say this because you're in the middle of the sea. I would like to greet them, I know their names, and may others add to those.

"I would like to greet those from that voyage, who have traveled on and will not take the same way back, all of them hidden in the wind. Maybe you see them, Diomedes, because they are with me. I sometimes hear them in the ear of the curled shell that is a snail. Everything invites us into that hum. Inside it hides the three-legged goat, whom we had heard; inside are our nurturers and builders, to whom the laws of the polis are the worst, the voiceless donkeys and

ROBERT PERIŠIĆ

mules, slave animals and people we don't recognize as people; that is the dull hum inside the shell ear. That is under the polis because it has raised its image high up.

"Your birds laugh under the sun, or cry, depending on who hears them. May they be laughing today, may they chirp, because the voyage we took from Syracuse, that distant dawn, is over.

"It has been my honor, Diomedes, to bring you news: the city is finished, as we have promised, Issa, our apoikia."

There was a silence in the circle surrounding Kalia, under the plane tree on Pelagos. There were raised heads with hard faces, shining eyes looking into the distance, a twitch of the cheek. He saw that not everyone disliked his speech. But still, a few of them, headed by young Kleemporos, had turned the corners of their mouths sharply downward. They glanced at each other.

Kalia looked at the tree above them: Who had planted it, and when?

They left gifts for Diomedes and vowed to build a shrine for him over there on the mainland, where no island stood in the way of the view to the other side.

Scatterwind

I ONLY RARELY go to Pelagos. And I go farther even more rarely. But I had gone, I had to see it, when they dug up the frozen town from the steaming ashes, under Vesuvius.

I witnessed a volcano's memory. It was quite different from my windy memory, this hard frozen image. That was the Earth. Compared to it, a wind is harmless.

They found everything, frozen by heat, but they didn't find any cats. Not a single one.

Then they thought, even some scholars, that at the time they didn't have cats.

There are no cats in Pompeii.

ROBERT PERIŠIĆ

Sica

ON THEIR WAY back, when they were approaching Komissa, a small boat filled with shouting people approached the celebratory ships. At first they didn't understand them, they pricked up their ears, and then Kalia thought he understood their shouts: "They're attacking Pharos! The Illyrians... they're attacking Pharos!"

He didn't want to repeat it until others had heard it too. They leaned toward the sound, Kalia and Kleemporos, who turned to him and said, "The Liburnians are attacking Pharos!"

"I heard Illyrians," Kalia said.

"We know who has a navy among the Illyrians!" Kleemporos said sharply.

There was much shouting on the ships, many voices, and they all meant the same thing.

"Did I offend you, Diomedes," Kalia mumbled, looking back.

"They waited for our celebration and then attacked, the sly pigs," he heard Kleemporos say.

Kalia watched the sea, the traces of light on it, he didn't look at the faces; he heard, in a slowed-down way, words full of wind: he heard that all of the rest of the Issean ships had gone toward Pharos. That there were thousands of Illyrians. "We are also heading to Pharos!" he heard Leonidas shout from behind him. That echoed strangely, as if Leonidas had forgotten to ask for permission. Kalia saw Kleemporos's face, which read: I should have shouted this. But he could only repeat the words: "To Pharos!"

Kalia had expected this, from his conversations with Arion. But they had waited a long time and it seemed that it wouldn't happen. He knew the Issa Liburnians would be in danger now. His people could be attacked also, unless he proved himself to be a real Greek in the battle. He looked back toward Diomedes in the wind, where he had spoken in the name of the polis.

That's it, I have become a citizen and the polis is asking for its taxes, he thought.

The ship's course had been changed, they were heading straight for Pharos. Arion's words rang in his ears: a man is the same as a soldier.

Kalia looked at the prow, where Leonidas, it seemed, stood taking on the cargo from the boat that had met them; something in his body language signaled that no one should approach him. But he caught Kalia's eye and nodded at him darkly. Kalia saw a glimmer of metal; they must have sent additional weapons from Komissa. The gamoroi had beautiful family knives and mákhaira swords, which they always paraded gladly. Kalia had nothing but those scissors of his because they had asked him to show up as he had arrived back then. He'd have to ask Leonidas for a mákhaira or a Liburnian sica.

The words must have already spoken to him, but Kalia hadn't heard them, and only now did he notice Kleemporos leaning into his face and spraying him with saliva as he heard, "So you say, above species?"

"Many species," Kalia said. "But I see you prefer the word 'above.'"

"I don't know in whose name you spoke," Kleemporos said.

They had a long way to go to get to Pharos. It appeared that the attack on Pharos had given Kleemporos some advantage.

"I spoke in the name of the whole island," Kalia said.

"Well, not in my name."

"There are so many speeches in your name," Kalia said.

He saw a hatred in Kleemporos's face, which was asking for pleasure. Kalia wished to move away from him, but he didn't want it to seem as if he was retreating.

Kleemporos looked straight at him. His father had mentioned Kalia to him several times, toward the end of his life. "You measure yourself too much against other gamoroi. We are not many here and I know them all," his father had said. "I know them all, I have watched them all, but you need to watch out for Kalia." Young Kleemporos found this odd because he'd never thought about Kalia. He was never with them at the school, in gymnastics or in philosophy. "But people like him," his father had said, "he was invited to Diomedes's, and everyone knows how he fooled us with the donkey—this is a quiet joke at our expense. That donkey is, trust me, more popular than you are. Luckily the fool doesn't care about the polis. But the fact that he doesn't care, the people like this too, because they think he isn't easily influenced. Keep that in mind. If there is an opportunity, get rid of him."

Young Kleemporos had always thought Kalia was unimportant. But now, after today, he saw Kalia could speak and was utterly rude. And Oikistes was half-dead. He had bitterly disappointed them by not announcing a successor. Did he really want this democracy thing?

The old wrestler had not chosen Kleemporos, and he had once upon a time chosen Kalia. He wasn't one of theirs, the old wrestler, the cheat, if he had ever belonged anywhere.

"We are going to Pharos, and then we'll see!" Kleemporos hissed.

Kalia was quiet, watched the sea ahead of him, thought about what it was they were moving toward. He was still hoping the attack on Pharos might be a false alarm. But it didn't seem that way, he felt it in his bones.

It would be so stupid if I'm killed by the Liburnians, he thought. *Should I have become a man? Did I have a choice? Miu and Mikro aren't participating in this. And if they from the mainland did conquer Pharos, and Issa, Miu and Mikro will be out of it. And if some come to kill us all, they won't kill them. They'll remain, because they are neither citizens nor human. They will remain even when we are gone. Walls cannot save Issa. They from the mainland outnumber us and they'll beat us, sooner or later. We'll have the likes of Kleemporos as our leaders and thus it cannot be any other way.*

But he had to fight together with them today, he saw. He hoped the Issa Liburnians would fight alongside the Greeks because if it was not that way, there would be war on the island, rather than on the sea.

Had Kalia been less occupied with his thoughts, he'd have looked more closely at the group of young gamoroi who awaited nearby. He might have noticed the exchange of signals between them and Kleemporos.

"We have to watch out for those who are sympathetic to the Liburnians," Kleemporos told one of them, casually, so Kalia could hear it.

When Kalia heard it, he thought that something might happen. There was something in Kleemporos's voice that reminded him of Pigras. Kalia touched his scissors in his pocket.

He found it strange. Was it just because of his speech? He couldn't know what old Kleemporos had said, just as he couldn't know that when they headed to Pharos, young Kleemporos thought that now might be the opportune moment to harm his competitor, charm him with treason— just like that, for treason, and make him get into a fight. No one would care about a traitor after the battle, a Liburnian toady, especially if a few gamoroi confirmed the same story. Kleemporos had, besides, always known how to get others to do his dirty work.

"Be careful with your dirty words," Kalia told him.

"We should watch out for the sails so these Liburnian sympathizers don't rip them up!" Kleemporos said, without his casual tone this time, and the young gamoroi surrounded Kalia, as if to protect the sails from him.

Kalia thought the next thing Kleemporos would do is shout that Kalia was destroying the sails, and then he'd be attacked by them, so as soon as the thought crossed his mind, he shouted, "Leonidas! A plot!"

"He wants to cut the sails!" Kleemporos shouted, but Leonidas saw that Kalia was surrounded and that he was being attacked. He saw blades. Several other sailors from Komissa ran with him.

Kalia had not been aware of how much he bothered the gamoroi, and Kleemporos did not know how long Leonidas had been waiting for such an opportunity.

Scatterwind

ALL SORTS OF stories went around afterward. Many were told in whispers. Because everyone knew the official version of the polis truth. Kalia died in the fight with the Illyrians. Young Kleemporos died in the fight with the Illyrians, as did his friends. Leonidas returned as a victor over the Illyrians. Someone might whisper, "And over the gamoroi."

Leonidas later explained to everyone, in a threatening voice, that those who said an Issean attacked another Issean, or that those who said a Greek went for another Greek, they were sowing division. There were people who said such things, and Leonidas moved them out of the city of Issa. And some he moved off the island. They were so brazen they said there had been no battle whatsoever with the Illyrians on that day.

A story is like the remains of a ship, when you come up for air. Such is a story when you propel it out of time, out of the virus of language: there are the ribs of the ship, the silence of the seabed, the algae, and the glance of a stranger.

Maybe one day I'll understand what really happened. As if anyone but me actually cares anymore. Perhaps I'll even remember it one day. Because there is this awful gap in my memory. It must be connected to Kalia's death. It could be the case that I fell into the sea. What else could have happened to me so that I don't remember? True, I don't recall ever falling into the sea, and still I somehow know that it's a catastrophe. Maybe I know that this is dangerous because I have fallen into the sea before. Perhaps it was that. Because some spoke of a hit that was heavy and it nearly toppled the ship. I could have caused this if I had fallen into the sea. Others said the hit was caused by an Illyrian ship, and that was the official truth of the polis. Maybe that is what happened, but I don't remember any of it.

My memory stops in the melee around Kalia surrounded by the gomoroi. I thought later that they stabbed him and pushed him over the edge, so I went after him, trying to do something because he was my favorite human, and if it hadn't been for him, I'd never have come to the Adriatic.

There was, later, a story that Kalia's dead body was taken away by the wind. Perhaps some saw it that way, if I had been trying to save him. Greeks sometimes saw odd things, more often than people do today, and I didn't trust them much. But if something similar had happened, it was clear to me that it could have only been my doing. I don't know how I could have carried him, where I would get the momentum from, what kind of force I'd have had to create to carry a body. Carrying things wasn't in my skill set. But it is possible I had tried to do something, so we fell into the sea together. I only know I never saw Kalia again, or his body. If I had, by some incredible coincidence, carried him off the ship, I know nothing about it, or where I might have left him.

I remember the crowd around him, the flashing of blades, Kalia holding his scissors, Leonidas approaching with a drawn blade, the shouts of his sailors....

I thought I was in some way connected to Kalia. I mean connected in a way that I died with him, or felt death, at least for a moment. Or I took something of his after his death.

It's true that I have his memory as if it were my own. In it, the image of the ship soundlessly turns into an image of Zoi, her hair down under a pale light, and I hear what she once said: it's a beautiful illness that makes one invisible.

I don't know what happened to me then, or what exactly happened to him, but I don't doubt that it's connected.

Kalia's body wasn't on the ship Leonidas went back on to Issa. But Kalia wasn't the only one missing. The very ship they'd sailed to Diomedes was missing. It sank soon after that hit, whether I had caused it by falling into the sea, or the Illyrian ship. They took over that Illyrian ship, which—according to the official polis version—was attacked by Leonidas, Kalia, and the Komissa sailors, because in that version Kalia died afterward, in battle.

The gamoroi are never mentioned in that attack. I guess they hadn't excelled in battle, since they all died.

They said that thousands of Illyrians died at Pharos. Leonidas returned on the captured Illyrian ship: it was a Liburnian ship, without any iron, tied together with ropes. Some said that Magas too was there, an old soldier like Leonidas, and the two of them took Issa back from the gamoroi. Some, those who were the descendants of the gamoroi and the Kleemporos clan, later quietly claimed—only I could hear them—that Leonidas had plotted all of it beforehand, back when the Komissa sailors were invited to follow the ship carrying the Issa elite to Diomedes. He had seen that he could get them all on one ship, in the middle of the sea. They said he knew already, from Magas, that the Liburnians would attack Pharos exactly on the day of the celebration, but he hadn't told anyone and used it for his plan and this made him a traitor, they whispered. We knew about Magas before, they said, we could have even caught him, but we thought he was preparing a Liburnian mutiny, which would have been good because we could get rid of the Liburnians since they still—after the original agreement—held too much of the land. We thought Magas cared about Liburnia, and not plotting with Leonidas and the Komissa lot to take over the polis and rule it. We were naive, and that is the fault of our strategists.

Then one of the remaining Kleemporoses would speak up, because the criticism was against them, and he'd say that some now, after the catastrophe, dreamed the big dreams of those two idiots. It was just a matter of things falling into place, that Leonidas saw an opportunity, and that our men were stupid to attack Kalia—this was how it started on the ship and Leonidas, once he killed one person, had to carry on. And we have to wait, and go back after it all falls apart, tomorrow or the day after, or after a number of years.

That's how they spoke and discussed, awaiting their return, the remnants of the gamoroi, exiled all the way to the mainland, to Tragurion and Epetion, to find their way or disappear, to found apoikias or die as heroes. Issa would support them in any case. I followed them, because I was interested in their stories, not just the truth of the polis where Leonidas, or so he claimed—and was even convinced of it—had brought democracy, and also the harmony between the Greeks and Liburnians who had all become Isseans. This last bit even seemed convincing, but I wasn't so sure about democracy, I didn't really have anything to compare it to.

Waiting

ARION SAT ON the ground. He saw flashes of fire in the eyes of those surrounding him; Miu and other cats from the necropolis were around him, and the people who waited lit the harbor with torches. There was still talk of victory.

Avita arrived, her legs full of scratches, she had walked in the dark. Mikro brayed quietly, like a wailing dog, when he saw her. She hugged him, put her forehead against his.

A turtle moved quietly in the yard.

An egg-white moonlight shone over the poor market.

Scatterwind

From this city, which longs for your courage, you sailed out
Came upon an Illyrian ship, and found your death there
And Harmo, your dear child, is now fatherless
Kalia, you hero, we have not seen such courage since

THEY FOUND A stone with these words and keep it in a museum now. They say this is the first writing on this side of the Adriatic. I think they mean to say that they haven't come across an older example. I didn't keep an eye on who wrote what, perhaps I ought to have done, but I felt a bit sick seeing monuments then.

I don't know if this was about the Kalia I followed here, because his son was called Darmo. That's a Liburnian name and the Greeks might have changed it a bit.

Or perhaps it was not my Kalia, but a different one whom I forgot. Because they named children after him, his and Darmo's descendants. And others on Issa. His name was remembered as long as their arrival was remembered, and

if this Kalia of the stone was a different one, it was still a
memory of the Kalia I traveled with.

And this was what was written in the stone:

Σ]ΗΣ ΑΡΕΤΗΣ ΡΟΛΙΣ ΗΔΕ ΡΟΘΗΝ ΕΧΕΙ

ΟΣ] ΠΟΤΕ ΠΛΕΥΣΑΣ ΑΝΔΡΩΝ ΙΛΛΥΡΙΟΝ

ΝΗΙ] ΕΠΙΒΑΣ ΕΘΑΝΕΣ ΠΑΙΔΑ ΛΙΠΩΝ Σ[ΟΥ]

ΦΙΛΟΝ Η]ΑΡΜΟΝ ΕΝ ΟΡΦΑΝΙΑ ΚΑΛΛΙΑ

[ΕΜΗΙ (Δ)ΑΡ]ΕΤΗΙ ΟΥΚ ΟΛΙΓΗΝ ΕΛΙΠΕΣ

Sand

MIU WAS MEOWING around Arion's shack. The door creaked open at dawn. Miu stood outside. Arion sat down on the bench by the door slowly, moaned quietly, and leaned against the wooden wall. There was long white hair growing around his ear and Miu looked at it.

"What have you to say, Miu?" he asked. "Never mind, I didn't sleep well either."

Miu sat outside, looking into the shack.

"You want to come in?"

Perhaps you'll find those I cannot find myself, he thought. *Perhaps I still have something of theirs. That's why I'm still here.*

"I wanted, Miu, so you know, to take a soft poison that makes you sleepy. But I can't while you're still looking for them. I'll bring you some food, let me just gather some strength. And because of Darmo and Voltisa, and Avita, I have to last longer, that's how it's turned out, Miu. You never know what the old hook can be good for in the polis." Arion laughed.

Miu touched his calf with the side of her body. She then sat beside him and looked at the sea.

Somewhere ahead of them in the darkness lay Pharos, and the mainland.

"He might be back still, Miu, you never know," Arion said. Miu turned her head and looked at him, and lay her head on her paws.

"I'll get you some food," Arion said, standing up carefully. When Arion came back Miu was gone.

"Are you there?" he asked, into the air.

Arion sat down again by the door. It was a warm night, a half-moon shone, late spring. He watched the pale shimmer of the sea, listened to the waves come and go through the hum of the beach. He snoozed off by the door. He was overcome with cold from a dream that was starting from a distance. When he opened his eyes, the light was bright, although the sun wasn't visible yet. A hedgehog was eating the food he'd left out for Miu.

The next day he heard a donkey bray from a height. The wind, a warm dry wind with sand, carried the sound; it lifted up the sound and the foam of the waves. There is sometimes such a wind, full of sand, they say it comes from far away down south, where the hills are crushed to powder. Up there, among the island's hills, is a valley full of this sand that accumulates in the depths that were once a volcano. Through it, rains go into an underground lake, and that is where the Issa water flows from.

Arion felt the tiny grains of sand stick around his eyes. He frowned. The day was blurry.

At dusk, a little boy turned up with a donkey. For a moment he thought he knew them from a long time ago. He rubbed his eyes.

"Who are you?" asked Arion.

"Arion, it's me and Mikro," the boy said.

"But..." Arion needed to collect himself. "It's Mikro and... Darmo?"

"It's me," the boy said proudly.

The Liburnians gave chores to their children early on and Arion thought the boy looked happy, even though he had lost his way a bit.

"Mother said I should go to you if it gets dark and I'm out."

"Good, good. Oh dear, this strange wind, you see it?" Arion said. "I'm half-blind all day."

"It gets into my eyes too," Darmo said. "But it's stopping, you see?"

Arion stroked Mikro, who watched and sniffed him. "Old friend, you're holding up well, the Liburnians are taking good care of you." Arion rested his head on the donkey's ear.

"He'd wandered off," Darmo said. "I was looking for him all day."

Ceuna arrived, having spent a few days at her sisters'. They were also working the land that Arion had gotten from the polis, in the countryside.

"Come and eat something." Ceuna had brought them a lentil and green bean stew with some chevon. Darmo didn't refuse.

"Mikro ran away, you say," Arion said. "You know, once Kalia wanted to run away with Mikro, and if I'd let him, you wouldn't be here."

"How so?" Darmo asked.

"Come on, don't confuse the child," Ceuna said.

"I'll tell you about it if there is time," Arion said. "Come to Issa more often, you'll forget your Greek in the village. And I have something for you."

Arion got up slowly and went inside.

"It's nice of Mikro to bring you over," Ceuna said.

"He doesn't normally run away even though he's not tied," Darmo said. "But this morning he wasn't there. He'd gone all the way up into the hills. I found him up there, next to the leaning rock, near a hole. I think there was a dead cat there, the one that belonged to my father."

"Miu? You saw her?" Ceuna asked.

"I saw her," Darmo said, nodding twice.

Ceuna sighed and closed her eyes. "Did you touch her fur?"

"No," Darmo said. "Should I have done?"

Issa sank into silence as darkness fell, a torchlight appeared here and there.

"May she rest with Latra," Ceuna said.

"I didn't know the cat well. Only when we went to the town house, which was twice, she would watch us from somewhere.

ROBERT PERIŠIĆ

She'd watch me and Voltisa like that. But she never came close. They said she lived at the graveyard, so I was a bit afraid of how she looked me in the eyes."

Arion listened from the door and said, "This sand in the eyes, it's from Africa."

He held a flute in his hand.

Later on, from the hill, a donkey's braying could be heard.

"He's run off again!" Darmo said, his arms in the air.

Arion, who'd let him go, told Darmo not to worry, because there were no wolves or poisonous snakes on Issa. Nothing could harm a donkey that knew his way around.

Scatterwind

THEY CAME AND dug. They used soft brushes to clean the bones, blew the dust off the ceramics. I always followed those who were digging because they were digging through my memory, unwittingly. No one had dug up the awful hole, which I don't remember, but I still followed them. So much time had passed and it was no longer considered a sacrilege to callously dig up graves. The bones were so old, separate from any form of remembered or felt life, that they had become science and archaeological heritage, and somehow I came to peace with the fact that knowledge taken from a grave was still better than oblivion.

I saw that this was a catch, a prize, which would be displayed behind glass, and they'd talk about it, tell stories. They were hunters of old deaths, but still: those soft brushes, like paint brushes revealing an image, the lips that blew away the dust—I watched them—perhaps there was some feeling in those careful moves, in the blowing at bones or at the remains of a wine skifos broken in time.

I saw the coast sink with time. Few but me could see it, but they knew it too, so I started to respect them and listen carefully. I heard them say the eastern coast of the Adriatic is sinking one millimeter a year and it was no wonder that no one could see this with a naked eye in their lifetime, except for those who jump through memory. It's the movement of the tectonic plates, they said, and deep under the Adriatic is the old African plate, because Africa is even bigger in the depths than on the surface.

A millimeter a year, this coast has sunk almost two and a half meters since I came here, following a ship to Issa.

Those soft brushes, like paintbrushes that reveal an image, the lips that blew away the dust, they were a good thing. They found people. And everything that had been buried with them—and there was plenty in the Issean tombs, beautiful things left for the afterlife of the deceased, which are there in the museums, alongside the bones; an illustration of the tomb under a glass cover: an Issean made of bones, and their things laid out around them.

They didn't look for cats.

One of them mentioned donkeys while he brushed Diomedes's pot on Pelagos, where I went along with them one time, and he was telling a young female friend about a finding, about donkeys in the tombs of Egyptian kings of the first and second dynasties, at the time when they—who had dug up those ten donkeys—were still not sure if those were wild donkeys. They looked closely then and discovered that those donkeys, buried near kings, ten years old at the time of death, were definitely not wild, which could be seen by the damage on their vertebrae, by the inflammation of their ventral ligaments, and by the partial and almost full degeneration of their spinal discs, their bent backs on all parts that were in line with external pressure above their shoulder blades and by the heavy use of their leg and foot joints. That is how the diggers can tell which animal was domesticated. These donkeys were royal and must have lived better than the rest, and were killed, apparently, as soon as the king died so they could serve him in the next life.

The one who dug around Diomedes's pot wanted to keep his friend's attention so he told her also of the village of the burial artisans in Luxor, by the Nile, where Sennefer from the time of Ramses III, which was around eight hundred years before Issa, which is when I was also in Africa, by the way, though because Africa is large and I wasn't in that part, I haven't a clue about the story. But anyway, this Sennefer buried five of his donkeys in his lifetime, and he named each one of them, and their mothers' names too.

They dug all this up, brushed with soft brushes and blew with their breath, and I got to feel for them because of it. Then he started telling her about Amenkha'u, a village policeman from this really old tyranny, who rented out his donkeys for a price of... But she interrupted him. I even saw that: love on Pelagos, a gentle mating of those who dug.

Diomedes's birds laughed.

Avita

"YOU KNOW, WHEN we came, everyone thought I was Mikro's owner."

Avita remembered Kalia's words, whose memory was starting to fade, whom she resented because he had disappeared. *Why didn't you defend yourself, why did you leave me like this?* she asked him in the night.

It had been a bad year, and no one from the polis helped them; Arion was gone too.

She thought about Kalia's words because there was that ship and she had to decide.

How could I be Mikro's owner? I left coins, I don't know how much it was, but still: How could I buy Mikro? From whom? I had left the money because of the polis. What did it have to do with Mikro that I left money for Alexandros? I left the money to some man, and no one asked Mikro anything.

She had told him then, *I don't even know who this Alexandros is.*

The smallest man in the world, Avita. Believe me, the smallest, but serious.

Why did you leave him money?

Because he was a man. Albeit the smallest.

That's what she remembered.

Mikro was weak, shivering, and she embraced him, and there was the ship, the one that passed by once a year, where one could sell an old donkey.

Virno was still alive and he dared tell her. "Think about it, Avita, because it'll be a hard winter. I know you love him, but he doesn't do anything anymore, and neither do those that Doris is taking care of."

Avita caught her breath as she answered. "But, Virno, he didn't belong to him. Neither did the land Teogen had left for him, he hadn't left it bare, but with those donkeys on it. I can't do it."

"I know, but you can when it's a necessity. No one will hold it against you. Consider it, Avita."

She knew Virno's voice belonged to the village, because hunger awaited.

I know where that ship sails. I should kill them, she thought. *I should kill him once and for all, him and his debts, and be the owner of an empty land. I should kill Kalia. Why don't I do it? What even makes him still alive?*

She was too tortured to do anything. Everyone told her it made no sense. He strained and was dying, and she could have sold him. She lay with him, in an embrace.

Scatterwind

A STORY, WHEN you come up for air, is like the remains of a ship. That is a story when it's propelled out of time, out of the virus of language: it's the ribs of a ship, the silence of the seabed, algae, and the glance of a stranger.

I watched Issa grow from an imagined picture, and then it, again, became an image.

I watched it sprout out of the soil and disappear in the soil like everything else.

On the stones cut by Teogen and Kalia, on the waterfront of their port, one can now walk in the sea up to their thighs, around a small peninsula where there is an amphitheater under the ground.

Sometimes I go up to where the city was. There is peace; vine, thorn, carob; no buildings; only the northern wall remains.

I always move along Teogen's vertical lines. I know the stone blocks and the drainage canals are there, inside the earth. The earth closed its jaws like the crocodiles' mother.

Sometimes I think about it like that: they are hidden inside. But still, I saw, time is linear. It only reverses in dreams. That's enough for me because I learned. I had time and I learned to snooze off in the summer heat. I learned to dream in the swelter, thick dreams, from which somebody else would struggle to emerge. But I think I've said it before: I am far from I.

When I go down the south walls, which aren't there, I see young men playing basketball above the graves of the Isseans; the asphalt, a basketball court, lines drawn out above the necropolis; a cat watches them sometimes. It is strange for me to watch this and I don't spend much time in Issa. I am more often to be found in Komissa, on the edge of Teogen's old land, on the discarded chair behind the wall.

Everything shivers, like on the edges of a flame. I rest on a velvet upholstered chair. It looks like a foldable chair, but it's not folded, it's broken. Bushes and weeds surround it on all sides, as if it's floating on plants. That is all hidden behind a concrete wall next to which cars park, sideways, and every driver parks so they don't open their doors on the side of the wall—because they have to get very close, not to stick out onto the road. It's all very narrow, which is why no one looks behind the wall where they park, although the wall isn't that high, and that is why Miu put her lair there.

I call her Miu because she looks just the same.

In those times, without a way to preserve an image, it was hard to recognize those who came back.

I don't have an image of Miu except the one in my windy memory and perhaps I just think she looks the same. Except this Miu doesn't meow. That is something they learn with people, and she had grown up by the road, next to the factory. She knows every inch of this place, she knows the traffic, the customs of parking, and what is good about cars; because neither people nor their dogs get under them, you can hide there and get good shade, although the engines have a particular smell, from the depths of the black earth. The best are the forgotten ones, that don't move, and there is one such car there, a red one—that is the best one, it hasn't moved the whole summer.

Across the road, on the edge of the half-sandy plateau, someone had forgotten a water tank from a ship, a white cube with rounded edges.

Under the road, surrounded by its wall, sat the fish-tin factory, which was the reason for creating this colony; the factory has been closed for some time, and they no longer know why they settled there. They were born there. The males wander off, but the females stay.

Nearby are also four rubbish bins, walled off on three sides: a yellow, blue, and two green bins. I watch them at night: they search through the plastic, through the glass. I watch them in the day: they're clean.

They die, but there are no bodies; there are no cats in Pompeii.

They were an independent colony for around a hundred years, which is how long the sardine factory lasted, here on the edge of Teogen's land, which had been taken over by Doris, and then Voltisa after her. Things go around in circles here like in music. I can hear the rhythm of life and death when I think with my ear, it is the music that almost no one else can have the time to hear.

There is always some kind of snail in the ear.

I listened to time, that curly song.

But then I have to snap out of it and be entirely in the present moment. The crickets speed up their song with the heat. Heavy bumblebees. People, their machines and radio presenters whom I unwittingly hear. The hissing of waves, the twitter of messages, the burdock of voices. I hear every-thing—it has an effect on me. I am not close to Miu here just because of memories. I like her frequency. I must balance myself out, otherwise I'd go crazy from the rubbish of the waves. That would not be good for the climate. Everything is quite wobbly already.

There are nervous currents at times, from above and below, irritable weather, followed by periods of deadness.

I saw a sea cucumber climb up a boat rope.

I get seized by a foreboding of the end, in the middle of the day, as if I could disappear from here. Perhaps that is why I get my desire to talk.

I speak from here, close to the rubbish, behind the wall. The ground climbs up behind me, there are gardens, intim-idating fences, and reserve spools of rusty barbed wire that the peasants robbed from the retreating army.

ROBERT PERIŠIĆ

A calico walks, a hole in her forehead.

A fig tree grows through a crumbling petrol can.

The people who walk around here, walk through a void. And without looking they see there is nothing there, except a way through, and they look farther, to the sea.

Only sometimes do I see the evident joy of existence, for instance when I am looking at the three of them nestled against Miu, sheltered behind the wall, on my broken throne, in the evening, when the heat dies down.

Just an occasional shadow wanders about the bare earth of the car park, around the narrow asphalt.

The path goes to the small spring by the sea.

You might come across two goats along the way.

My apoikia.

ROBERT PERIŠIĆ was born in Split, Croatia, in 1969. In 1988 he moved to Zagreb, where he studied Croatian literature and became a freelance writer, penning literary criticism, poetry, plays, and fiction. His most widely translated works are the novels *Naš čovjek na terenu*, (Our Man in Iraq) and *Podrucje bez signala* (No-Signal Area), both of which have received international critical acclaim. His 2002 collection *Užas i veliki troškovi* (Horror and Huge Expenses) was also published by Sandorf Passage. Perišić's time on the Adriatic Sea island of Vis, ancient Issa, inspired *A Cat at the End of the World*.

VESNA MARIC was born in Mostar, Bosnia and Herzegovina, in 1976. She left at sixteen as part of a convoy of refugees. She went on to work for the BBC World Service and now writes and translates. Maric's memoir, *Bluebird*, was published by Granta in 2009, and was longlisted for The Orwell Prize. Her first novel, *The President Shop*, was published by Sandorf Passage in 2021.

About Sandorf Passage

SANDORF PASSAGE publishes work that creates a prismatic perspective on what it means to live in a globalized world. It is a home to writing inspired by both conflict zones and the dangers of complacency. All Sandorf Passage titles share in common how the biggest and most important ideas are best explored in the most personal and intimate of spaces.